fifth Life of the catwoman

a Novel

KathLeeN DexteR

B

BERKLEY BOOKS, NEW YORK

A Berkley Book
Published by The Berkley Publishing Group
A division of Penguin Putnam Inc.
375 Hudson Street
New York, New York 10014

Copyright © 1996 by Kathleen Dexter.
Text design by Tiffany Kukec.

PRINTING HISTORY
Llano Press trade paperback edition / August 1996
Berkley trade paperback edition / November 2002

Visit our website at
www.penguinputnam.com

Library of Congress Cataloging-in-Publication Data

Dexter, Kathleen.
    Fifth life of the catwoman : a novel / Kathleen Dexter.—Berkeley trade pbk. ed.
      p.   cm.
    ISBN 0-425-18618-0
      1. Women—Fiction.   I. Title.

PS3604.E88 F44 2002
813'.6—dc21

                                                                                      2002071690

PRINTED IN THE UNITED STATES OF AMERICA

10   9   8   7   6   5   4   3   2   1

For my good Sicilian boy

fifth Life
of the
catwoman

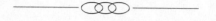

SUMMER

Not a whisper of a breeze had ruffled a single cat whisker in days. Dust hung suspended in the air without drifting, without falling. Cottonwood leaves forgot the steps to their summer dance, shimmy-shiver, side-to-side. Even the cicadas held their song secret, waiting. On the third evening of the stillness, the CatWoman went to the tortoise-shell.

Who's coming? she asked silently.

Paws, face, chest, tail—the tortoise-shell had a bath to finish and was not quick to reply. *A man,* came the answer at last as she rolled onto her back, inviting the woman's hand to rub her belly.

How did he find the way? asked the woman, rubbing her hand absently over the autumn-colored fur.

He knew the way, purred the cat.

But how?

Ask him when he gets here tomorrow. He's camped a few miles east.

There was no need to ask how the cat knew this, or to wonder why she herself knew from the stillness that her world was holding its breath, trying not to be discovered. Like me, she thought.

You're sure he'll come this far?

He's heading for the cottonwoods, was the reply. *He's thirsty, and he knows he'll find water here.*

The CatWoman looked overhead at the ancient trees that were luring a stranger to invade her private world, even while holding their leaves still and silent. The stand circled the low mud house like a collar, sending their roots under the building to the courtyard where a spring bubbled from a stone cairn. Some of the roots broke out of the ground, half-buried under grass, giving the courtyard the look of a pond frozen green and still just after a big splash. The trees were several houses tall, spreading wide over the house and courtyard in one direction, the sage and piñon desert in the other.

So my oasis isn't as invisible as I'd hoped, sighed the CatWoman.

The tortoise-shell rolled over and sat up to look at her with a long, slow blink. *It was never invisible. That's why you found it.*

⊙⊙⊙

Sleep teased and eluded the CatWoman that night. Far past the time when she otherwise would have been dreaming, she paced the well-worn paths in the dull slate floor of the house—to the bedroom, through the sala, to the kitchen, back again—and paced anxious figure eights around the courtyard, interrogating the unconcerned cats lounging here and there.

Have you seen a man camping nearby? she asked.

He's carrying a big pack on his back, said the silver tabby.

He sings when he walks, said the apricot siamese.

He has a dog, said the old calico, disgusted.

He ate tuna for lunch. This last, volunteered by a small orange and white spot-cat, caused a brief commotion.

Did you get some? they all asked simultaneously.

No, said the spot-cat, *I was afraid of the dog.*

Why didn't any of you tell me about him? asked the CatWoman impatiently.

They all stared at her with the same unreadable expression. *We thought you knew,* the calico spoke up.

No, I didn't know. Did anyone see how he got in?

The same way you got in, shrugged the tortoise-shell.

The comment brought the CatWoman's pacing to a wide-eyed halt. *But that means I'm not the only one—*

Did you really think you were?

"Yes," she croaked, her rusty voice stumbling ungracefully into the night on legs rarely used. "Yes, I did."

A few hours before dawn, she set out silently through the arch of the courtyard gate and up a trail cut into the hillside west of the house. Halfway up the hill, in a tight grove of olive trees, was a small, stone-lined warm spring. She slipped in without a splash, sitting low till the water nuzzled her chin. The moon had set already, but by the light of the stars her night eyes could see the outline of cottonwoods below, the house hiding under thick branches, and the surrounding gardens and orchards, all a hazy blur in the still night. It was an oasis she'd had all to herself for nearly six years, and now that solitude was about to be broken.

I have to get rid of him quickly, she thought, but had no idea as to how she might do it. She had no way of defending the place against intrusion; indeed, she had never even prepared herself for the possibility. She assumed no one but herself would know how to find the entrance to a mirage the way she had learned to do— how many years ago?—from her mother.

This wasn't the first mirage she had opened, only her very favorite one, as it shimmered above a forgotten mesa too wonderful to leave. Not only had someone been here before her to build the house and plant the orchards, but they had left their touch of magic on the place itself that kept the winters mild and made the flowers bloom early in the spring.

And they had left the cats—nearly fifty of them, she estimated once, though they were rarely all in one place at the same time, so she wasn't quite sure. Some, like the tortoise-shell, made themselves distinct from the others by hanging around a lot. The rest came and went, seemingly in shifts. She imagined them on a constant, rotating patrol across the many miles of mirage-mesa, keeping an eye on everything. Surely they must have seen her hiking in, like they saw the man approaching now, and spread the word among themselves from behind piñons and sage. Did they take note of what she ate for lunch as she hiked toward the cottonwoods, she wondered, like they noticed the tuna today? No doubt they did, storing the information away in the same impenetrable vault of feline reticence that would have swallowed the news of today's intruder had she not asked them for it outright.

She rolled over on her back to float, staring up through the olive trees where leaves shone silver in the starlight. "How could anyone possibly know the mirage trick?" she fretted to the leaves. For that matter, why would anyone have any use for it? Her mother only taught it to her as an afterthought, insisting it wasn't nearly as useful as knowing the right herbs to put into a tea for bringing down a fever, or knowing the right words to say to make the mud dry up overnight around a house, or even knowing the right way to touch a tree to make it sleep through a drought. It unnerved her to think that in the whole world, another person would have this gift and would use it on *her* mirage.

Perhaps the thing to do would be to stay out of sight, she thought. He can get some water and leave, and never know I'm here. That seemed terribly unlikely, though. The house was obviously not abandoned, the way it had looked when she found it years before, with stones tumbled from the terraces and weeds choking the rosebushes. And if the man had even half an eye, he would see how well-kept the orchards were—far too fruit-heavy for untended trees. No, it would be obvious *someone* lived on this patch of fertile ground in the middle of a dry mesa. All the Cat-Woman could truly hope would be for the man to leave quickly and not poke around too much. For the first time in lifetimes she wished her gifts were greater than they were, for she would sleep much more soundly if she could somehow seal the entrance to the mirage behind him. But while opening a mirage took no more effort than opening a walnut, closing a mirage was a complete mystery to her.

The midnight stars were sitting low on the horizon by the time she got out of the water and walked down the trail in the shadow of the hills, taking care not to send any noisy rocks down ahead of her. There was nothing to do but wait, so she took up position by a window in the bedroom. She didn't have to wait long.

As she expected, the man showed up within an hour of sunrise. She heard him before she saw him, out beyond the ring of cotton-woods and probably still a quarter mile away. He wasn't following the runoff stream where the two springs, cold and warm, joined to run together toward the big river in the gorge to the east. The sound of his footsteps came from north of the stream's path and the CatWoman suspected he hadn't seen it. But he had definitely seen the cottonwoods towering lettuce-green and lush above the dark piñons and was hiking without hesitation toward them. Next to the sound of his footsteps was the sound of dog paws in the sand.

A sudden break in the rhythm of the footsteps told her he was within view of the house. Though she had no window on that side for spying, she could well imagine the look on his face as the entire oasis revealed itself, for she remembered vividly her own first view. The cottonwoods would suddenly become, to his eye, not just a gathering of color but a majestic canopy over a low adobe house. His eyes would then travel down to notice the arched entrance to the courtyard, around which the house sat in an embrace. He would notice the cut in the courtyard wall, where the cold stream ran downhill and away from its hidden source. And noticing the wall, he would surely see the delicate fresco design following the ridge—cream-colored birds flying nose to tail, meeting at the top of the arch.

Footsteps told her the man was walking slowly again toward the house, through the sage as it met the skirt of wildflowers, past the east orchard full of young fruit, through the terraced bank of roses in early bloom, up the last stone steps to stop at the courtyard entrance. He had walked slowly, as if admiring every flower, tree, and trickle in the stream, bathed now in a morning glow halfway between silver and gold. The tiniest of breezes came up just then through the cottonwood leaves, adding a shimmer to the glow. Just enough, thought the CatWoman in dismay, to make him fall in love with the place like I did.

"Hello?" he called out after a moment. She said nothing, standing out of sight. He called out again, stepping close enough to the archway to see inside, then said, "Ooooh—wow!" under his breath. She knew what he saw here, too—the frozen splash of the grass, the spring bubbling from its cairn, thick vines of morning glories open full blossom to the early sun, a deep roof shading a porch—and cats, everywhere. Nearly all of them this morning, the CatWoman had noted in surprise.

"Hello?" he called out a third time, stepping inside the courtyard and motioning for the dog to stay outside. As the dog whined in answer, every cat eye on the porch widened perceptibly. The man scanned the courtyard scene slowly, then walked to the spring to fill a canteen. One eager dog paw stepped inside the courtyard and then immediately retreated as fifty cat voices suddenly hissed in unison.

"Too many cats for you, Oso?" The man laughed.

A memory flicked through the CatWoman's mind when she heard the dog's name. She'd had a dog once named Oso, when she was very little, that first time . . .

A very long time ago, she thought.

The dog whined and stayed put just outside the archway while the man drank long and full straight from the spring. She saw him loosen a tie in his hair and put his head into the water for so long it seemed he had no intention of emerging—until he suddenly swung his head back up, back into the sunshine, shaking like a dog. The spray from his hair reached the cats and a sudden fifty-cat protest broke the serenity of the scene.

I'm sorry, but you don't know how good that feels!

The CatWoman gasped. The comment surely hadn't come from any of her water-shy companions, yet she'd heard it clear as she now heard fifty cat faces being rubbed dry. Who *is* this man? she wondered. There was something hauntingly familiar about him. It wasn't so much how he looked, but rather how he was— *who* he was—

"Who he used to be—" she whispered.

—and suddenly the CatWoman was seeing another sunbaked courtyard, so many miles and years in the past. A hot morning glaring off flagstone, climbing roses on white plastered walls, a fountain—and a young girl laughing and squealing as her older brother dipped his head into the cool water and shook himself, splashing her over and over again. *Try it, Josefa!* came the voice, echoing up through the caverns of her memories. *You don't know how good that feels!*

You don't know how good that feels . . .

Her mind went back to the man before her, sitting quietly now surrounded by cats, water dripping from the black hair on his shoulders to the stones below. There was nothing about him that was familiar, nothing in his appearance to suggest he might once have been that teasing boy, nothing to entice her to call out to him. Yet she knew if she watched him any longer, she would do just that. She inched back into the darkness of the bedroom, hoping to send him away with her thoughts. After a moment, he stood, gathering his pack and canteens and waving to the circle of cats. "Ciao to you all," he said out loud, bowing grandly.

The dog outside pranced eagerly as the man approached, clicking toenails on the stones underfoot. Just as he reached the archway, the pull of the CatWoman's memories overwhelmed her plans of the night before, and she called silently, *Julio?*

The man stopped short and spun to look in her direction, eyes squinting to pick her face from the shadows as she stepped slowly into view. He walked warily across the grass to stand in the shadow himself and stare at her through the window.

"Who *are* you?" he whispered.

"I'm Josefa."

◯◯◯

"Your hair is darker," said the CatWoman as she and the man sat eating the last of the cherries he'd brought in his pack. "I wasn't sure it was you."

"What tipped you off?" he asked, incredulous.

"You spoke to the cats the way—" She hesitated. "—Mamá showed us."

"Ahhh," he chuckled, "no one's ever caught me doing that. Though I've heard a couple other people do it along the way."

"You *have?*"

"Here and there. I've never spoken to them about it. I just took it to mean there must be a few others out there in our—" He spat a cherry seed across the grass. "—predicament."

A wave of memories rose to sweep the CatWoman under, and like a reflex she fought to keep herself from falling into them like she had fought so often before. They came as a confusing collage, jumping forward and backward through time—herself as a child, as a mother, as a young girl, as a child again—memories of other sunbaked houses, of crowded tenements, of neat clapboard houses in a tight group on a river somewhere—memories, her very oldest, of a woman holding her face between two big hands and whispering something urgently into her ear before being dragged away. This last memory turned her stomach upside down and she spat out the cherry she'd been eating.

"Bad cherry?" asked the man.

"Bad memory," she mumbled. "Where did you go after they took Mamá? I never heard anything about you again."

"I found a ship ready to sail and never looked back." She heard him fondly cradling the memory. "Those were the good old days—just go hop a ship and march with madmen, looking for gold. Ha! So where did *you* go?"

"I—stayed," she replied vaguely and could feel, without looking at him, that he expected her to elaborate. As a welcome distraction, the tortoise-shell separated herself from the crowd surrounding them and hopped onto the man's lap to lean heavily against his chest. His hands, rough against the sleek fur, were the thick hands she remembered from other lifetimes, on farmers, on blacksmiths, on herself.

"She's after your food," she warned him.

"Shameless, huh?" He lifted the cat by the shoulders to look her in the eye. "You're not shameless, are you?"

"She is. She's also the most talkative one of the bunch. She's the one who told me you were coming."

"Oh really? How did she know?"

"I don't know. I've wondered that since I've lived with them."

"How long have you lived here?"

"Six years." She let her gaze wander to the trees overhead, where sunlight on the leaves had slipped slowly downward, over the house wall and into the courtyard. Once again she could feel that he expected her to elaborate, but instead she added, "I really should have a hat on," and got up to walk indoors.

To her uneasy surprise, the man cradled the tortoise-shell in the crook of his arm and followed her into the house, standing just inside the sala, eyes wide as he scanned the ancient room. He ran his foot over the slate floor, finding the depression that hinted of a thousand years of feet padding from bed to kitchen and kitchen to bed. "Who lived here before you?"

The CatWoman fetched a hat from a peg and turned to go outside, hoping he would follow her lead. "I don't know." Though she walked back to sit on the stones by the spring, the man stayed where he was, running an admiring hand over the carved timber of the doorframe and the heavy double doors, stained dark at the latch from the oil of untold generations of hands.

"Mind if I look at the rest of the house?" he asked.

The CatWoman looked up sharply as he spoke the very words she had dreaded hearing. Her uneasiness must have been obvious, for even as she started, awkwardly, to say, "No," he looked at her directly, saying, "Yes, you *do* mind."

"No—go ahead—it's just—" She dipped her hand into the spring and counted the ripples floating away. "—I'm not used to having someone in my house."

The man hesitated just a moment before setting the tortoise-shell down. "I promise I won't touch anything," he said in the flat tone of one who has just realized his welcome is perhaps not so warm as he had assumed.

The CatWoman chewed on her lip as he disappeared into the house, not so much wanting to follow him as to hurry him through his tour and send him on his way. Hardly the proper sentiment to extend to a long-lost—brother? she wondered. What is he to me now? Nothing. I don't owe him any sort of sentiment. He's trespassing—

He's fine, the tortoise-shell broke into her thoughts, as if reading them carved into the lip she'd been chewing. She glared at the cat without comment, then walked out to the terrace of rosebushes where she found the man's dog lying in the shade, tail in the runoff stream. As she began nervously picking stones from the soil, she wished he would hurry his way through the house, but her ears could easily hear his footsteps inside and he was taking his time. Like I did, she thought, the first time I went inside.

The house was actually quite small, only three rooms. But the details in every window frame, every post, every curve of a plastered wall were so lovingly carved and molded, one couldn't help but stop to admire. She recalled how it had seemed to her like a dollhouse that first day; and yes, it was very old, this much she knew. What held it frozen in such a timeless state of good repair, she didn't know. The roof never leaked, the plaster never cracked, the paint and fresco never faded. Whatever magic had been breathed into this place was far beyond anything she herself could bring about. Of the fifty cats and their nine lives each, not one of those lives had been lived when this magic was being worked. She knew nothing more about the builder than the masterful craft work left behind.

Footsteps on grass announced that the man had left the house, and as he stepped through the courtyard arch, the dog jumped up to greet him with a tail spraying droplets left and right. "I've seen all the old houses in town," he said, ruffling the dog's ears. "They just don't compare to this. You've got a real treasure."

"Yes," the CatWoman answered as she continued to sift rocklets from the soil, sweeping her hand too close to a rosebush and pricking herself. She swallowed a startled cry by putting the cut quickly to her mouth.

"Are you okay?"

"It's nothing—"

"I don't mean the finger." The man's voice was baited with concern. "I mean—you've been alone out here all this time, haven't you?"

"I'm fine," she said, pulling her hand back out of her mouth and resuming her unnecessary attention to the rose terrace.

"Don't you get lonely?"

The CatWoman felt herself go rigid. She turned at last to stare at him as, somewhere beyond the courtyard wall, two cats could be heard arguing over a lounging spot. "No, I don't," she replied stiffly over the muffled yowls of the feline wrestling match, followed at last by a thump as the loser jumped to the tiled floor and stalked off to find a new spot.

With the thump, the concern in the man's eyes hardened and fell away. "Well, Oso and I better be going now," he said. A wave of surprise and relief caught the CatWoman in the back of the knees as she realized she wouldn't have to run him off after all. "It was nice to see you—Josefa—" he added in an awkward search for courtesy to fill the stilted moment, and then moved as if he might hug her.

"Yes—Julio—" she stammered, interrupting the hug as she reached stiffly to shake his hand. But the gesture was met only by an offended look that wilted her effort and her words, "It was good to see you—too—"

He tipped an imaginary hat to her instead and, without another word, hoisted his pack onto his back and turned to follow the runoff stream away into the sage, his dog close behind.

The CatWoman let out a long breath, not realizing she'd been holding it, and felt deflated. I need some sleep, she thought.

⌒⌒⌒

When the CatWoman woke from her nap, the heat of the day had passed and the cicada song in the cottonwoods told her it was early evening. She hadn't meant to sleep so long. Her hair stuck to her forehead and neck when she sat up and her clothes were creased with sharp, damp wrinkles. The floor felt delightfully cool in contrast as she walked barefoot through the house and outdoors.

I don't know how you do it, she said in general to the cats in the courtyard. Having hair just on my head is even too much in the summer.

She splashed herself thoroughly at the spring, not caring that she got her clothes wet; the desert air would dry them soon enough. When she leaned over the spring's pool to look for her reflection, she caught her breath as she found another one—a young Josefa in a laughing pantomime, dipping her head into the water so she could shake and spray back at Julio. The CatWoman ran her hand over the water to touch that laughing face, but it rippled away leaving only her own, softened into a wistful smile. Without thinking, she dipped her head into the water just as the man had done and held herself there until she heard the faint echo of childish laughter. Then she stood up to shake like a dog, prompting the day's second chorus of cat protest as her shaggy hair sprayed the entire courtyard.

The CatWoman laughed then—laughed and laughed until the tension of the morning shook out of her. With a long "Ahhh," she sat down in the grass and ran her hands through the cool green, surprised when one of them came upon a feather. When she picked it out of the grass, she found it was attached to a leather thong with a second feather at the opposite end. Clumsy stitching held the feathers in place, with finer stitches of a different color seemingly added in repair. The leather was soft with age and use.

"He'll miss this." She sighed, remembering the man untying his hair at the spring while she hid indoors. As she twirled a feather in the western light, it shimmered from black to blue, to green, to black again—a buffalo bird's feather. Rats, she thought, her momentary relief fading. If I don't get this back to him, he'll come looking for it.

She looked around at the assembled cats. *Would one of you please do me a favor?* she asked silently. Several dozen faces stared at her blankly. *I need someone to take this thong back to that man.* Still the faces were blank. *Anyone?* They all blinked in unison and none volunteered. *Can I bribe you somehow? Catnip?* Not a word. *What's wrong? Didn't you like him?*

The tortoise-shell spoke up from her perch on a beam under the porch roof. *We liked him. We didn't like his travelling companion.*

I forgot about the dog.

That's because you're only part cat. If you were all cat, you wouldn't have forgotten the dog. Cat snickers murmured through the courtyard at the analysis.

That man is part cat, too, said the CatWoman. *He was my brother once—in my first life.*

I can't even remember my *first life,* spoke up the old calico with a snort. *And when you get to your ninth, you won't remember your first either.*

I doubt that, replied the CatWoman. *It was unforgettably bad.* She looked at the feline assembly once more. *So none of you are going to help me out with this?*

Why don't you take it back? asked the spot-cat. *You're not afraid of the dog.*

The CatWoman looked again at the thong. The fading light had shifted, the feathers no longer held any blue or green. *It's nothing fancy. He probably won't miss it.*

Don't count on it, came the tortoise-shell's voice.

The CatWoman stared at her, knowing she was right. With a "Well, then," she went inside to get some shoes and set out to follow the runoff stream.

The stream widened eventually to a pond where she found the man's small camp, though she didn't find the campers. She waited beyond a ridge of piñons until she was sure the man wasn't there, then walked quickly over to lay the thong out at the head of the bedroll where he would be sure to find it. She surprised herself by being slow to leave, instead looking around at the few things lying about. The man's spilled pack looked huge to her and she could easily imagine how heavy it must have felt, hiking toward the cottonwoods with empty canteens. She recalled how weary she had been the day she first found the spring, and how grateful she'd been that the house was there with a bed inside. The sight of the man's bedroll on the sand with no soft mattress underneath gave her more than a slight twinge of guilt.

After all, he used to be my brother—

She cut off her thoughts when she realized where they were headed. Making sure the thong was in plain sight, she set out upstream and back to the house, nearly bumping head-on into the man as she stepped around a thick piñon. His hair was wet and he had a small towel around his neck. Both of them jumped back in surprise.

"I—uh—found a thong in the courtyard—" she stammered, embarrassed at being caught. "It must be yours. I set it out on your bedroll."

"Thanks—I didn't know how I was going to get that back from you." His voice held in it the same tone she'd seen in his eyes when she tried to shake his hand earlier. "I've been up at your warm spring," he added. "The cats said I could use it—that you were sleeping—"

"*They did?*"

"—so Oso and I were trying to walk quietly."

That's why we didn't hear each other just now, she thought. *We both know how to walk like a cat on the prowl.* "No—you didn't disturb me."

He relaxed enough to nod politely but said no more, walking past her to continue down the path to his camp. The CatWoman opened her mouth to speak, not sure why she would want to say anything more, or just what it was she meant to say. After all, she heard herself thinking again, *he used to be my brother—*

"Are you hungry?" she called after him, amazing herself.

The man stopped to look back in surprise. "Yes." Even at that distance, she could see the hint of a grin sneak into his eyes, though nowhere else on his face. "For anything besides dried stew."

"I have—" She pictured her pantry. The gardens wouldn't be producing for a few weeks yet, and it would be at least that long before the earliest fruits would be ripe in the orchards. "—potatoes. I could fry up some potatoes. If you'd like."

"Anything is better than dried stew."

"I'll be back with some potatoes then."

She had already turned to make her way back to the house when she heard him ask, puzzled, "Back here?"

It was well over an hour by the time the CatWoman returned with a pack full of food and dishes. She found the man leaning up against a rock with a book in his lap, the dog sprawled next to him. Both he and the dog stood up when she appeared, but she waved him away as he went to take the pack from her.

"I can manage it." She unloaded their dinner onto a cloth he'd spread on the ground next to a campfire already hot and ready for cooking. "I don't have much this time of year. If you were here a month from now, I'd have eggplant and apricots."

"Are you inviting me or warning me?" he asked lightly.

"No—" Much to her chagrin, she felt herself blushing. "—I was just—telling you." She turned to begin peeling potatoes and eventually heard the rustle of a page as he went back to his reading. She was curious about the book, but decided not to ask about it. She was curious about the thong, too. In fact, she realized as she chopped potatoes, there were several things she was curious about but was thinking she probably wouldn't ask. Isn't curiosity what killed the—

"Over in town I know people who would sell their own mother to have a warm spring on their land." He spoke from behind her. "If you ever sell this place, you'll make a bundle."

She stopped chopping. *Sell* it? She looked at him and found his eyes were clearly grinning at her. "That's not—possible." At her words, the grin fell from his eyes and was replaced by something she didn't recognize. He went back to his reading and she to her cooking, and when she served the food at last, they ate in long silence.

"Well?" the man asked with his last bite.

"Well, what?"

"Well, why are you here, bearing potatoes? You obviously didn't feel like cooking for me this morning when we met."

The CatWoman felt herself wince inside, remembering the guilt creeping into her at the sight of his bedroll. "Curiosity, maybe."

"Like a cat." His voice was flat. "What do you want to know?"

I want to know what I'm doing here, she thought. "How did you get in?"

"Did you think Mamá only taught her tricks to you?" He tossed a pebble over her head and into the shadowy pond. "Next question."

It took her a moment to think of one. "Why did it take you three days to get here? It's not very far."

"I camped on the gorge rim for awhile. Next question."

"Why are you rushing me?"

"Because I'd rather find out why you're really here. Next question."

"Why do you think I'm here?"

"You're lonely."

She bristled. "How would you know? You don't know me. You barely knew me when we were related and that was four hundred and seventeen years ago."

The man whistled. "Four hundred and seventeen—*you're keeping track?*"

"Aren't you?"

"Not *that* closely." He shook his head and walked to the pond where he splashed water on his face. With his back to her, the Cat-Woman saw his hair was tied again with the thong she had returned and, in the light from the campfire, the feathers lay flat black and dull against his faded shirt. "You're right." He sighed. "I hardly knew you then, you were so much younger."

"Did you make the thong in your hair?" she asked quietly.

"No, my great-grandson made it."

"You have a *great-grandson?*"

"You'd never know it, looking at me, huh?" He laughed to himself and returned to the fire. "Actually, he's not related to me this time around, but his mother's father was my son—last time." He untied his hair and ran the soft leather tenderly through his fingers. "That was the first and last time I'll *ever* be a soldier."

"You were killed?" Her voice cracked and her mouth went dry as somewhere deep inside her the memory beast awakened.

"Uh-huh. The only time I've died young, though. I've lived long enough to know my grandchildren every other time. And now I'm a teacher—headmaster, actually—at my great-grandson's school." He twirled one of the thong's feathers between his fingers, just as she had done when she found it. "He made this for me when he was twelve. I really appreciate you bringing it back."

"What if I hadn't?"

"I would have crept in like a cat tonight and looked for it."

Hisses and crackles from the dying campfire were all that was heard in the moments it took for the CatWoman to consider this—that he would have been prowling around her courtyard among the cats, too silent even for her cat ears to hear. It was not a comfortable thought.

"So I think you're lonely," the man said at last, leaning back to look at the stars while she watched the liquid flames. "And I think you just wanted to hear another person's voice—someone who's living through what you're living through."

The CatWoman felt the memory beast pull slowly back into its cave at his soft voice. "How long will you be camping here?" she asked, her voice barely louder than the flames she watched.

"Only as long as I'm welcome," he replied.

"You're welcome."

"Thank you."

She left soon after that, making her way easily through the night to her dark house. Sleep was the last thing on her mind after the day's long nap. But no sooner had her head touched the pillow than a dreamless sleep floated her down the quiet night river till morning.

⟨◯◯◯⟩

The CatWoman didn't see the man again for three days, though the cats kept her well informed of his activities. It seemed he was exploring the mesa in all directions. He found the hot spring a few miles to the north and the salt cedar marsh feathering its runoff. He spent a whole afternoon sitting atop the tallest of the sandstone buttes to the west, doing nothing more than enjoy the vista. He sang to the coyotes each night, lying in the moonlight long after his campfire died, and, quite suspicious to the cats, the coyotes sang back. Sometimes, they said, the man would even wake in the middle of the night to strike up this sagebrush opera anew, long after coyotes and cats had gone to sleep.

Intriguing, the CatWoman found herself thinking. She had kept close to the house during this time, not sure if she was trying to avoid meeting him on a trail somewhere or trying to be easy to find should he seek her out. By the third evening she knew she was trying to be easily found, but no one was looking for her.

Is he still here? she asked the tortoise-shell as darkness fell around the house and its sheltering cottonwoods.

Yes.

I'm surprised he doesn't come by here.

Maybe he doesn't feel welcome.

I told him he was.

To camp, yes. To visit? No. He knows you're skittish about having him here.

The CatWoman's sigh was lost on a small breeze tiptoeing into the courtyard from the south. *I suppose I'll have to go invite him.*

Better hurry. The tortoise-shell spoke with eyes at half-mast. *He'll be leaving tomorrow or the next day.*

How do you know?

He's running out of food.

Morning glories were just opening to the sun's eastern glow when the CatWoman reached the man's camp the next morning. He was already up and tending a pot over a fire. She had from habit been using her cat walk, and he was startled enough to nearly spill the pot's contents onto the fire when she said from behind him, "Good morning."

"I didn't know anyone got up as early as I do." He gestured with the pot. "If you'd like some coffee, we'll have to share this cup. I'm all out after this."

"No, you drink it. I have some at the house." She forgot the invitation she had rehearsed as she walked, blurting out instead, "I hear you're out of food."

"Those cats don't miss a thing." He laughed. He seemed to be altogether past his sober mood of a few nights ago.

"You can eat at the house tonight." When he didn't answer, but merely raised his eyebrows at her, the CatWoman heard her awkward non-invitation echoing in the silence of his non-reply. "If you'd like," she added.

"Yes, I'd like." He poured his coffee into a tin cup. "When should I be there?"

"I don't have a clock. Late in the day."

"I'll be there."

As she left him to drink his coffee, his eyes were telling a joke in a language the CatWoman didn't speak.

∞∞∞

With no rain in over a week, the orchards and gardens were needing the CatWoman's attention that day. Throughout its long, slow arc, the sun watched her direct the cold spring's runoff into an intricate series of channels that wove a spiderweb down the hill from the house. Irrigating was a job she looked forward to all winter long—wading and shovelling new paths for the water as each terrace and orchard was quenched. It was slow work and long work, as what began in a stream ended in a trickle at the foot of each tree. There were times when the CatWoman had to remind herself the water was actually there, hidden as it was under the mat of orchard grass. Then suddenly, she would look up late in the day and, in the sun's lowering angle, the still water would look like a glass floor under the trees, telling her the work was done.

The glassy sheen hadn't quite hit the east orchard yet when the man's voice startled her. "You look like a barefoot contessa."

"Is it that late?"

"It's late in the day. Don't hurry."

"This orchard is nearly done—you can wait up at the house."

He leaned on an old cherry tree, heavy with still-young fruit. "I'd rather help."

"I don't need help—"

"I figured."

The CatWoman looked up at his quick retort. There was that joke in his eyes again, making it seem he was grinning when he wasn't. She went back to shovelling a little self-consciously until he wandered off to look at the other orchards. Once she relaxed again into the work, it went quickly, and soon she was walking up to the house. The man caught up to her and took the shovel from her hand, and when she began to protest, "I can—" he laughed and put up a hand to stop her.

"I *know* you can. I'd like to earn my supper."

When they reached the courtyard, the CatWoman went into

the house while the man stayed on the porch, negotiating with the cats for a place to sit. *So, are you growing roots on that banco, or what?* she heard him ask. *You've been in that same spot since I was here a few days ago.*

No, I haven't. I was in your lap when you were sitting at the spring.

It must be the tortoise-shell, thought the CatWoman, walking into the pantry.

At the spring? I was sitting at the spring?

Don't you remember? You put your head in the water and sprayed us all.

No, I don't remember it. Gee, I hope I'm not getting sunstroke. I'd never remember where I put those cans of tuna I was saving for you.

Tuna? came a chorus from all cats present.

Have a seat, said the tortoise-shell, and the CatWoman heard her move aside.

The pantry was still sparsely stocked. Potatoes. She gathered a handful and carried them out to a small circle of stones in the courtyard where she set about arranging kindling on ground already well-blackened from previous fires. The man was comfortably seated with feet up on a stool and the tortoise-shell was on her back next to him, getting a belly rub. As the CatWoman stepped back from the heat of eager flames, he offered, "I'll watch the fire, if you want to go wash up."

She looked down at her muddy legs. "I didn't realize what a mess I am."

"Nothing like having a second pair of eyes around to let you know how you look."

"True," she said, feeling self-conscious again and not noticing if the joke was still in his eyes. Slipping through the house and out the back door, she climbed the path to the warm spring to wash off. When she returned, she sat in front of a small mirror in the bedroom, brushing her damp hair and trying to see herself through a second pair of eyes in the fading light of the dark old house. She lit a candle.

In each of her lives, her hair had been one dark shade or another. In this fifth life, her hair was the same as the tortoise-shell's, gliding smoothly through all the shades of autumn—from the brown of dry leaves to the gold and red of those still to fall, from the grey of branches about to sleep to the glossy black of charcoal when those branches are burned. She had lived through years of ridicule as a child this time, because of her odd hair, and had learned to keep it short and under a hat. Since living alone on the mirage, though, she'd let it grow out and only wore hats to keep the sun off, or when she ventured into town. The cats found her hair quite ordinary.

Ordinary was the word she would have used to describe her face, not her hair. It was unremarkable, even as seen through a second pair of eyes. Sun and wind were obviously waging a constant battle with the home remedies she had lavished on her skin through years of tending gardens and orchards. What she saw in the mirror was an impasse—skin neither rough nor smooth, but softened and glowing slightly in the candlelight after a day outdoors. Her eyes were a green-gold she had never seen on any human, except for the man outside who was once her brother.

The thought of his eyes pulled her thoughts away from the mirror, and she dressed quickly. Her hair was still damp as she stepped outside and she could feel it stand slightly away from her in the hot, still air. The man was now seated on the grass by the fire pit where, even in the twilight, she could see him grin as she stepped beyond the shadow of the porch.

"I put them on—they'll be ready soon." He gestured toward a goatskin she'd seen looped over his shoulder earlier. "Do you have any wineglasses?"

"You carry wine when you *camp?*"

"Hey—it's the only civilized way to dine."

The CatWoman smiled back in spite of herself. "I haven't had a glass of wine since I went to town last spring." She gathered wine-glasses and dishes, and a cloth to spread on the ground. "Where is your dog?" she asked as he poured the wine.

"I told him to stay at the camp. He feels a little outmatched by the cats." He handed her a glass and lifted his own. "To wine and potatoes," he said grandly.

"To wine and potatoes," she echoed, and raised the glass to take a long, slow sniff of the wine's breath. Eyes closed, she let the wine-breath whisper through her nose into her head as a breeze whispered its way through the courtyard, rippling the cotton-wood leaves overhead and breaking what was left of the day's heat. Cats who had spent the day stretched in the shade now curled slightly for the cooler evening ahead. Cicadas were in mid-concert all through the trees, singing the darkness in.

"How often do you go to town?" the man asked.

"Twice a year. There isn't much I end up needing that I don't grow here myself."

"I'll bet you're a hit with the commune crowd."

She looked at him, puzzled.

"Missed that phase in history? Never mind. What did you do before you moved up here?"

She sighed. "Looked all over for a mirage I could live on."

"You have the money to do that?"

"Had." The wine and firelight began to sing a soft duet inside her head. "I used the money to buy a ticket away from people. A hundred mirages later I found this one, so here I am."

"And your family?"

"I haven't seen them in years."

"Don't you think they miss you?"

She felt herself stiffen. "I doubt it. I was a bit of an—oddball."

Sudden laughter startled her out of the evening's muted symphony. "I'm not surprised, with hair like yours," he chuckled, as she froze with wineglass midway to her lips. "I've been an oddball myself every time too, without the markings. Except my eyes—they attract some attention."

"Mine, too," she agreed, as she finished the wineglass' path a little stiffly.

"And before you opened mirages?"

"I went to college. Majored in history."

"So did I. A natural choice, don't you think?"

"It was a joke," she said, disgusted. "All the books talked about were wars, as if nothing else happened in the world. What *really* happened—what *I* lived through—was never in the books. I used to write papers about what really happened and ended up arguing for a grade with some idiot who learned history out of a book."

When the man didn't respond, she looked to see a teasing sparkle in his eyes that she was ready to believe was only the firelight, until he said, "I'll bet you're a terror in an argument." Vague second thoughts about inviting him to dinner wove themselves into the duet in her head, making a trio. She reached for the shovel to fuss with the fire.

"The potatoes are probably done," she said, noticing the sparkle died somewhere between his comment and hers. The first potato she unearthed was a bit undercooked but edible.

"I love teaching history," he said as they ate. "When the door's closed, I get to put the books aside and tell the kids *my* version, based on experience. I don't tell them that, of course," he added.

"Do you think it does any good?"

"Yes, I do." He took a last bite and set his plate aside. "Or I wouldn't do it."

The CatWoman set her plate aside as well, pulling her knees up as a perch for her chin. In the flames before her, she saw thousands of previous fires in her lives—for heating, for cooking, for company. The trio in her head struck a discord as she saw that other, terrifying fire she'd known once, and the dissonance woke the memory beast once again. She fought to put it back to sleep. "I don't see how you can talk about it," she said.

"I *love* to talk about it."

"I get—seasick—if I remember too well." Her voice sounded, even to her own ears, as four hundred years' tired. She leaned to put fresh wood in the fire pit as the air put aside its daytime touch and was now cool on her bare arms.

"What name were you given this time?" he asked.

"The CatWoman."

"That's perfect—but no, really, what's your name?"

"Kat. K-A-T." She absently coaxed a flame from the bed of coals. "Don't ask me if they were onto something. I doubt it. They weren't that kind of people. I haven't used the name since I've lived out here." She stopped her hand in mid-poke and sat back on her heels, silent a moment. "When you live alone, away from people, what's a name? I'm a woman who lives surrounded by cats. The CatWoman." Darkness had settled around them, making the embers glow even more orange-hot in the fire pit. She let the drone of the cicadas settle around them as well.

He lay back on the grass, staring at the splattering of stars thrown against the night. Far beyond their circle of light, coyote pups were being called to their den. "Yip yip-a-you too!" he called under his breath, then rolled on his side to ask, "What's your last name?"

"Why?"

"I want to know if we're related."

"Well, I suppose it would be unlikely—given the number of people who've been born since we—" Again the cicadas' song fell around them as she drifted off.

"Since we were brother and sister," he finished for her.

"O'Malley. Kat O'Malley."

He rolled back onto the grass again, laughing a deep, hearty laugh. How many years had it been since she'd made someone laugh, since she'd sat talking with someone? A tiny flame, orange and hot as the embers between them, shot through her and faded. For that instant, she felt she'd missed out on something precious. "What are you laughing at?"

"Nothing, nothing, it's just—" His laughter slowed to a chuckle. "—I was born this time into a family who never once said anything good about the Irish. That settles it, then. We're definitely not related." He chuckled at something from that history she didn't share with him, and again the feeling came to her of having missed out somehow. The symphony in her head went discordant once again.

"What's your name?" she asked, trying to turn her attention away from what was now an annoying crescendo inside her.

"Angelo diVita. Italian on both sides. And yes, I've eaten well this time around."

"Oh?"

"Sure. The Italians taught the world how to cook. And—" He leaned close enough to her she could smell faintly the wine on his breath. His voice was low and conspiratorial. "—and the Irish failed the final exam."

She wondered uncomfortably if he could smell wine on her breath, then wondered why she wondered. "What do you mean?"

"See for yourself," he said, nodding toward the fire pit without taking his eyes off hers. "Potatoes. That's all they know how to cook."

A flush rose in her, singeing her cheeks as she was suddenly aware she'd been leaning toward him, her eyes not on his eyes but on his mouth as he spoke. She sat up stiffly and looked away, burying her gaze in the embers. From the corner of her eye, she saw him hesitate a moment, then lean back on his elbows. The cicada song receded as a breeze played through the cottonwood trees and the cotton folds of her skirt, which she gathered more tightly around her knees.

When he spoke, his voice had a distinctly impatient edge. "You've been away from people too long. You don't know when you're being teased."

The edge in his voice sliced through the wine and crescendo in her head, making the hairs bristle on the back of her neck. "I liked Julio better," she said tightly, and got up to leave. She wasn't three steps beyond the emberlight when his own tight voice held her back.

"I'm not Julio anymore—and you're not Josefa. That life is *over*."

"You act like you *like* this!" she spat, spinning so quickly she startled both herself and him. "You make it sound like you're having *fun*, like it's some *lark!*" She waved her hand and imitated his voice. "Yes, I guess I'll have *Italian* this time, they eat so well, and you know they taught us all how to cook. And after that, gee I don't know—maybe I'll have *Chinese!*" She stalked off toward the house, the symphony in full forte in her head, pulling up short at the crash of glass shattering on stone.

"Yes, I AM having fun!" The cottonwoods trembled overhead. "I've been having a DAMN GOOD TIME!"

She glared icily at him across the dark courtyard. "You broke my plate."

"Good! Now maybe you'll break out of this cocoon of yours and go get some more." He reached for a wineglass.

"Don't break my things!" she hissed, running across the grass to gather the wineglasses quickly into her hands and out of his reach.

"What, may I ask, is wrong with having a good time?" His voice had dropped, the trees were still. "How many *centuries* has it been since you thawed out a little bit?"

She caught her breath at the sting of sarcasm, and the symphony abruptly halted. The air around her felt electric in the silence, even crackling slightly. "How many do you think?"

"About four."

"About four," she echoed.

He shook his head. "You can't tell me you let four hundred years go by—"

"*Let* them go by!"

"—without having some kind of fun somewhere along the way. What the hell have you been doing all this time?"

"What have I been *doing?*" She hated the shrill in her voice and could do nothing to stop it. "What have I been *doing?*" Every muscle in her body was tensed and, like a spring unwinding, she spun toward the circle of embers and smashed one of the glasses against a stone, spraying shards against her bare ankles. "Let me *enumerate* for you!"

"Your hair—" His voice sounded suddenly concerned as he stood to take a step toward her, but she put up her hand to stop him.

"One! I was burned at the stake for a witch because my own mother taught me the very dangerous art of bringing down a fever without saying any prayers. Two! I was drowned as a witch after I had an argument with a man who went and got himself so stinking drunk he couldn't find his way home and he accused me of casting a spell on him. Three! I was stoned to death by a mob who thought there was something a little 'witchy' about a girl who was so well-liked by cats." She was crouched, panting, holding the one wineglass to her breast and her free hand out to keep him away. "And four! I died in childbirth with my *thirteenth* child because the jerk I was married to wanted a son at any cost." She staggered slightly, caught her balance. "And you come in here out of four *hundred* years of nowhere to tell me I need to be around people more!"

The crackling in the air around her had built to a roar, neither symphony nor cicada song, pounding through her head like an angry surf. While her entire body shook with each breaking wave, his was perfectly still. Neither said a word for a very long moment. Then he whispered, "You had *thirteen girls?*"

"Yes!" she screamed, smashing the last wineglass into the tiniest of airborne arrows, all above and around them. The sound of the exploding glass punctured her, deflated her, and she swayed on her feet feeling suddenly sick. He caught her from falling, but she pushed herself away, standing alone and still until the echo of the smashing glass and the roar in her head died down a bit. With a long, hoarse breath shuddering out of her, she whispered, "I had *thirteen girls,*" then stumbled through the dark courtyard and into the house.

She heard no footsteps behind her, and if he left the courtyard, it must have been very late, long after she'd fallen asleep exhausted from the pounding in her head and the pitch and roll of her memories.

∞∞∞

You look awful.

The CatWoman rolled over to see who'd spoken. It was the tortoise-shell, perched like a ship at anchor on the pillow she hadn't used all night.

"You're no help," she answered out loud, then stopped with a groan. The pounding in her head was gone, leaving a hammered-out chamber that echoed her every word. Wrapping the blanket over her head to shut out both light and sound, she asked silently, *Is he still here?* and found even the thought-talk echoed and rattled inside her.

Yes.

The CatWoman rubbed tentatively through her hood, where each and every hair felt as if it had been yanked out by the roots. She pulled the blanket away to make sure her head wasn't bald.

That was some glass of wine, she said to the cat, who only smirked in reply. *Why is he still here?*

Ask him yourself. The tortoise-shell got up to stretch first her front legs, then her back legs, then turned and hopped off the bed. *He gave us tuna for breakfast,* she added, just as her tail disappeared with a twitch through the cracked door.

"Tuna?" The CatWoman pulled herself up slowly, holding on to the windowsill above the bed. Morning was already shaking hands with afternoon, from the looks of the shadows outside in the courtyard. Her feet found the floor just as her eyes found the skirt she'd worn last night, crumpled now and lying half under the bed. It took several minutes to get dressed, with one hand busy holding the pillow to her aching head. She let her feet guide her along the worn depression in the cool floor from bedroom to kitchen, where she found the man sitting with arms crossed on the table in front of him, watching her with what she supposed was a silent chuckle.

"You look awful," he said.

She winced at the sound and sat down on the banco along the wall. "I've been told that—already—once today—thank you." She leaned back gingerly to rest her head against the pillow and the soft plaster.

"Do you want something?"

"What's good for a hangover?"

"I don't think you have a hangover."

She shifted the pillow so she could see him, trying to sound a skeptical "Hmm," but managing only to sound like she was in a lot of pain.

The chuckle in his eyes nearly spilled out onto his face, but she saw him rein it in. "Have you ever—" he began, then stopped. "Of course you haven't."

"Have I ever what?"

The eye-chuckle broke free of its rein. "Had an argument in front of a mirror."

The CatWoman closed her eyes. "You make no sense at all to me," she whispered. "But I've been told you have some tuna."

"Had. I gave it all to the cats."

"Rats," she whispered, then giggled at the sound of the rhyme, then moaned with the pain of the giggle. "Why do you ask?"

"You really don't know?" She waved her hand and shrugged. His chair creaked and she knew, with her eyes closed, that he'd leaned away from the table, stretching his legs out across the dark floor. "You've had it rough," he said softly. A few minutes of silence waltzed between them before he added, "And I've only had it rough some of the time."

"Do you see now why I stay away from people?"

He didn't answer, but instead she heard him stand and move his chair across the floor to the banco. He moved her hands off the pillow and began to massage her head ever so gently, until she felt herself relaxing away from the headache. "You don't have a hang-over," he said after awhile. "You barely had two sips of wine before that glass fell out of your hand—"

"Fell! Ha!" she laughed, eyes still closed, and her head didn't echo quite so badly this time. "That's helping."

"What? Making you laugh?"

"No—" She reached up to stop his hands and held them, shyly, for just an instant before she sat back again and let him resume. "Yes."

"You know, I had a lot of time to think last night while I was trying to find a comfortable position in the grass."

"You didn't go back to your camp?"

"No. I thought I'd better stay. After all, I'd just led you into your first screamer argument in six years and I was feeling responsible." The CatWoman knew, if she'd taken off the pillow, she would see that joke laughing out of his eyes again. "So I lay there rolling

over every few minutes, thinking two things: One, I was right—
you're a terror in an argument."

She groaned.

"And two—you're uniquely qualified to teach history."

"Not unique. You're qualified in the same way I am."

"So we both are. But I was thinking about you, and thinking
it's a long shot, but—would you come teach history at my school
in the fall?"

She took off the pillow and looked at him as if he'd lost his
mind. "You've got to be joking."

"No—for once, I'm not."

"You said I don't know when I'm being teased. Are you teasing
me now?"

"No."

She shook her head. "Well, I think you're crazy."

"That's possible, but besides what you think of me, what do
you think of the idea?"

"It's crazy." He started to speak but she cut him off. "And no, I
won't do it."

"You're passing up a golden opportunity here."

"I found my golden opportunity when I found this mirage.
That's all the opportunity I need for this lifetime."

"I'm offering you the chance to mold the next generation. And
hey—after all you've been through? Seems like you'd have a keen
interest in doing that."

The afternoon aged gently as the CatWoman held his gaze,
considering. He truly didn't look anything like the brother she'd
once had. In fact, it was hard to imagine this face on that brother,
riding the fine horses their father had trained. Nowhere on this
face was the haughty look of a young caballero, decked in silver
that jangled heavily against the wiry, leather-clad body of a not-
yet-man. The face in front of her now looked as if it had seen life
from the ground this time, and maybe many times before this.

"You know, Kat—if you'll allow me to use the name—"

"Go ahead."

"Good. It suits you." He put the pillow back on her head and began to massage again. "I think you're wasting away out here. You're young—"

"I'm four hundred and twenty-three."

"You know what I mean. *This time*, you're young, you're intelligent, and you're wasting all your gifts on a herd of cats and a home that doesn't even exist."

The CatWoman felt the same heat rising inside her that she'd felt the night before. "It's not a waste. It's the first time in five lifetimes that I've been able to live out of the reach of mobs." The heat singed her throat and choked her voice. "Do you have any idea what it's like to be *stoned to death?*"

His hands slowed and his answer was long in coming. "No. It must be horrible."

"It's—beyond horrible." The memories shot suddenly through her, icicles after a heat wave, making her shiver.

"And may it never happen to another person. Ever."

"Ever," she whispered. "No one."

His voice was barely louder than the buzzing of hummingbirds out the window as they shopped the morning glory vines. "That's why I teach, Kat." He pulled the pillow off her head and set it in her lap. "So that no one will be stoned to death, or burned, or drowned ever again." The icicles began to melt, the heat wave slowly cooled. "You know, if everyone were going to live nine lives, they'd be a lot more careful about what they set in motion in their first eight." He brushed her pillow-tousled hair back from her face. "I'm going to leave tomorrow. You don't have to give me an answer before I go."

"But I *have* given you my answer," she protested.

"I'll be back in a month. You can give me a final answer then."

"But—"

He moved his hand over her lips. "I won't listen till you've slept on it for a month. Besides," he added, running his finger slowly down the ridge of her nose to rest over her lips, "I want to collect on the eggplant and apricots you were promising me."

She shook her head. "I was warning you," she said, her voice muffled under his fingers.

He grinned. "Hey—I *knew* you could tease back."

Early the next morning, the tortoise-shell announced that the man and his dog were gone. A week earlier, the CatWoman would have greeted the news with immense relief. Today, she felt just a touch melancholy.

I don't understand me, she mused as she heated water to wash her face.

It's territory, the tortoise-shell explained. *You feel your territory. He stepped on it and you felt it. You'd feel it even more if you had fur and whiskers.*

What do you mean "if" I had fur? I do have fur. The water was hot and she began washing her face. *I didn't get this hair from my human side.*

You're blessed, the cat replied, sitting up to wash her own face as well. *Not all cats get such beautiful coloring. And certainly no humans do.*

No one thought I was blessed when I was born. More like cursed.

Humans don't appreciate variety.

"That's no joke," the CatWoman mumbled.

Cats don't mind when their kittens come in all colors. The more the better.

Well, people could learn a lot from cats.

The tortoise-shell finished her face and began to wash her chest. *True. But people have been living with cats and not learning from them for a long time. I suspect they're not capable.*

Nor would they learn from someone who's part cat. Julio's idea is ridiculous.

The tortoise-shell interrupted her bath to look up at the Cat-Woman. *I heard him say his name. It's not Julio.*

Angelo, then. The CatWoman splashed the last of the soap bubbles from her face and reached for a towel. *I still think of him as my brother.*

But he isn't. You start over fresh each time. And the ones who survive are the ones who never forget that. The tortoise-shell went back to preening her chest. *For example, I haven't always been a tortoise-shell, but if I kept thinking of myself as the cat I was seven lives ago, how could I survive? I'm not a panther now—*

You were a panther?

The tortoise-shell gave a prim nod. *Big and black.*

I didn't realize cats—switched around—

We're all cats. She sneezed a delicate cat-sneeze. *The point is, even though I haven't forgotten myself as a panther and all I needed to know about living in the jungle, it's of no use to me now. I'm a tortoise-shell. I live in the desert. If I ever forgot that, I'd be dead.*

What's it like to be a panther? the CatWoman asked into the soft pile of the towel.

The tortoise-shell didn't answer. She stopped preening and crouched slowly, paws tucked under. Her eyes narrowed, and the CatWoman heard her breath change from the near-silent whisper of a house cat to the guarded, cavernous echo of a much larger cat. The adobe-softened light of the kitchen faded nearly to black as it became the evernight of the jungle. The CatWoman soon felt the cavernous breathing come from her own chest, and with each breath, she tasted every droplet of air for the scent of creatures lying hidden in the damp and dark. She felt the sleek weight of muscles tensed and ready to pounce, ready to spring into that darkness. A growling rose in her stomach behind the tension, behind the tasting, and drove her eyes and ears and nose to be keen in a world darker and damper than the CatWoman had ever imagined. Food. She needed food. The growling came in bursts, never letting her attention wander. Food. She heard from some corner of darkness the waddling of soft feet, their steps muted on the moist, rotting jungle floor. The tension in her muscular legs shifted noiselessly, her entire heavy body focussing on the waddling noise. Her breath nearly stopped, absolutely silent now as it passed shallowly through her opened mouth. With no light filtering down through the trees above, her eyes still found their target, driven by the growling inside her. Tense—crouch—taste the air one last time—the CatWoman felt her huge body spring loose, riding the unleashed tension now, out and away and onto the unsuspecting creature, stunned and dead by the sheer weight of the fall. Blood and sinew filled her mouth, slowing her body, slowing her heart, filling her stomach at last until the growling stopped and she felt heavy with sleep . . .

. . . sleep . . .

The image disappeared as a dream at dawn, and the Cat-Woman saw before her the tortoise-shell she'd known for six years, yawning. "What did you *do?*" she whispered.

I showed you the world through my eyes.

But how?

With my eyes—and the breath, said the cat, making her way leisurely to the floor and out into the morning brightness. *Every good story begins with the breath.*

A week later, as the full moon rose over the mountains on the east side of the river gorge, the CatWoman realized she had lost track of her usual timepieces: the risings of sun, moon, and stars, the daily rhythm of cicada songs, the openings and closings of morning glories. The moon reminded her she had lately been marking time not by the cyclic rhythms of her world but by the syncopation that had stepped so suddenly onto her mirage.

It's been eight days since he left, she thought.

As always on a full-moon night, the CatWoman was sitting in the courtyard at the fire pit, small flame-fingers poking at the darkness before her. She hadn't slept through a full moon since she arrived on the mirage-mesa, looking forward to the coyote songs that would keep her out under the stars till dawn. This month, however, the full moon took her by surprise. She had passed the last week slightly out of step with the waltz of her world, which danced on without her nonetheless. The waxing moon fattened fruit in the orchards and enticed greens to reach high and wide beyond the garden soil. Roses opened from bud to flower, one satin petal at a time, bringing to crescendo the first rose chorus of the season. In the past, the CatWoman had anticipated each of these swellings and reachings and crescendos. The timing of them had become, in six years, second nature to her. Now, she found herself surprised each morning since the man had left his syncopation reverberating in her world—the apricots were riper than she'd expected, the eggplants were fuller, the roses were already in their first prime.

And the moon was full. Again.

My mind is somewhere else, she mused. A pair of smoke grey kittens were draped on her lap asleep. They were still too young to speak except in image-jumbles the CatWoman couldn't understand, but they could understand her when she called them from the porch to join her. A few assorted adults were at anchor just beyond the circle of firelight, staring at the flames as she did, mesmerized and thoughtful. Among them was the old calico, the one in her ninth life. Try as she might, the CatWoman could not picture her as anything but a crotchety old house cat. The thought of her as a panther made her giggle.

Have you always been a calico? she asked the old cat.

Flames reflected hypnotically in the calico's eyes as she turned slowly to reply, *No, I was a cinder siamese once.*

Were you ever anything big?

I was a bobcat, twice.

It was a difficult image for the CatWoman to conjure. *The tortoise-shell told me—showed me—I don't know how she did it, but she showed me what it's like to be a panther.*

She's an exceptional storyteller. Better than most.

It was a story? But it seemed so real.

The calico grunted and turned back to the flames. *Of course it was real. She really* was *a panther.*

Coyote yips bounced faintly along the edge of the mesa. The CatWoman closed her eyes and forgot the old cat, letting the coyote song fill her as it grew steadily louder, fuller. She could see in her mind's eye the cluster of coyotes, scraggly now with their winter coats gone, singing each other into a lively moonlit party to send the full moon along its path. There would be old ones showing off their voices for the young ones, mothers nursing pups, pups wrestling and tumbling over one another in the dirt. One voice, more eloquent than the rest, separated itself in the CatWoman's mind—this would be the one of the pack with the most stories to tell. The other voices faded out, leaving this one to solo for a moment before rejoining with an emphatic chorus. Coyote mischief and coyote jokes sang out across the mesa in story after story until finally, with the moon at its highest, the solo-chorus-solo died down, the last tale ended, and the pups were put to bed. The new silence woke the kittens in the CatWoman's lap just long enough for them to re-settle upon each other before dozing off again. She stroked them until they purred in their sleep, and she thought she heard one of them say, *Ahh.*

Into her mind came an image of the man, Angelo, singing with the coyotes when he was camping at the pond. What did the cats call it? An opera. He was striking up midnight operas, and the coyotes *sang back to him*. Maybe they like his stories, she thought, smiling in the dark at the idea. She heard again in her mind that solo coyote voice and put Angelo's face on it, laughing and crying and surrounded by a chorus. Then as suddenly as it had begun, the coyote voice was gone, Angelo's face was gone, and into her mind came a lone mourning cry, soaring across the vast, dark plains of her imagination. Lost love, lost children, lost hope—the cry wailed across years and miles and lifetimes, one long, lonely note. Before the CatWoman could identify the sound, that note flew her out to the full moon to look back on the mesa, the house, the courtyard, the campfire—and beside the campfire she saw a wolf, head thrown back in a howl.

The CatWoman's eyes shuddered open. The kittens in her lap were sitting with heads up, ears intent on the mournful aria. Every cat ear in the courtyard was trained on the cry, riding it as it wafted over and over through the night air.

I didn't know there was a wolf on the mesa, she thought, staring into the shrinking flames of her campfire so intently the flames and the wolf's cry became one. Flickering inside the circled stones was the lonely singer, head back, eyes half shut. The CatWoman lost track of the courtyard and the cats, even the fire, as she felt a cry rise inside her to match that of the flame-wolf. She didn't know if what she heard was herself or the wolf, or a song her mind had conjured, aided by the full moon at its peak. All she knew or felt was the pulling of this song from so deep inside her, pulling out into the lacquer night. At last the song changed, tipped back toward earth to float and land, leaving the mesa again in silence. The flame-wolf faded with the song's descent, her head leaning forward again, and she turned to face the CatWoman. With the last flicker of the image, the CatWoman saw the wolf's eyes, and realized they were her own.

She felt suddenly desperately alone. She hugged the two startled kittens and buried a choked sob in the bundle of their fur.

∞

When the moon reached its third quarter, the air on the mesa was as dry as the CatWoman had ever felt it. There had been no rain for a month, and she was irrigating at least one garden or orchard every day. The work kept her busy and tired, and left her sleep thankfully free of dreams and images. She was throwing herself body and soul into the farming, hoping to catch up to the rhythm she'd lost the week before. Every shovelful of dirt was artfully dug, every trickle of water hand-led to each tree. Each and every leaf was studied carefully for signs of change, each flower for signs of fruit, each fruit for signs of ripeness. The gardens and orchards became her university.

It won't work.

The tortoise-shell's opinion came at the CatWoman from below as she was seated halfway up a large cherry tree, examining the reddening fruit. *What won't work?* she asked absently.

This game, this pretense.

Game?

The gardens will get along without all this muttering and puttering. Pay attention to what's distracting you—it's more important.

I don't need advice from a cat.

Everyone needs advice from a cat.

Is that so? Well then, advise me, dear cat. What should I be doing?

Deciding whether or not you're going to stay here.

"Of course I'm going to stay here!" the CatWoman gasped.

Then why are you dreaming about taking Angelo up on his offer?

I am not! I haven't dreamed in a week.

You've been talking in your sleep about it.

I don't talk in my sleep.

I'm in a better position to know that than you are.

The CatWoman sighed and held her hand to her eyes as if the close scrutiny of fruit were tiring them. The tortoise-shell turned to leave. *I see you're in no mood to discuss this,* she said, walking away. When she was past the edge of the trees and stepping onto the path, the CatWoman called out to her.

"Wait—" The cat turned and sat where she was. The Cat-Woman could barely see her through the fruit-heavy branches. *How long have I been talking in my sleep?*

Nine nights.

Since the full moon—never before that?

Never coherently before that.

The CatWoman leaned her forehead onto the branch in front of her. The image of the flame-wolf passed briefly through her. *What did I say? I don't remember any dreams.*

The first night you said you were a wolf.

The CatWoman closed her eyes.

The next night you were a coyote, the tortoise-shell continued, *and after that you were asking me how to be a panther. On the fourth night you said you had a story you wanted to tell, and you've been trying to tell it ever since.*

"What story?" She heard herself whisper the words even as she thought them.

I don't recall word-for-word. You didn't get it out very well.

What story?

About a young woman who found out how hot fire can be—that's how you start, and—

That's enough. I know the story.

The tortoise-shell walked back to the cherry tree and climbed the trunk to sit at eye level with her. *Tell me the story.*

The CatWoman's autumn-colored hair rocked side to side as she shook her head. *I can't leave here—*

Tell me just the beginning of the story.

—this is the only place I've ever been safe—ever—
Tell me what it's like to be a little girl—
I'd rather live alone forever than be killed by a mob again.

—with a mother who could bring down a fever—without saying any prayers. The CatWoman heard the tortoise-shell's voice come from years away. *Let me see your eyes—and start with the breath . . .*

The CatWoman opened her eyes and gulped for air. She saw before her folds of coarse cotton, stained and yellowed, and smelling of sweat and horses. All around her was the smell of horses and hay in various stages of sweet and rot. Beyond the smell and the cotton, she heard a contralto voice singing softly, "Pobrecita mijita, brillarás como estrellita, cantarás en voz dulcecita, mañana, mañana, mijita." She lifted her head just enough to see over the folds and saw a big-boned woman seated at a table, silhouetted by the flickering of a candle. "Mamá," she called in a tiny, raspy voice. The woman moved from the table to sit on the edge of the bed. Her large, cool hand lay on the CatWoman's forehead a moment, pushing damp hair away from her face. "Josefita pobrecita," cooed the low voice. When her big hands grasped the CatWoman under the arms to pull her from the blankets, her body felt like a rag doll. The woman held her crooked in one arm, rocking gently. "Duérmete," she whispered, over and over again, rocking and stroking her damp hair until the Cat-Woman felt herself lose hold of the smell of horses, lose hold of the feel of big arms around her . . .

The image faded, and her gaze focussed once again on the tortoise-shell before her, perched on the limb of a cherry tree on a hot, cloudless day. She felt dizzy, grasping the cherry limb with a white-knuckled clutch. The drumroll of her heart would not slow easily, and she hung on to the branch until she shuddered a last long breath and sagged against the tree.

What was she singing? asked the cat.

The CatWoman wiped beads of sweat off her forehead as the

big-boned woman had done in the memory. *It was a song she made up for me when I was sick—you'll shine like a star, you'll sing—I was five. There was a fever going around.*

And she kept you alive?

The CatWoman nodded, exhausted. *No one liked her, and they turned on her when their children died and hers didn't. Called her a witch.*

Was she?

The CatWoman sat silent, a soft breeze carrying a fine film of summer dust that settled around her as the leaves stilled. *She was a woman with—gifts.*

Which she gave to you.

Some.

Why did she give you the nine lives?

The CatWoman tried to squeeze her eyes shut, as the memory beast reached out of its cave to close its claws around her throat. Her world rocked with the image of her mother slicing her palms across the blade of a crude knife—two times, three times—eyes burning with the fire of desperation until, bloodied at last, those palms reached for the wide-eyed faces of her two children. Inside that embrace, sticky with blood and stinging with tears, the words were whispered with a terrifying urgency—*"Te doy el gato, las vidas del gato, la oreja, el ojo, el corazón del gato. Lo que te doy, nadie te lo puede quitar!"*—only barely ending before the angry crowd outside the house broke through one of the door planks—

The crashing of the door was as far as she ever went, except in her dreams, when the hand on the rudder of her memories seemed to be someone else's. Awake now, the CatWoman slammed the door shut again and the image shattered. She heard the tortoise-shell wince in the shower of image-shards.

"She cursed me," the CatWoman said dully, opening her eyes to the midday desert sun. "With the last breath she ever gave to me, she cursed me with these nine lives."

The tortoise-shell's eyes widened. *You really think she meant it as a curse?*

The CatWoman shook her head wearily. *She thought the mob would take me and Julio, too. All she did was give the mob more chances to come for us.*

Holding tightly to branches with what little strength she had left, the CatWoman climbed down the tree to sit heavily in the grass. She let the hot sun sink through her skin and begin to fill emptied places inside her.

I can't leave here, she said, weaving her fingers into the grass, *no matter what I'm saying in my sleep.*

The cat said nothing.

∞∞

It was on the night of the new moon that the summer's first thunder threw open the door standing wedged between the Cat-Woman and her dreams. A flood of suddenly familiar images washed into the house, into her sleep, into her slow awakening, until she vaguely realized the tortoise-shell was right. She *had* been dreaming about leaving, about taking Angelo up on his offer, and the dreams were—

"Pleasant." The word tasted exotic on her lips as she mouthed it into the flicker of a lightning flash. When the crash of thunder followed moments later, cool slate slid under her feet and the doorway to the courtyard arched overhead. She heard cats considering the weather somewhere in the hot, electric night.

It's about time.

It's not time.

You don't think so?

Another week, at least. Not enough pull in the air yet.

But it's a good sign.

It's a good sign.

The CatWoman passed wraithlike through the courtyard into

the dark piñons. Talc on stone pushed between her bare toes, hot breath of the storm danced capriciously with her hair. Each flash of lightning pulled sparks from inside her to burst on her skin, only to douse them a moment later with waves of thunder, echoing west to east. From no direction could she taste rain, only a hot, dry tease. A week, she thought dreamily. A good sign. The talc under her feet eventually changed to sand, and with yet another flash of lightning the CatWoman saw olive trees more silver than green in the crackling light, next to a pond more mirror than water. The mirrored lightning blinded her a moment and she stopped. She recognized the lingering image burned into her closed eyes—the trees, the pond. This was where Angelo had camped. She lay slowly down, eyes still closed, curling into the sand with her knees hugging her chest. The sand cradling her cheek vibrated faintly, as if the thunder were coming not from the sky but from somewhere deep underground, fighting its way to the surface through millennia of stone and rubble.

"When it reaches the surface, the rain will fall." The CatWoman's whisper drifted through and around her, curling on the wind. Lightning tried to cut through her closed eyelids—she nestled deeper into the sand, waiting for the thunder to struggle up toward her again. Flash and rumble, flash and rumble. She had no idea how long she lay there before they blended to a lullaby and she stepped into her hidden dreams.

She was neither wolf, nor coyote, nor panther, but herself, sitting cross-legged at the front of a vast hall of sleepy-eyed faces, unaware of her. When she opened her mouth to speak, out came the long howl of a wolf, arching over the sea of startled eyes. With a second howl, the sea of faces sat forward and the howl turned to a laugh. *Yes, it's a good story, isn't it?* She raised her hand and long ivory-colored claws reached out from her fingers, one by one, each emergence sending a shiver of fear through the faces before her. *It's the story of a cat.* She pulled the claws in and the faces relaxed. *I am fifty cats.* She giggled. *I have fifty cats. I live with fifty cats.* The faces before her were perplexed. *I AM KAT, with fifty tales.* She laughed at her own joke and saw the perplexed faces begin to nod off, drift away. She reached to pull them back to her with her voice, sending the scream of a jungle panther into the hall. From the farthest corner came an answer, a low-pitched echo scream that met hers somewhere high overhead. Angelo's face pulled out of the crowd as he crept noiselessly toward her through the sleeping faces.

It's a good sign, he said.

It's a good story, she answered.

Another week, I'd say.

Not enough pull yet.

Angelo stopped moving toward her, and he and the faces began to fade. Somewhere nearby, the CatWoman heard coyotes yipping.

Yip yip-a-you too, Angelo whispered, and winked at her. With the wink he was gone, and she listened to the coyotes, reaching for their story, until the grate of sand against her cheek woke her up.

The sun hadn't reached the pond yet, but was threatening. The CatWoman rolled over, confused, expecting to find a dark ceiling above and finding an olive canopy instead. She lay still, watching fingers of sunlight come slowly through the olive leaves, one tendril here, one tendril there, until she recalled enough of the night's storm and dreams to know how she came to be by the pond.

"I must be out of my mind." The bluejays in the olive trees ignored her soft voice. She clutched cool sand and let it trickle onto her belly, handful after handful, watching the sun rise behind the olive leaves, until she stopped herself with a short laugh. "And in her fifth life, she lost her mind."

On the precise morning when the cherries and apricots, along with a handful of radishes and one precocious eggplant, reached the zenith of their sweetness and stretched eagerly to be plucked—on the precise afternoon when prisms of impending rain chased the dust from the air on the mesa—on the precise evening when the thunder rumbled its way to the surface and called the summer's first rain down to meet it—precisely on this day, Angelo hiked back onto the mirage-mesa only to find the Cat-Woman was gone.

She's tempted. That's the problem. Rainwaterfalls cascaded from the canales off the porch roof and into the stone channel that carried the rain to meet the spring water in the runoff stream. The rain had already stopped, but the cascade continued in an ever-diminishing flow, splattering onto the porch floor and onto the tired hiker stretched on the banco, cat on his chest. No other cats were present on the porch, perhaps because of the splattering rainwater, perhaps because of the large dog lying near the man's drooped arm.

Well, if she's tempted enough, she's got the job. He stroked the tortoise-shell's sleek autumn fur with one hand while scratching the dog's floppy black ears with the other. *But I need to know. I can only stay a couple days.*

She's camped at the hot spring. The rain will bring her back.

You sure?

The tortoise-shell's slow blink told him he was impertinent to doubt her.

∽∽∽

With the nearly full moon at its apex on a black silk sky, the Cat-Woman stepped noiselessly through the arch separating the open mesa from the embracing house. In the moonshadow under the porch roof, she saw the man and dog, as she'd expected she would. Her clothes had long since stopped dripping, leaving her completely silent as she stepped across the grass to the porch and stood looking at her sleeping visitors.

Angelo, she said to his cat-self.

Kat? The human in him slept on.

I want the job.

Good. Without moving a muscle, his face seemed to grin. How does he do that? she wondered.

"There's one condition," the CatWoman called out through the doorway into the kitchen.

"How do you cook a decent meal on this thing?"

She put aside her comb and stepped away from the big mirror in the sala, her stay at the hot spring still stubbornly tangled in her hair. Maybe I should cut it all off, she thought.

"What's the one condition?" she heard Angelo call, just at the same moment she called out, "What do you mean how do you cook on it?"

She walked into the kitchen to find him kneeling in front of the old cookstove, head inside the open oven door. "I mean," came his muffled voice, "it's a handsome piece of casting and the enamel's held up beautifully, but how do you *cook* with it?"

"You're serious?"

"What serious?"

"You never cooked on one of these?"

"No, my stove uses gas."

The CatWoman rolled her eyes. "Obviously, you never cooked till this lifetime."

"So call me a chauvinist," he egged her with a tease in his eyes. "Say it—chauvinist pig."

"A product of your times."

"No, c'mon Kat. I was the worst kind. I made my wives all slave over hot stoves and wait on me hand and foot—"

"Did you really?"

"—and all I ever did was sit down at the bar all day and drink and play poker—"

"No—"

"—and leave them to run the farm and raise the kids and do the laundry and fill the cistern and—"

"You sound like the guy I was married to last time."

Angelo stopped with a sigh. "I was kidding."

The CatWoman looked out the window over the dry-sink, out over the sage carpet spreading north, pungent and slightly steamy after the night's rain. "I wish *he'd* been kidding."

A moment of silence, of unshared history turning its page, crept slowly between them and out the window to drift over the sage before Angelo asked, "What's the one condition?"

The CatWoman pulled her eyes away from the history and back to the present. "I want a closed classroom. No visitors."

"Not even me?"

"Well, maybe you. But no one else."

"We can manage that. I think."

She opened a door on the side of the stove. "This is the firebox. There's some kindling on the porch, and you're better off starting small." She rubbed her hand along the cream-colored enamel edge, recalling vividly the enamel stoves and sinks and tubs of her past, stained and pockmarked from too many years of unkind use. None had ever been this smooth, this creamy. Again, she pulled her thoughts to the present and looked at Angelo, sitting on the floor. He'd been staring at her, and, realizing this, she turned uncomfortably away. "What are you going to cook?" she asked.

His reply was slow, as if he too had to pull his mind to the present, to the question. "A feast. In honor of your willingness to take a chance." He dragged his backpack across the room and began to loosen its various straps and ties.

"How much of a chance am I taking?" the CatWoman asked dubiously, eyeing bundle after bundle, as he unpacked an incremental feast of foods she hadn't eaten since slipping into her spare life on the mirage.

"For someone like me, it wouldn't be much of a chance at all," Angelo replied, unwrapping one of the packages with special care. "It'll only be two days a week, back to back. In fact, for any other teacher, this would be a piece of cake. For you?" The odd, green-gold eyes lost some of their familiar grin. "You've been living like a hermit for six years. Even two days a week in a classroom is going to be a big change." Shedding the last layer of wrapping, he transformed the padded, shapeless bundle into a pair of delicate wineglasses, proffering them up like a magician. "A gift."

"You carried crystal in a backpack?"

"I did."

"What if I'd decided not to take the job?"

"So they'd still have been a gift."

She took the glasses hesitantly, their delicate curves in pronounced contrast to her calloused farmer's hands.

"What made you decide to do it?" he asked.

"My dreams," she said softly.

Angelo groaned and covered his face with his hands. "I don't believe it," he mumbled. "I'm outnumbered." He stared out at her from between his fingers, and she laughed at the silly face he made.

"What's wrong?"

"Nothing. You're just going to be a *hit* with the commune crowd." He walked outside to gather kindling. "I should talk," he called back to her. "I dreamed last night you stood right here and said you'd take the job."

"Did you?" The CatWoman grinned slowly to herself.

When the rain came that evening, it brought gusts of wind that rattled the windows and sent cats scurrying underneath anything that could be gotten underneath. Even Oso seemed nervous, whimpering with each flash of lightning or roll of thunder. The CatWoman and Angelo sat listening to the storm in the kitchen, with Oso under the table and the last of their feast on top.

"I guess I won't need to irrigate tomorrow," sighed the Cat-Woman, looking out the courtyard window. The cottonwoods above seemed to collect the rain and hurl it in sheets against the old roof. "That's good."

"Good?"

She shrugged. "Maybe I'm getting old. It seems like more work this year than before."

Angelo looked at her sideways. "Don't give me that *old* stuff. You can't be a day over twenty-nine. You're just understimulated."

The CatWoman blushed, and the combination of blood and winesong in her head was almost unbearably warm. She stood to put her face into the gust of storm coming through the window. "I'm nearly thirty-two."

"So I err on the side of flattery."

"I don't know what it's like to grow old. I've never been old."

"*Never?*"

"Thirty-eight is as old as I've ever gotten." She shifted her eyes from the waving cottonwoods to the solid adobe wall, as she felt the memory beast try to pull on her stomach. The nausea was only slight. My time at the hot spring helped, she thought.

"Was that with the thirteen girls?" he asked.

The CatWoman nodded. She stared at the courtyard wall in the drenching storm until her eyes pierced its very heart and wrapped themselves firmly around a good-sized brick within. "Angelo?" she asked, reluctant to take her eyes off the anchor they'd found. "Can I tell you a story?"

"Of course."

The CatWoman turned to look at him. She took a long moment to breathe in, then let her breath out shallowly in a quick pant-pant-pant-gasp, pant-pant-pant-gasp. The adobe wall faded, and she saw in its place a painted plank ceiling, once white but now blurred with three generations of burned lamp oil. Pant-pant-pant-gasp. I hate that ceiling. I don't want my baby to live under that ceiling. Pant-pant-pant-gasp. The air she breathed tasted of blood and urine and sweat and too many people living together and too many clothes unwashed and too many children needing food and not enough food to give. Pant-pant-pant-gasp. Too many faces with too little hope, hovering around—when will this be done? When will you be finished? I need you. I'm hungry. Pant-pant-pant-gasp. I don't want my baby to be hungry. Pant-pant-pant-gasp. I don't want my baby to live like this. Pant-pant-pant-gasp. I don't want my baby to be tired. Pant-pant. I'm so tired. Pant-pant. I'm so tired. Pant—

Gasp—

Ahh—

Ahh—

Someone kicked a chair hard enough to break it. "Fer the *luv-a-christ,* woman! It's another blasted girl!"

Ahh—

Gasp—

I'm so tired. I'm so tired . . .

"I'm so tired," the CatWoman heard herself whispering into the storm. She was standing at the window, swaying on shaky knees. Angelo came up from behind to steady her and stood with his arms around her until she stopped panting. His warm, fast breath in her ear brought her back to the present.

"Why don't you sit down?" he whispered, and walked her back to her chair at the table to settle her into it gently. He looked at her in awe. "Mamá taught you to do that?"

"No." She took a few long, slow breaths and felt her heart slow back to normal. "I learned it from the cats."

Angelo stared at her a moment longer, then sank into his own chair to look somewhere into the unfocussed history beyond the room. When his eyes finally focussed on her again, he shook his head. "Boy, were you married to a *jerk*."

⟨◯◯◯⟩

Two storms in two days were enough to drop several bushels of fruit in the orchards. It was also enough to make mud of the less sandy patches of mesa surrounding the house. It was a slippery time they had, the CatWoman and Angelo, gathering fruit for cleaning in the stream and carrying it up to the house. Oso's efforts to follow them only left him muddy to the belly, with orange, sticky feet where he'd stepped on fallen fruit. Angelo was orange and sticky as well, and left his fruit baskets on the porch banco where he'd slept rather than take the mess indoors. The CatWoman managed to avoid the mess plaguing the other two until the very last basket was on its way to the stream for washing. Perhaps she was moving too quickly, wanting to finish one chore and begin the next—perhaps she was thinking of the job ahead of her off the mirage-mesa instead of thinking about her footing. Perhaps she just wasn't thinking at all, for when she came to the last muddy stretch with her last basket of fruit, she slipped and dropped the fruit ahead of her fall, managing to land right in it. As luck would have it, she had an audience, all of whom burst into peals of silent laughter.

Orange goes well with your hair, dear, laughed the old calico, perched high enough in an apricot tree to be out of Oso's reach. Not that any of them needed to avoid him—he'd shown great deference to the cats during his stay, and they were hiding less and less frequently from him.

Damn, swore the CatWoman. Her entire left arm and hip were covered with sticky orange pulp, while the rest of her sat squarely in the mud. *What a waste.*

You won't miss that last basket, came the tortoise-shell's voice from somewhere overhead. *You'll be gone for the winter anyway.*

No, just a couple days a week, the CatWoman corrected her, looking around for something—a rock, some grass—onto which she could scrape the goo from her hand. *I'm sure you'll be able to fend for yourselves. I seem to recall you were all fat and happy when I showed up six years ago.*

We've never *been fat,* protested a grey tiger cat.

Oh, what I wouldn't do to be fat—once in my lives, sighed the apricot siamese.

I was fat once, the tortoise-shell bragged. *I was a bookstore cat once—a fat, lazy grey tabby. Everyone who came into the store brought me treats.*

*Ohhh, to be fat—*the apricot siamese crooned the refrain.

Listen, the tortoise-shell advised them all, *if you must live with humans, live in a bookstore.*

In the pause following this pronouncement, the CatWoman heard several cat faces being turned in her direction. When she looked up from her feeble attempts to separate herself from the fruit mash and mud, she saw a dozen pairs of cat eyes glaring at her. *Don't look at me,* she said. *I don't own a bookstore.*

Why don't you *bring us treats?* the apricot siamese asked in a tone that was unmistakably accusatory.

Now wait a minute—I do bring you treats.

We'll never get fat on a can of tuna twice a year, grumbled the grey tiger.

You know how hard it is for me to get my own food up here, much less treats for you. That's a long haul.

You should go to town more often so you wouldn't have to carry so much, the apricot siamese admonished.

I don't want to go to town more often.

Then why are you taking this job? asked the tortoise-shell.

"Not because I want to go to town more often," she muttered, sinking back into the mud.

"Hey! Orange goes great with your hair!" Angelo's voice came from behind the CatWoman, up toward the house.

I know why you're taking the job, the tortoise-shell snickered.

Before the CatWoman could demand an elaboration, the apricot siamese butted in. *Well, don't waste the opportunity. Bring tuna every week.*

Angelo's squishy footsteps drew near. "Are they giving you shopping lists already?" *Shame on you,* he added.

Shame, nothing, grunted the grey tiger as he jumped off his branch and stalked away. *You've brought us more treats in one month than she's brought in a year.* The rest, all but the tortoise-shell, seconded the comment and followed, leaving the CatWoman to stare after their departing tails.

"Was that a mutiny?" Angelo laughed.

The CatWoman shook her head. "I'm not sure *what* that was." She looked at the tortoise-shell. *What did you mean?* she asked, but the cat only blinked dumbly and bathed her face.

"Cats!" she muttered under her breath, and began anew her attempts to stand. "They want me to be a pack animal and keep them fat on tuna," she complained as she walked to the runoff stream. The water was chilling, and while it took the muck and mud off, her skin was still sticky. "I'd like to see one of them—just once—put out the kind of effort it takes to pack in food on a bicycle—"

"A bicycle? You go to town on a *bicycle?*"

"How else am I going to get there? I can't drive a car onto this mirage, and a horse would draw too much attention down the main road. Besides, I never learned to ride very well." The fruit pulp had, by now, glued her clothing to her skin. "I need a bath," she groaned, and turned toward the trail to the warm spring.

"Do you want to hike to the hot spring?" The CatWoman hesitated, surprised by the suggestion. Before she could turn to respond, he added, "I would go as your brother." When she turned, he was grinning from eye to eye with his hands half-raised.

"You're not—my brother."

"We have both heaven and hell to thank for that."

"No—I don't want to go up there—I left too many nightmares when I was there the other day. I'd rather wash up here."

"So I should beware of demons in the water if I go?"

"No—" She turned to retreat up the hill. "I doubt they would bother you."

Angelo looked down the muddy slope to where the spilled basket lay. "Why didn't she just dry up the mud?" he said to himself. "I thought she knew how to do those things."

Because you're distracting her, came the tortoise-shell's voice from the orchard below.

Am I? He grinned. *I couldn't tell.*

She's slow. I'm surprised she admitted she wants the job. The cat stepped out from the orchard shadows and made her way up the hillside toward him. *And she's like a mule—the harder you pull, the slower she goes.*

I already figured that out. Angelo retrieved the forgotten basket and the small quantity of fruit that hadn't been ruined.

On his way back past the cat, she added, *But whatever you do, don't give up. We need someone like you in her life.*

What? Like a second pack animal?

The tortoise-shell blinked her eyes demurely.

Kat was right—you are shameless, he chuckled, and carried his muddy load up to the house.

<hr />

The CatWoman was up all night cooking and canning fruit, which, she explained to her sleepy guest, was the best time for cooking on a woodstove in the summer. "You'd know that if you'd ever used one," she chided, to which he replied, "There are just some things you can't count on a chauvinist to know," as he retired to the porch banco. Oso surprised them both by staying in the kitchen after Angelo went to bed, following the CatWoman out to sit under the stars while each batch cooked. The storm brewing on the horizon in the afternoon was snagged on its trek by the mountains far to the west, and by midnight, even the last of those clouds had slid quietly off the night's edge. The moon rose early to lacquer the silken sky and inspire the storytellers living hidden in the sage. The CatWoman listened for the wolf's voice but never heard it.

Do you have a story? she asked Oso as she stirred the night's last batch of fruit. The big black head came up off the floor and cocked to one side. *You understand me better than I understand you. Does Angelo talk to you like this?* The floppy black ears perked forward. The CatWoman sat down, feeling in her feet the whole long day of getting fruit from orchard to stream to kitchen to pot to jar. *Does Angelo have nightmares?* she asked thoughtfully, but Oso left her then. Looking out the window, she saw him lick Angelo's sleeping face. His sleeping human-self reached a hand into the furry neck, and Oso lay down.

The CatWoman leaned out the window and peered at Angelo's dark face dreaming on the banco an arm's length away. *Angelo,* she said to his cat-self.

Yes, Kat.

Do you have stories?

Lots of stories.

Tell them to me sometime. His hand twitched in the pile of Oso's fur. Oso groaned softly, settling into his first real sleep of the night. The CatWoman was about to return to the stove when Angelo's voice drifted through the window to her cat-self.

Kat?

Yes, Angelo.

Why are you afraid of me?

The question surprised her. She stared at the sleeping man—he was sleeping, wasn't he?—his olive brown skin and black hair, his muscular arms and rough hands, his face with its nose right off an ancient statue. She stared at the man who was enticing her to leave the only safe place she'd known in five lifetimes, and she thought, how could anyone be afraid of a man who can grin in his sleep?

I don't know your stories, she said at last.

Once again she saw a hint of a grin pass over his face, while not a muscle moved. *I'll tell them to you sometime.*

How *does* he do that? she wondered yet again, then finished her work and went to bed.

The final day of Angelo's second visit passed quickly, with the CatWoman asleep till midday while Angelo and Oso hiked to the hot spring. "We ran off all the demons," he teased as they ate dinner. "It's safe to go back there now."

"I'll do that," she replied absently, wondering why a mantle of melancholy had settled around her as the afternoon aged into evening. Probably because I was up all night, she mused. But I slept nearly all day—

"It was tough, though. Took us all morning."

—and that's just the apricots. I still have cherries and tomatoes to do—

"There was one who looked suspiciously like the jerk you were married to—"

—probably ten more nights of work, maybe twelve—

"—so I took the liberty of decking him cold on your behalf."

"You what?"

"I decked him."

"*Who?*"

Angelo teased her with raised eyebrows. "You weren't paying attention? I risk dog and limb defending your honor with a drunken brute from the very pits of hell, and you repay my chivalry with *inattention?*" He rose grandly, sweeping a napkin off the table to clutch to his heart. "Mi querísima señorita, you cannot know the *pain* it does my poor heart to find that my efforts to save you from wraithful torment would go thus disregarded." The CatWoman giggled, and Angelo dropped to one knee to reach for her hand. "There is not a breath I breathe that hath not your name upon it, not a beat of my heart without the beat of hope that one day your eyes will look fondly upon me." He pressed her hand over his heart. "And should the gods of heaven and hell be so unkind as to deny me this small request, I shall retreat forever into my heartbreak—" He bowed his head. "—and surely die of sorrow."

She burst into laughter. "Which life was that from?"

"My second."

"And the señorita?"

"She married me." He held her hand just a bit longer than she expected he would, then let it go, and sat down across from her again. The CatWoman watched him drift in his thoughts before his eyes focussed back upon her.

"What was she like?" she asked.

"You really want to know?"

She nodded.

Angelo leaned forward onto his elbows and thought a moment. "She was poor," he began, "and very proud—"

The CatWoman reached over and touched his arm lightly, stopping him. For the first time since she'd met him, Angelo looked genuinely surprised. "Let me—see your eyes—" she said hesitantly.

Angelo shook his head with a short, self-conscious laugh. "I don't have that gift of yours."

"The tortoise-shell says all cats do. That means you, too."

Angelo looked as if he might protest, leaning back in his chair and out of her reach. She soon saw his eyes glaze over, however, and knew he wasn't seeing her anymore. She heard his breath very suddenly go shallow and fast, and felt a rush of blood racing through her from a heart whose pounding came in surges. She found herself watching a crowd of dancers out under a hot sun where the dust was thick and the sound of clapping and whistles and shouting nearly drowned out the feeble stringed instrument out of sight, sawing a tune. The beat of the pounding heart within her rushed every time a certain dancer swirled near—a girl, perhaps fifteen, in faded yellow skirts and no shoes. Over her shoulders hung a large scarlet shawl that she'd coyly wrapped over her face until only her eyes, dark as midnight, could be seen. Each time the beat of the dance brought her close, she would wink one of those midnight eyes and toss her head so that the shawl fell slightly away from her hidden face. And with each glimpse of her face, the CatWoman could feel her heart race, and her breath go shallow, and her stomach plummet in dizzying freefall—

The image ended abruptly. She saw Angelo across the table, looking a little pale and breathing fast. "I need some air," he said hoarsely. The CatWoman led him outside to the grass where he lay down and closed his eyes until Oso walked over to lick his face.

"It's okay, Oso." He laughed weakly. "It's just a time warp." He wiped his hands slowly over his face. "Whew—that takes a lot of energy!"

"Telling a story?"

"No, being sixteen." He rolled slowly to sit up. "You'd think I'd remember it, after being through it so many times." He ran shaky hands through his hair. "Ah, how a body does forget." When he looked at her, she realized the grin on her face must be like one of his own. "What are you smiling at?"

"I liked that story. It wasn't a nightmare—like mine."

Angelo grinned in a woozy sort of way. "Yeah, and if I ever get past the novice dizzies, I may tell you another one."

"It took me four days at the hot spring to get past the dizzy part."

"So those are the demons?" The CatWoman nodded. Angelo sighed. "I'm sorry I have to go back to town. I'd like to take some time and do the same myself."

The CatWoman stared at a blade of grass she'd been twining absentmindedly between her fingers. "I'm sorry, too," she said softly. In the unusual silence of his reply, she looked up and added, "Would you really have decked my husband?"

"Cold." Even in the fading light, the hard glint of gold in his eyes told her he wasn't kidding.

"Good," she said. "Then my story was a good one."

"And would you have fallen in love with the girl in the red shawl?" he asked her, eyes still intent and shining.

"Head over heels," she answered feebly, remembering the dizzy rush and the midnight eyes.

Angelo's eyes slowly softened to their familiar grin. "That's just what I did."

The CatWoman was well aware of Angelo's departure the next morning and needed no cats to report it. She couldn't pretend not to know the source of her melancholy, falling on her again now like rain, like mildew, like all things wet and clinging. While Angelo wasn't looking, she slipped two jars of apricots into his pack, then found herself feeling silly and embarrassed when he discovered them.

"They're a gift," she faltered.

She's training you to be a pack animal, the tortoise-shell snickered, watching the scene from her usual perch until a pillow tossed her way sent her scampering off, tail high.

"I'll be back to pack you out in three weeks," Angelo said. "I guess you don't have a calendar."

"Just the moon."

"Then I'll be back at the first quarter moon. I'll know by then where you'll be staying and what you'll need to take. Shouldn't be much." His eyes took on a tease. "It better *not* be much. I'm not sixteen anymore." As he hoisted his pack onto his back, it seemed to the CatWoman that Angelo would say something else. But whatever might have been on his lips remained unspoken and, instead, he reached to brush her hair gently back from her face before giving her a quick grin and a wink. "See you," he said. Then he and Oso headed southeast until the sage and piñons swallowed them from her view.

And, hours later, the CatWoman needed no cats to report to her that they'd stepped off the mirage-mesa, for at that very moment she was drowned by a wave of loneliness unequaled in three lifetimes.

◯◯◯

Under the waning moon of the following week, summertime slipped its grasp on the mesa and the first finger of autumn tiptoed in. Each afternoon saw a tall, grey column of rain march across the desert floor, drenching all in its daily path. Each sunset gilded the edges of hills and made baroque riot of the orange and purple clouds to the west, while the occasional rainbow danced like a showgirl before the mountains to the east. And each morning, while summertime slept off its evening Mardi Gras, autumn slipped into the dawn air, looking for a place to settle in awhile.

Already, thought the CatWoman, walking to the warm spring

before dawn. Seems like I was just planting seeds a few days ago. She felt a hint of autumn gliding along her face and arms, sleek-edged and intent. Gone for a moment was the pregnant luxury of summer air percolating upward from a ripening earth. The Cat-Woman had always noted this changing of the dawn air with the slightest pang of regret, as if it were possible that one year the swellings of summer might go on and on. The plump, lazy summer air would push back autumn's surreptitious advance and hold the sun hostage, never to shrink southward. There would be no curling inward, no harvesting, no gathering indoors of all the bounty needed for lean times ahead. Summer would stay comfortably slumped over the pillows of piñon and sage and mountains, drowsy in the hot sun. And school would never start.

Listen to me, she thought as she stepped into the dark pool. I'm dreading school like any ten-year-old. She ducked underwater, then began rubbing soap into her wavy, multi-colored hair, wondering for the eighty-third time in a week whether she'd made the right decision. For all her calm words to the cats, she had a butterfly ballet inside each time she tried to imagine actually standing in front of a room full of students. Still and all, Angelo could not have put the matter more precisely; she *did* have a keen and admittedly selfish interest in molding the next generation. She may have found a mirage to hide out on and the means to do so in this life, but what about the *next*? And the several more after that? What if history were to turn back to the way things were—she shuddered—in her third life, with no possibility of escape or seclusion, no means to do anything with her life but beg or steal her next meal?

"*That's* a story I should tell," she mumbled.

Which one? came a voice from the shadows. The old calico stepped silently from under an olive tree to settle on the stone wall of the pool. Her silhouette against the faint dawn looked just a shade fuller than the CatWoman expected, and she wondered if her coat might already be preparing for winter.

Did you feel the air change? she asked.

Of course, said the old cat.

The light in the east pressed up against the mountains there, slowly backlighting them with the glow that would become the spotlight of sunrise. There had been a double rainbow the evening before, shimmering before those now-dark mountains—two great arches spanning the entire valley east of the river gorge and making all beneath them glow a yellow-white. The CatWoman knew that the feet of those rainbows landed to either side of the town there, even though she could not actually see it. The mesa on her side of the gorge rose gradually like a long swell on an ocean floor, only to be cut abruptly by the river's path and rise only half as high on the other side. The town across the gorge lay in a wide valley, hugging the eastern mountains. When people over there watched the sunset, they saw only the spine of the gorge rim backed by the faint blue of the western mountains on the horizon, and seemed to have little or no interest in what lay between. When the CatWoman watched the sunrise, all she saw were the eastern mountains and the spine of the gorge rim cutting off their base. It was easy for her to pretend there was nothing else there.

Have you ever run into someone—some cat—you've known before? she asked the calico.

Never. But I met a cat once who had that happen.

Only one, in nine lives?

Just one.

The CatWoman tried to calculate in her head what the odds were of her meeting Angelo four hundred and some years after that first time, and stopped when the numbers became unimaginable. *It's amazing.*

It was obviously meant to be, so take advantage of it.

How do I take advantage of it?

I have no idea. You'll have to figure that one out yourself. I just know the world only rarely goes to such great lengths to beat the odds.

The CatWoman ducked underwater to rinse her hair, then resurfaced with a sigh. *I'll have to cut off my hair.*

Why?

Because it's not—because it gets me into trouble. It's not human to have hair like this. The dawn took on a seasick green cast just for a second as she remembered the endless taunts of her schoolmates and Draconian efforts of her family to color, cover, or camouflage her other-than-thoroughbred looks. She saw in a vivid flash the looks of wary detachment from her parents, as if her father couldn't believe she was truly his child and her mother couldn't believe something so odd could come out of her body. *There's no hiding that this isn't human hair.*

But it's beautiful hair. Can't they see that?

The CatWoman shook her head slowly, shoving the memories aside before they could take hold of her stomach. *No, they can't. They just see someone who's too different.* She stood up and let the hint of autumn bite softly at her skin a moment before getting out and drying off.

The tortoise-shell will be insulted, the old cat chuckled, *but she'll get over it.*

What does it matter to her?

A lot. You're the only other one on the mesa with her coloring, and that makes you like—sisters, I suppose would be the human way to put it, though that's not quite it exactly.

Well, the coloring will still be there, said the CatWoman as she slipped into her robe. *There just won't be so much of it.*

I don't think she'll see it that way, replied the cat, hopping down from the stone wall with the groan of the aged, *but I may be wrong.* And the two of them walked down the path to the house, with hints of autumn slipping between and around them one last time before sunrise woke summertime at last and cooked up a hot morning.

∞∞

New moon and four days, new moon and five days—the Cat-Woman found herself so aware of the countdown to the first quarter moon she didn't need to keep written track. The approach careened toward her some days and away from her others, as she was alternately dreading her departure from the mesa and eager, in some way, to get on with it all. For two nights running, she slept fitfully between dreams of classrooms overgrown with weeds where the students should have been and orchards so fruit-laden the branches were breaking, crashing to the ground before she could gather the fruit into her pantry. On the sixth night after the new moon, the CatWoman woke in a sweat from a dream of herself as the child she'd been in this fifth life, with a circle of sneering faces around her calling, *Heeere kitty-kitty-kitty.* With laughter still ringing in her sleepy ears, she felt her way through the dark to the old desk in the sala, fumbled through drawers until she found a pair of shears, and cut her hair off. She stumbled back to bed without lighting a candle.

The first time she woke the next morning, it was to a sudden shriek from the tortoise-shell. *What did you do?!*

The CatWoman sat bolt upright at the sound. *What happened?* she gasped.

Your hair is gone! wailed the cat.

Her pounding, panicked heart made it difficult to slump back against the pillows. *You scared the daylights out of me,* she scolded, and rolled over to pull the bedsheets firmly between herself and the morning's first light.

The second time the CatWoman woke that morning, it was to an unexpected knock on the open front door that, once again, set her bolt upright, heart racing. "Kat? Are you here?" When she recognized Angelo's voice, her heart slowed, but only a little. How could he be here already? she wondered, jumping out of bed and into one slipper, then searching frantically for the other. I must have slept half the day away.

"Yes—I'm here—" she called out the window. The second slipper eluded her and she left the bedroom without it, rushing around the corner into the sala just as Angelo stepped through the doorway from the porch. "You're here early—" she started to say, then stopped. Something had halted Angelo in mid-stride and he stood staring at her—or at something behind her, she thought at first, so she turned to look back where she'd been. By the time she looked at Angelo again, his deadpan voice gave away none of the laughter streaking the corners of his eyes.

"Am I allowed to laugh?" he asked. With that, the CatWoman recalled the night's dream and put her hands to her cropped hair.

"How bad is it?" She nearly bumped into him as she hurried to the big mirror. "Oh no—" The left side hugged her ear, the right side her shoulder—there were bangs falling from eyebrow to cheekbone, depending on which way she turned—curls coiled skyward from the top of her head—and the whole mess looked like she'd slept on it. "That's awful." She giggled.

"Did you do it with your eyes closed?"

"Sort of." She dug out the scissors and quickly snipped until she was at least balanced left to right. As she put the scissors away, the tortoise-shell walked in from the kitchen, arched her back to hiss, and stalked out to the courtyard.

"Nothing subtle about that cat, is there?" Angelo laughed, bending over to pick up a handful of fallen hair, no fewer than a dozen shades of color dangling between his fingers. "You really didn't need to do this. Your hair would have blended right in with the crowd at the school."

"Not unless my students are cats, which you never said they

would be." She made a cradle of her nightshirt and gathered all the hair she could find, taking it out to toss into the sage.

As she stepped back inside, she found Angelo ducking his way through the kitchen under her low-hung bunting of strung apricots, snitching a dried tomato from one of the many racks spread about the room. He pursed and smacked his lips. "Oooh, Kat, I can hear angels singing. Are you sure you're not Italian? Adopted maybe?"

"I'm sure," she retorted. "Where's Oso?"

Angelo moved several racks aside to clear a seat for himself on the banco. "I rode a bike this time—had to leave him at home." He leaned his head against the cream-colored wall and looked at her with a tired smile. His eyes questioned her silently before he asked out loud, "Still want to do this?"

"Yes."

"Are you nervous?"

"I'm having nightmares, I'm so nervous. But I still want to do it."

Angelo sighed, his eyes closed, the question gone. "Good." He smiled. "We leave tomorrow."

If he heard the CatWoman gulp, he didn't show it. "What do I need to take?"

"Oh, three quarts of tomatoes," he replied, his face soaking in the sunlight streaking through the window on the opposite wall. "A handful of dried ones would be nice too, but hey—I don't want to overburden you."

"Am I being hired as a teacher or a cook?" she quipped.

Angelo opened one eye at her. "Not bad for a lady who didn't know a tease from an insult when I met her." He sat up to reach for another tomato. "Some clothes," he said between bites, "enough for a four-day stay."

"*Four days!* I thought you said—"

"Just this first time," he interrupted her. "You have to be at school on opening day to meet the parents and the board of directors." He paused to lick sticky tomato from his fingers. "And you know, you'll make a better impression on the board if you show up with both feet shod," he joked, nodding at her slipperless left foot, "though half the parents would forgive it of you and none of the students would even notice."

The CatWoman felt the lightness of her mood, brought on by the teasing she'd missed in the last three weeks, begin to dampen. She had prepared herself for facing a room full of students, but not a crowd of adults. "I *have* to be there?"

"Attendance required by the boss. No way out."

"But *you're* the boss—"

"That's right."

"Oh."

"Besides, my bringing you in out of the blue is causing some stir on the staff, and I think they need to meet you as soon as possible. Settle them down a bit."

"What's the problem?"

"Oh, it's the usual why-hire-a-stranger stuff. Small-town attitudes, that's all."

His words sent the great bulk of her enthusiasm diving from her heart, through her stomach, down her left leg, and out her unshod foot, leaving her to fumble for a chair. "Angelo," she said, trying to level her shaky voice, "that's exactly what I *don't* want to be in the middle of."

"It's not a big deal. You just need to be there to meet these people on day one, and then on day three you start teaching." At her wide-eyed look, he added, "It'll be a closed classroom. No visitors. Not even me, if that's what you want." She nodded, not seeing him with her wide eyes, but seeing rather the circle of small-town residents who once stoned her for being a stranger, though she'd lived among them all her life. "Kat." She half-heard Angelo's voice over the shout of the crowd in her vision and the groan of the memory beast in her stomach. "*Kat—*" she heard him say again, and the feel of his rough hand against her cheek broke the memory's hold, letting her shake herself to the present. "Kat." He was squatting eye to eye with her, his voice a whisper. "If I really thought there might be trouble for you, I'd never lead you into it. You have my word."

"Okay," she said hoarsely, getting up to build a breakfast fire. "Okay, so I need four days of clothes. What else?"

Angelo replied from the pantry, where he was inspecting her canned laborings on the shelves there. "That's it."

"No towels? Pots and pans?"

"Just clothes. And tomatoes. I wasn't kidding about the tomatoes."

"Where am I staying?"

"Near me." Angelo leaned out to add, "Do you mind?"

"No," she answered, and when he leaned back into the pantry, she added under her breath, "Sounds like I'll need to."

The day's tin-rain-soldier began its march early, pushing a glaring heat across the mesa that caught the CatWoman in the garden, picking anything she thought might ripen in the next four days. When she stood to toss her now-short bangs from her sweaty face, she saw the tortoise-shell sulking in the shadows of cornstalks, very expressively saying nothing. *You don't understand what I'm up against with this hair,* she told the cat, no apology in her tone. The cat let the comment fall dead in the furrows between them and the Cat-Woman resumed her gatherings, ignoring the sulky presence until the vanguard of the day's rainstorm chased her up the hill.

As she ran into the courtyard, she found Angelo with the skeletons of her bicycle and the buggy she used for cargo standing upside down on the porch. "It's obvious you were born into money, Kat O'Malley," he was mumbling, sitting surrounded by wheels, gears, and brake parts, cleaning a chain link by link. "Were you just going to throw this chain away when it got too dirty to bend?" To his one side, laid out on a faded cloth, were all

the pieces he'd cleaned, arranged in an order she could compre-
hend at a glance. To his other side was the much larger assemblage
of as-yet-unattended parts—also grouped, but not so neatly.

"Are you sure you know how to put it all back together?" she
asked, shaking raindrops from her head and clothes.

"The sincerity of your tone makes that an insult, my dear," he
growled playfully. "I know how to put it all back together."

"Do you know how to cut hair? My butchering job seems to
have cost me one feline friend."

He looked up. "You want it *shorter*? Hair isn't my specialty."

The CatWoman waved her hand at his concern. "I don't mind.
Just get it short and level in the back so I can cover it up."

"Are you going to cover it forever?"

"Forever as long as I'm off this mesa."

Angelo's silence surprised her, sitting with a cleaning cloth
lying still in one hand and an unreadable look in his green-gold
eyes. "You have the most beautiful hair I've ever seen on a
woman," he said after a moment, his voice nearly drowned out by
the growing rainstorm. His comment startled the CatWoman out
of the usual rhythm of their banterings, and as she could come up
with no reply, she ducked into the house. When she returned with
scissors and a chair, her poise was gathered once more about her.

"I take that as no light compliment, given your age and the
extent of your travels," she said lightly, handing him the scissors.
"But, feline and human opinions be damned—I know what I'm
doing. I want it really short," she instructed, sitting down with her
back to him. "It has to fit under a bandana."

"Maybe I should tell you about the school before I cut."

She shook her head. "No, tell me *while* you cut."

He worked slowly, cutting and re-cutting until she could feel
none of the sway or pull of long hair but only the spring of short
curls against her head. "The school isn't like any you or I ever
went to," Angelo began, leaning close to her ear as he worked so

she could hear him over the raindrops splattering noisily on court-yard stones and grass. "It was built by the communes about fif-teen years ago, when everyone was running away to live in the desert. Were you there then?"

"No, I only lived there a month before I moved out here."

"It was a wild time," Angelo continued, "and basically, the school and the students there are the fruits of those wild times—half the students, I should say." They both jumped at a sudden silent flash of lightning, and Angelo held the scissors still until its thunder had rolled over the house and out into the piñons. "When I was first hired to teach, no way in hell would the locals send their kids to such a school. But that's changed over the years. The communes are dying, the runaways are middle-aged. The students you'll be teaching are the last of that era." In the wake of a second lightning flash and thunder drum, the rain-soldier's feet came stomping through the oasis as if to flatten orchards and gar-dens instead of nourish them. Angelo stopped trying to talk over the roar and finished quickly. "Come take a look," he called, lead-ing her into the sala to stand in front of the mirror. "Will that do?"

There wasn't much left of her at all, it seemed to the Cat-Woman, once the waves of wild-colored hair had been reduced to tight curls haloing her face. The lack of hair made her eyes more prominent, but she decided they could pass as merely exotic, instead of odd. She pulled a sweaty bandana from her neck and tied it tightly over her head, stuffing all curls inside except a few renegade red-brown bangs. "It's perfect," she announced, smiling at Angelo's reflection behind her own.

"I could have shaved one side of your head and painted it green, and these kids wouldn't even notice," he said. "They've lived their whole lives with stranger sights than you could ever give them."

"Too late now, the deed is done." She pulled the bandana off and leaned toward the mirror. "I think you even took a few years off my face with those scissors."

Angelo cupped her chin with his hand and turned her face for exaggerated inspection. "You're right—it's uncanny. You don't look a day over four hundred."

"Now, that's *not* a compliment," she scolded, heading into the kitchen. "Were you planning to dine with the cats tonight or with me?"

"I tell you, Kat," he called after her. "You do learn fast."

⚬⚬⚬

You'll wrinkle up like a raisin. The tortoise-shell's voice came out of the shadows of olive leaves, damp with steam from the warm spring.

You're speaking to me again?

You've been here twice today.

The CatWoman sighed in the light of the nearly-set moon, sorry the cat interrupted what might have been the beginnings of sleep. She shifted from floating on her back to leaning her arms and chin on the stone wall, looking east over house and cotton-woods and mesa. The gorge rim rose solid and blue-black in the night, a great dinosaur sleeping downstage from high mountains. She envied the sleeping dinosaur like she envied Angelo, snoring on the porch banco as she paced restlessly through the house and finally up to the spring. At one point in her pacing, she had nearly struck up a conversation with his cat-self, just for company, but thought the better of it. One of us had better be ready for the ride tomorrow, she'd decided. *What do cats do when they can't sleep?* she asked the tortoise-shell.

Cats don't ever have trouble sleeping. You get that from your human side.

"Cat-side, human-side, inside, outside," chanted the Cat-Woman, smirking invisibly at the sliver of sense in the rhyme. *I seem to have gotten the worst from each.*

You shouldn't have cut your hair—

The CatWoman groaned.

—but at least you cleaned it up. It looks decent now.

The CatWoman's eyebrows rose in the dark at the not-so-veiled offer of reconciliation. *Thanks*, she said.

Angelo says you're worried for nothing.

When did he say that?

Tonight.

She slid back to sink her shoulders underwater again and away from the midnight air, cooler now with each passing evening. *Angelo means well*, she said slowly, *but he'll never see things the way I do. He's never been killed.*

I thought he said he had.

You're right, you're right. He said he was a soldier last time. But that's different. He's never been killed—by his own kind. She got the words out without waking any beasts inside and thought that was a good sign for the eve of her departure. Behind her, beyond the hill that housed the spring, she could tell the moon was setting, turning the night-clock past midnight. The piñons fell to flat black below her, the sage lost its slightly silver cast. The CatWoman watched as the last of the moonglow escaped the world between the eastern and western mountains, leaving it to float on pure starlight until dawn. The whole of this world was silent, and into this silence she told the cat, *When I was in my second life, my family had a flock of ducks—dozens of them, all different colors. I used to feed them. That was my job, and I loved it. I remember thinking back then that it must be wonderful to be a duck—waddling around, puttering around—I'd watch them for hours, out on the water, gliding around so effortlessly. And then one day, when I was—about thirteen, I guess, I noticed one of the ducks was losing its feathers, a few here, a few there. It was so sudden, just like that—bald spots showing up on this one duck but not on any of the others. Of course, I thought maybe the duck was sick, but then I walked out one day and saw the rest of the flock pecking at this duck, and plucking it alive, and biting the bald spots till they bled.*

By the time I moved the duck out of the flock, it was too late—it died anyway. Olive leaves began to rustle above her as a midnight breeze scurried across the mesa, chasing the memory of the moon. From every direction came a soft whooshing of olive leaves, piñon needles, sage blossoms, combing the breeze as it passed through them. *Angelo says I'm worried for nothing,* said the CatWoman into the dark and muted song, *because he's never had his own flock turn against him. I have.*

Then why not stay here where it's safe?

Because I'm still only in the fifth of this nine-life curse. I have to make things safe for the next time, in case I can't find a mirage.

It's not a curse to a cat. That's your human side.

Cat-side, human-side—what a juggling act, she said dryly, as the midnight breeze shuddered loose a trio of leaves overhead, depositing them silently on her shoulder, her nose, and her newly cropped hair.

∞∞∞

"Got everything?"

The CatWoman blinked at Angelo in the morning glare, standing astraddle his loaded bicycle with her buggy attached. "No," she said, hoarse and bleary-eyed from watching too many hours of the night go by. "*You've* got everything. Why didn't you put the buggy on *my* bike?"

"Because I'm a gentleman of the old, old, old school, you might say. And don't tell me you can pull it yourself—I know you can." He grinned in his disarming way, blocking any further debate. "Did you say good-bye to the cats?"

"The cats are sleeping through this momentous event," she replied, and swung her leg over her own bike. "They have no sense of history in the making." She gave the pedal a kick, spinning it effortlessly backward on its newly cleaned and oiled shaft.

When it came to a stop and she poised her foot upon it, she looked up at Angelo who still hadn't budged. "Well?" she asked.

"Still want to do this?"

"Still want to do this." She nodded, and stood on the right pedal to push off ahead of him down the trail leading away from the house. As the last trees in the east orchard passed behind her, the CatWoman heard a cat voice sliding down the hill after her, calling, *Wait!* When she glanced over her shoulder, there were fifty cat faces peering over the courtyard wall, calling in unison, *Don't forget to bring us treats!* The sound of their voices, and of Angelo's laughter behind her, shook the night's worries and cobwebs from her eyes and heart, and she rode to the east with a much lighter load than she had expected she would.

faLL

N oise.

It was always the noise, first, to set Kat on edge whenever she ventured into town. Aside from the thunder of late summer and the winds that shepherded winter in and back out again, the mirage-mesa kept its hypnotic lullaby at pianissimo. Her ears were so attuned to the melody, she could hear cherry blossoms drop their petals in the night, hear the moment when piñon cones opened wide enough for gathering nuts. In the seasons when the wind was still and the thunder slumbered at the center of the earth, cat purrs and coyote yips might be the only sounds she heard for weeks, and these would seem sometimes to roar in her ears. Kat had never walked so far to north, south or west that she'd left the reaches of the lullaby, and she wondered if perhaps the mirage had no end in those directions, but drifted on in a sleepy forever. But to the east, the lullaby extended only to the bridge at the bottom of the gorge, and there it ended abruptly.

The east side of the river gorge had no lullaby. When a breeze blew there, it didn't just comb softly through sage blossoms and cat whiskers, as it would on the mirage. The same breeze on the east side would begin in the long slope of sagebrush spreading from gorge to foothills, but would soon hit a fenceline, a barn, a windbreak of trees. It would bounce off a car heading north up the road to town, only to ricochet off another heading south, and another, and another. The breeze would wobble its way between houses, would shimmy and bounce off shop doors being opened for a day's business, would get stepped on by feet bare or booted, moccasined or manicured. And with each bounce, ricochet, or shimmy, another ripple of sound would break on the pond that was the town, crossing the last ripple, multiplying itself into ever smaller and faster ripples until they filled the entire east valley to the foothills like a huge, vibrating bowl of gelatin.

And noise.

Kat was sure it was more the noise that kept her awake her first two nights in town than it was her anxiety about the first day of school. Even at midnight, in a thick-walled house surrounded by an overgrown plum orchard, miles from the center of town, Kat felt the low rumble smothering everything in the east valley, the inescapable pulse of lives bumping against other lives. When she did sleep, she dreamed earthquakes and thunder and endless avalanches. She missed the animal calm of the cats, wishing at least one had come along to purr her to sleep. When Angelo misread the bags under her eyes as fear for her own safety in a strange place, she was only too glad to accept his offer of Oso as a nighttime companion. Thereafter, she slept, if fitfully, with his big black nose breathing calm onto her drooping hand.

The house was quaint and squat, and in bad need of plaster. It sat half a stone's throw from the dirt road, hidden in what might have been a plum orchard at one time but was now more like a thicket. Kat guessed it was probably a fruit shed years ago, stiflingly short on windows but perfectly adequate in every other way. One room served for cooking, sleeping, and sitting, with a small bathroom attached recently. "Indoor plumbing? That's a step up," she had said that first day. "How did you find this?"

Angelo pointed out the window at his own house on a ridge above the dirt road and wild thicket. "It belongs to my landlord. I fixed it up in trade for rent. It's going to be a cold house in the winter, but if it's ever too cold, come up to my place. There's a path." Kat could see faintly a switchback on the steep hillside.

"You're a builder?"

"In the summertime." He waved his hand at the outside walls, blotchy with mud patching. "I ran out of time on this one, but I'll get it done before the snow flies, especially since you're here to lighten my load."

"I didn't know I was."

"Yeah—you're taking over my history classes. I'll just be the headmaster now, instead of trying to do both."

Angelo's words didn't register with her at the time, nor did they come to mind as she lay for hours tossing and turning on a bed that seemed to vibrate with the valley's hum. But they rang out in neon fanfare the next day when she was introduced to parent after parent, and more than one of them said, "Oh, too bad—my child was looking forward to having Angelo again."

"Didn't they know you were bringing in someone new?" Kat asked Angelo later.

"The last time I saw any of the parents, even *I* didn't know I was bringing in someone new. That didn't happen till I met you."

"And now I'm replacing everyone's *favorite teacher*? Angelo, I don't think you could have found more ways to stack the cards against me if you'd tried."

"Relax, Kat. The kids are going to love you. I know it."

Some of her prospective students appeared at the school that day, but those who came seemed to have been dragged, forced to end their vacation a day early by conscientious parents. They stayed outdoors when they could, so Kat only caught an occasional glimpse of them. They appeared to her like any other group of teenagers she had seen in this fifth lifetime.

Not so the parents, who could at best be described as a disparate and accidental grouping. In the space of her first hour, Kat shook hands with a woman dressed like a bank executive, an elderly couple in threadbare church clothes, at least three women in gypsy-like skirts and no shoes, a man in irrigating boots with mud drying on them, a hurried woman in a nurse's uniform, and a thick-muscled man in fringed buckskin, a knife the length of Kat's forearm strapped to his leg. "I'm Mountain Man," he had boomed at her, walking into the room with the gait of a grizzly bear. By midday, the tapestry of faces swam before her and the names blurred. Her clearest thought all day was of her bandana—is my hair covered? She tugged on it constantly, worrying nervously at tendrils again and again as if their escape might be the death of her. She could see by day's end why Angelo had thought her bandana obsession unnecessary; half the parents and several of the other teachers looked to her like circus performers. The batiked gypsy skirts appeared over and over, as did multiple nose-rings, ankle bells and moccasins. Feet were nearly as apt to be bare as shod in this group, and more than one shoulder was adorned with a bird. What was lacking was any self-consciousness, and while Kat began to suspect Angelo might be right about her hair seeming perfectly normal to this crowd, they were only about half of the parents she met. The rest looked like they would definitely notice her odd hair, so she fidgeted till day's end to keep it hidden.

She began to categorize the unexpected names rather than remember them: those named after heavenly bodies, those named after the four elements, those named after plants and stones and earthly phenomena, and those with names common in distant cultures but not given at birth here. A hybrid of these categories swirled into Kat's room near the end of the day, a slow-motion whirlwind of bright shawl and dangling fringe, hair the color of the harvest moon rising, all accompanied by a soft tinkling of hidden bells. The woman seemed to bring with her into the room a Saharan breeze, a harem scent. Her carriage was that of one used to giving orders to those she might consider lesser beings than herself. Later, Kat would remember cringing slightly at first sight of her. At the time, all she could do was stare at a woman who would have been considered strikingly beautiful in each of Kat's five lifetimes.

"I'm Layira Moonfire, and you must be Eli's new history teacher. I'm on the board of directors, so you'll be seeing me a lot. Eli just hates it that he won't have Mr. D again—that's what he calls him, it's so precious—so you may have to put up with some pouting. They'll probably all pout. Have you been teaching long? This group needs a strong teacher, you know—"

The voice came out like a bird's—not at all what Kat expected—up, down, singsonging its way quickly from thought to thought, with no room for Kat to reply. By the time the woman swirled her fringes and her scent back out of the room, Kat realized she had only managed an "Mmm" and two "Yes's" before the woman was gone.

"You're not alone. Layira never lets anyone talk," Angelo said later as they sat eating supper at his house on the ridge. "She's the queen bee of the commune crowd."

"I'm not surprised she's the queen," Kat mused. "I felt terribly plain next to her."

"She looks just like her grandmother—my wife, last time. What a shame she didn't inherit her grandmother's temperament, and brains."

"*She's* your granddaughter?"

"Was. And her son Eli is the one who made the thong for me."

As flamboyant and unexpected as Layira and half the parents were, however, the day's encounter that stood out most prominently in Kat's mind was her meeting with Mu, a fellow teacher whose son would be in her afternoon class. She had been looking out one of the classroom windows, feeling her sleepless night heavy upon her as she waited for the next wave of parents to appear and wondering about a peaked something-or-other she saw to the west. Had she been so tired and wondering so intently that her cat ears didn't hear the footsteps, or had he deliberately tried to sneak up on her? Certainly both, she thought later, since her ears rarely missed anything louder than silence. Whatever it was, in one moment she was alone with the western view, and in the next she was jumping like a cat with its tail under a rocker, as two hands suddenly squeezed her waist from behind.

"Gotcha!" someone whispered in her ear.

It was a full minute before Kat's heart slid down out of her throat to allow her to speak, but the man didn't let her obvious discomfiture impede him in the least. "I'm Mu," he said smoothly, "and someone tells me you're Kat, but—" He held his hand over his eyes, standing quietly for a moment. "—I see your face with another name," he went on, his voice fairly slithering between his lips with the grace of a sidewinder. When he pulled his hand from his eyes, he asked, "Don't I know you?"

"I don't think so," Kat replied, with what voice she had.

"Ahh, well—perhaps in another life then?"

"Your naïveté is showing, Kat." Angelo laughed when she described to him how she'd been speechless after Mu said this. "Mu's an ass. You can bet he says that to every woman."

"Well, I did start to wonder—especially when he told me he could see a Jupiter moon in my eyes and wanted me to guess which moon was in his."

"What did you say?"

"I said moons weren't my field—that maybe he was looking for the science teacher."

Angelo howled when she said this, slapping the table and

laughing till his eyes were damp. "Ahh, if I didn't dislike the man so much I might feel sorry for him. I'm glad I don't need to worry about you holding your own with him."

"How much will I have to be around him?"

"Not much. His schedule only barely overlaps yours. He's the science teacher, by the way."

"Uh-oh—"

"A mediocre one at best. I was hoping to high heaven he would leave when I got the headmaster job, but—no such luck."

"He didn't want to work for you?"

"He wanted to be headmaster. He's been at the school longer than I have—thought the job was his by right. He would have gotten it too, but two of his cronies on the board of directors left on a vision quest and the balance of the vote shifted in my favor."

"So you don't exactly have a popular mandate."

"I'm not the darling of the commune crowd, if that's what you mean. It's more like a love-hate relationship. But I have to admit—they do care a lot about their kids, and as long as I do right by them, they leave me alone. I think they'd rest easier if they could claim me as one of their own, but—what can I say?" He shrugged. "That kind of life just isn't for me."

It was midmorning on day three before Kat realized her time would now be subdivided into weeks, and those weeks into days, and that the maddeningly idle day she had mulled through yesterday was a Tuesday late in August. She hadn't used the names of days since moving to the mirage-mesa, as they mean nothing to a farmer. Now, she realized, she would need to keep close track, would need to carry a calendar back to the mirage with her lest she lose track of the days and miss her classes. Wednesdays and Thursdays would become the axis around which her weeks would spin, and on this hot morning, at the center of her new axis, Kat was having a hard time believing she had agreed to set her life spinning in such a way.

Her pacing began at sunup: first, to all ends of the plum thicket, then up the path to Angelo's empty house at least four times, and then even down the dirt road a bit under the pretense of making sure her bicycle would have no trouble with it. At the moment she thought she would surely go mad with waiting, the clock hands showed her it was time to tighten her bandana and go. She sent Oso home and pedalled her bicycle west down the dirt road, feet pumping to the rhythm of her churning stomach.

Angelo had driven her along the route, but they had passed the trip in conversation and Kat hadn't noticed the details she now saw from her bicycle. The road threaded along between the ridge where Angelo's house sat and the valley of old orchards where Kat's house sat. After awhile, it crossed the main road leading north to the town, and thereafter it was paved and somewhat wider. The fields here looked more vigorously well-tended, the houses somewhat modern—a contrast to the dirt end of the road, where the orchards were thick with the neglect of the arthritic, and the houses were crumbling gently back to the earth from which their bricks had come.

Beyond the last of the well-tended fields, the road turned again to dirt and led eventually to the school, a cluster of small buildings sitting alone on a slight rise. Behind the school and to the west stretched the saged drylands considered useless by the valley's old-time residents—no good for farming, little good for grazing. It was here that the communes sprawled in ramshackle arrangements of scrounged materials and inexperience, dotting the barren landscape with suggestions of transience.

Kat coasted her bicycle off the dirt road and through the school parking lot. Beyond the lot was the yard, a dusty circle of beaten ground and gaming equipment, all surrounded by wooden tables and benches. The entire school population was exuberantly taking in the last of summer's air over lunch, clustering here and there by age, by activity. It was more confusion and noise than Kat had been around since her own days in school, and while her cat-self was ready to skitter under the nearest clump of sage, her human-self told her to stay put and get used to it. It's only two days a week, she reminded herself. And it's important.

The students under the sun varied in age and ethnicity, but in no other way did they appear to be the wild and offbeat grouping the parents had seemed. From their clothing and hair and manner, it would be hard to tell who might be the banker's child, the gypsy woman's child, the child of a man with an arm-length knife strapped to his leg. Most seemed to be cloaked in the style of the current generation: well-fed and well-washed. Kat saw no limps, no eye patches, no heads that looked to house lice, no clothing that didn't fit except out of deliberate affect. No one laughed with closed mouth to hide rotting teeth, no one was without a lunch, no one sat out because they spoke a different language. Kat saw her fifth lifetime hanging easily from the shoulders of these students, a well-tailored suit of historical privilege moving gracefully with their every gesture. She stood momentarily enchanted watching this group that would have been impossible in any of her other lifetimes and wondered if they had any inkling of how historically unique they were.

Kat's eye didn't pick Angelo out from the crowd until he stood and walked toward her, looking relieved, as if he hadn't been quite sure until now that she would actually show up. He gave her arm a quick squeeze and whispered, "Have fun—" before announcing lunchtime's end.

She rode the wave of students into her classroom, arriving not ahead but in the middle of them, differentiating herself only in that she remained standing while the rest flung themselves into a variety of gangly seated postures. The desks she had moved to the perimeter of the room two days before, making room for scrounged pillows and more comfortable chairs, had been reset into rows now all a-tangle with extended arms and legs. While Kat was noting how uncomfortable it all looked, a "Shhh" went through the group and the last of the lunchtime boisterousness came to an end. Twenty-one fourteen- and fifteen-year-olds sat staring at her staring at them.

"Aren't you—uncomfortable?" she asked, then heard how ridiculous an introduction it must have sounded, and between that and her nerves, she giggled. A few of the students looked at each other, a few laughed with her, but most just sat and watched, waiting. Kat thought of the dream she'd had of the sleepy-eyed faces coming to life when she showed them her claws. These eyes weren't at all asleep, making her think wistfully of her mirage and the cats who only barely paid her any heed. "Please," she said, "make yourselves comfortable." There was more subdued laughter this time, and many of them turned to each other with silent dares in their eyes. After a minute of self-conscious shuffling in the room, a boy wearing camouflage fatigues and heavy black military boots stood up, got a pillow from the pile in the corner, and lay down on the floor out of sight behind the desks. All eyes swung toward Kat, to watch her reaction; when she had none, the group suddenly exploded with action and laughter. In half the time it took them to be indecisive, Kat saw the entire room transformed. There was now a generally open area in the middle full of reclining bodies, with desks piled to the perimeter, much as she had arranged it originally. Some of the students remained in desks, some slouched into the half-dozen chairs, the rest made a few dogpiles on the floor that quickly toppled with earthquakes of giggles. When everyone had more or less settled in, another "Shhh" went through the group, making Kat wonder who had appointed themselves deputies in charge of silence and order. Once again, twenty-one faces looked at her, only this time she saw the mischief in their eyes, daring her now to scold them for taking her offer seriously. The mischief was familiar to Kat; she'd seen it in faces this age through four centuries, in several cultures, in all languages. There's something about this age, she thought as they continued to wait for her reaction. They're like coyotes.

That ludicrous thought—seeing herself, part cat, willingly stepping into a den of coyotes—broke the clutch of Kat's nerves and made her laugh aloud. The students watched uneasily as she failed to deliver the scolding and, instead, settled into an over-stuffed chair she had saved for herself. When she sat forward, she had the sense they did too, that their ears had perked toward her.

"I'm Kat," she said, noticing her voice held none of the tension she'd felt building up for weeks toward this moment. "O'Malley," she added. "And I'd like to tell you a story."

∞∞

"Well, except that I completely forgot to call roll, I think it went okay," Kat announced as she stepped into Angelo's house that evening.

"I may have to fire you for that," he called from the kitchen. "I was going to quiz you on all the kids' names."

"No dessert for me, then." She shrugged, stepping through the low arch from the sala. Angelo was pressing garlic into a hot frying pan, Oso at his feet.

"The kids didn't give you trouble?" he asked.

"No, not at all. I couldn't figure out why they were being so good."

"I primed them—"

"I should have known."

"—but not enough to take all the credit, not by any means. You're just one of those teachers that kids take to." He added onions to the pan and the biting steam made Kat's eyes water. "Which I had a feeling you would be. Also, everyone's curious as hell about you. You're the first new teacher in the school in four years, so that was working in your favor. Once they get used to you, they'll start testing you."

Kat snitched a mushroom from a pile on the cutting board. "I think they were testing me today," she said between bites, "and maybe I'm fooling myself, but I think I passed."

" 'Pass' wasn't the word I heard in the parking lot—'cool' was what I heard."

"They talked about me after school?"

Angelo slid the mushrooms out of her reach when she tried for another. "Hey—you Irish girls need to show a little more respect in the kitchen," he said, dumping the mushrooms into the frying pan and out of her reach. "Of course they talked about you. You've just stepped into one of the tightest communities on earth. You can bet they pass around all kinds of information about teachers."

"They said I was *cool?*" Kat's hands went absently to her covered head for the twenty-dozenth time since arriving in town.

"Cool. And I didn't hear one word about your hair, so you can take that thing off now."

"No, I'm going to *sleep* with my hair covered as long as I'm in town. I don't want anything to go wrong." When Angelo raised a curious eyebrow at her, she added, "It was fun. I had fun today. I don't want to mess it up."

His smile was broad and slow as he folded his arms and leaned against the counter. "Do me a favor, would you Kat?"

"Sure, what?"

"At the end of February, when the kids are cabin-crazy and the heat doesn't work and all the teachers are threatening to quit because of the mud in the yard—do me a favor and remember that it was fun today." He sighed. "It would make my job a *lot* easier."

"You mean, it all goes downhill from here?" She grinned.

"No, things are fine till winter starts to melt. Then the bottom drops out for about six weeks." He turned back to stir things on the stove. "I'm convinced it's the mud. Since I've been headmaster, I haven't made it through a mud season yet without spending half my time keeping someone from strangling someone else." He looked at her sideways. "Of course, with *you* around, the mud wouldn't have to be such a problem—"

"No, Angelo, I'm not going to—"

"Just the mud trick! I never learned that one—"

"No, Angelo. No hair, no mud trick, no curing sick babies. I'm just teaching. I don't want anyone paying attention to me. Except the students."

Oso sighed loudly and groaned himself into a new position with his head on Kat's foot. "See?" Angelo laughed. "Even Oso thinks you're hard to get along with."

"No mud trick." She sat on the floor and moved Oso's heavy head to her lap, stroking a slow finger up the ridge of his nose until he nearly purred. *You like that?* she asked silently, but his only reply was the roll of a half-lidded eye.

"He doesn't talk. I've tried."

"Too bad." She sighed. "I'd like to hear his opinion."

"On mud? He hates it. Sticks to his paws."

"No, on fifteen-year-olds. I felt like I was in a room full of coyotes today."

"A cat in with coyotes?" Angelo laughed.

"Exactly. I've never had anyone pay so much attention to me, unless they were staring at my hair, which they weren't."

"What were you doing?"

"Just telling a story, most of the time. By next week, after they've done some reading, there'll be other things to do. But on the first day, what else is there?"

Angelo jumped back from the stove's splatter and turned the

heat down. "Well, that's it then. You're an incredible storyteller and you had them in the palm of your hand the way you had *me* that time—"

"I didn't do it *that* way—not like I did it for you."

"Probably better not, either, if you don't want to draw attention. The parents may look wild, but they have their limits. I've run into a few." Angelo moved her aside a moment so he could fetch a pot from the cupboard behind her. "So what kind of story were you using to enchant them?"

"I told them about you and me—well, not exactly you and me. I told them about Julio and Josefa, who lived in a time and a place when there was no school to end the summertime."

"And you had them eating out of your hand with that one." He grinned. "What I don't understand is why you've been hiding out on that mirage all this time. Anyone with cat blood who can charm a den full of coyotes—"

"I didn't *charm* them. I just told them a story I thought they might be especially interested in."

"Same thing." Angelo filled the pot with water and set it over a flame, then slid down to sit by Kat on the floor, Oso between them. "What did you tell them about Julio? That he was an insufferable teenager with a good eye for a horse and couldn't write his own name?"

"Pretty much." She smiled. "Angelo, when did you first learn to read?"

"Last time." His eyes squinted faintly as he tried to bring the departed world into focus for himself. Kat caught a fleeting glimpse on the far wall of a stub of pencil too small for the rough hand clutching it, but it faded before she could see what the hand was writing.

"This is my first time," she said softly, still staring at the far kitchen wall. "I wanted the class to start out with a sense of that—how important it was, because we couldn't have it." Oso shifted his head, trying to rest it on both their laps simultaneously but finally settling it on Angelo's with his tail draped over Kat's knees. "I tried to teach myself to read last time. One of my little girls was too scrawny to work, so she got to go to school for awhile, and I'd try to read her schoolbook at night when they were all asleep. But I never quite got it figured out." Kat bit her lip at what felt like tears pushing from behind her eyes, then shook them off and smiled. "But I could write my name. My daughter saw to that. She didn't want her mama being *too* illiterate, so she taught me how to write my name." Angelo was nodding beside her, seeing his own times while she narrated hers. "I couldn't spell 'dog', but I could sign my name like a queen." Her hand painted the letters with a flourish upon the garlicky air. "Regina—Rose—Klimek," she whispered. "It meant a lot to me, to be able to sign my name."

The pot on the stove was beginning to hiss, but Angelo didn't budge. "Julio Amadeo Duque Castaña," he said slowly. "I always wondered what it looked like, but I didn't know anyone who knew how to write that time."

Kat pulled a pencil from her pocket and scratched it across the tile floor. Julio Amadeo Duque Castaña, she wrote in her most calligraphic hand. "That's what it looks like."

Angelo stared for a long time at the script, faint on the dusty brown of the tiles—stared as if trying to find an old face on a new friend, then traced the letters with his fingertip. He reached for the pencil and wrote Josefa Mercedes Duque Castaña next to the first name, his script wide and bold and not so ornate. Kat took the pencil back and wrote Regina Rose Klimek, to which Angelo responded with Christos Papadimitriou. Kat had to scoot to the side to make room for Feliciana Alegre Morales Luna, and by the time Angelo added Thaddeus Carter Brown, the lead had spent itself on the rough floor and he had to sharpen the pencil with his pocketknife. The two of them crawled from one end of the kitchen floor to the other to read the last of the names: Epifanio

Bolívar Rios, Ivy Church, Angelo Vittorio diVita, and Meghan Katlin O'Malley.

Oso had chewed through two whole dream-bones and the air was thick with evaporating water before either of them spoke. "It looks like the neighborhood I grew up in this time—a whole different world on every block," said Angelo. "What's the order on your names?"

"Josefa first, then Feliciana, and Ivy, and Regina, and Kat."

Angelo nodded. "And I was Julio, Epifanio, Thaddeus, and Christos before I was Angelo. I've never looked at them together like that." He stood to tend to the forgotten dinner while Kat stayed on the floor, looking at the names and combing her fingers through Oso's fur. "Keep it up," said Angelo eventually. "If that's what you're like in the classroom—keep it up."

"*Meadow* Million Flowers Buckman—?"

Kat was only three names into the roll call and already she regretted not glancing at the list before reading it cold. It was hard to keep the question mark out of her voice.

"That's me," came a voice from Kat's left. There was nothing in the girl's appearance to suggest a million flowers, unless it could be said the spikes in her hair resembled a zinnia in full bloom. A variety of sharp-ended objects pierced her ears and nose in a way that made Kat's knees hurt at first glance. She was clearly the extreme in the room. No trouble remembering *her* name, Kat thought.

"Rey Cortez."

"Here."

"Ann Marie Dennler."

"Annie."

"Anan—da—Ananda—Da—"

"AnandaDava Shakta Dugan." The voice coming to her aid was

leaning against a pillow propped on the back wall, but Kat wasn't sure by the time she looked up if it had come from the dark-haired boy with the surprising grey eyes or from the doe-haired girl next to him.

"Are you called anything for short?"

"Nope," said the boy, eyes twinkling, whereupon he was elbowed by the girl and hissed at by some of the others.

"Angelo said not to—" someone admonished him, and he raised his hands in surrender.

"Okay, okay—I was just kidding."

"Nanda," said someone in the back. "His name is Nanda."

Kat sighed and missed the coyotes of yesterday. She was already thoroughly out of tune with this more subdued morning class, and all she'd tried to do was call roll. She looked for the next name on the list, saw it was Aspen Grove, and tossed the paper into the trash. "Just tell me what you want me to call you. That's all I need to know."

Zoe, Rey, Nanda, Marta, Annie, Aspen, Travis—without context except faces, the names slid easily into place in the group. Meadow, Gregorio, Victoria, Sky—the offbeat grouping she'd seen visibly in the parents was reflected invisibly here in the names. Dakota, Agate, Simon, Joaquin, Kali, Elektra, David, Sundar. The last to speak was a boy sitting to the side, seemingly not part of the group.

"Eli Papadimitriou," he said quietly, the only one to give a full name.

"That's not his name," protested the girl named Agate. "It's Moonfire. Eli Moonfire."

"Eli Papadimitriou," he repeated in the same soft, deliberate voice. The thong-maker, Kat thought. The great-grandson. The child of a woman whose every step is accompanied by hidden bells. Eli came with a context.

"Papadimitriou it is," she nodded to him, then looked to the whole group to add, "and I'm Kat O'Malley."

"*Aspen Grove?*" she asked Angelo as he walked her out to her bicycle after the class.

"Now you have no room to talk, Ms. O'Malley," he laughed. "In your second life you were Feliciana Alegre Morales Luna, and that means Happy Happy Mulberry Tree Moon if you want to get technical about it."

"It's different."

"No it isn't," he chided. "How did it go otherwise?"

"Oh, fine—once I got the names out of the way. And I met Eli," she added. "He gave his name as Papadimitriou, but someone said it's supposed to be Moonfire."

"Legally, it's Moonfire." He sighed. "Layira had his name changed when she changed hers. But for the last couple years he's been claiming Papadimitriou, and he told me he plans to change it back as soon as he's old enough."

"That's how you knew she was your granddaughter. It's not a common name."

"Not around here, it isn't. She was Chrissy Papadimitriou when I first met her." He watched skeptically as Kat bent to tie her skirt into a knot for riding, then swung her leg carefully over the bike. "Are you sure you'll be able to get back to the mesa okay? I can give you a ride to the gorge rim if you just wait till my lunch hour."

"I do this all the time," she said lightly. "Besides, I can't be dependent on you and your truck. You've got your own work to do."

"Then let me at least show you the shortcut," he said, pointing up the road toward the first commune buildings. "See that track cutting off there? It's an old road—a little rough, but it goes straight to the gorge. You won't have to double back toward town to catch the main road."

"A shortcut? That sounds heavenly." She smiled. "See you next week." And she pushed off down the dirt road with a buggy full of dirty laundry behind her, eager to leave the town's rumble in her wake and go soak in her warm spring.

◯◯◯

It didn't happen as the CatWoman stood at the bottom of the river gorge staring at the rickety footbridge and pulling together with her eyes the second, sturdier mirage-bridge floating above it. Nor did it happen as she walked her bicycle and buggy up the mirage-slope on the west side of the river, drinking in the sudden quiet of the place after four days of the east valley's noise. It didn't even happen when she saw the cottonwood salad spring to view a few miles ahead of her as she rode through the sage. But when she rounded the edge of her east orchard and saw fifty cat faces peering expectantly at her from walls, from trees, from porch roof, it happened. She realized what she'd forgotten to do.

The cats must have read the realization on her face. Led by the apricot siamese, they all started to hiss, then turned tail high and stalked away, leaving just the tortoise-shell perched on the arch into the courtyard.

How could you forget the tuna? You were in town for four days.

The CatWoman pulled off her bandana, letting her hair try to spring to life after being so tightly swaddled. *I was distracted.*

The tortoise-shell just shook her head and, finally, she too walked along the ridge of the wall to disappear into the shade under the porch roof. *Humans!* she muttered, before she was completely out of sight.

"Cats!" muttered the CatWoman in response.

The oasis looked surprisingly unchanged. Everything sat right as she left it, except for the drying apricots and tomatoes, which had pulled away from each other since she'd seen them last. The orchards still looked healthy, the garden bountiful. The cats were still plump and well-fed, though she knew they would never admit to such. There was nothing on the mirage to mirror the eons she felt had been passing while she was in town, and the CatWoman decided she would see that as comforting. She wasted no time in unloading her bike and buggy, then went straight up the hillside to the warm spring to soak away the pulse of the town. Looking down over the house and orchards and gardens, she felt comforted indeed that it was all still there, all still the same.

⊂⊃⊃⊃

"History," Kat told her afternoon class the next time they met, "is nothing more than a collection of stories about people and how they've lived. You and me. Your grandparents and mine. Your parents—"

"I wish *my* parents were history," groaned a long and lean boy named Sean, sparking quick laughter and some agreement from the others.

"Oh, but they are." Kat smiled. "Maybe not in the sense you mean it, but they *are* history, and so are you. There's no separating anyone out, because every single life that's ever been lived has added to the history of the human race in some way—whether it's mentioned in a history book or not." Kat had only just learned their names an hour earlier and was unsure of at least half of them at the moment. She turned to one whose name stuck out in her mind to ask, "Soukishna, who are some of the people who *are* mentioned?"

Soukishna reminded Kat of a mouse—mouse-brown hair, mouse-brown eyes, long fine-boned fingers, and a face completely dwarfed by glasses. "Presidents," she suggested.

"Queens," someone added before Kat could remember the name to go with that face.

"Generals," came a husky voice from the boy who wore camouflage fatigues again, like last week. His name, Kat recalled, was Shanti, and he was Mu's son.

"Presidents, queens, and generals," she echoed. "I couldn't have put it more precisely. So why them? Why not us?"

"Because they do the important stuff." Diego's answer was almost impatient, as if he couldn't understand why Kat wouldn't know this.

"All of it?" she asked him.

"They make the laws and tell us what to do—and they can put us in jail if we don't," he explained, but Shanti corrected him.

"Generals don't make the laws. They win the wars."

Adelmo took issue with this. "That's not what my grandpa says. He says it's the soldiers who win the wars, and the generals just wear the medals and don't do anything dangerous. And they don't dig latrines." He snickered.

"Did your grandfather dig latrines in a war?" Kat asked.

"Uh-huh."

"Is his story written in the history books?"

"Are you kidding?"

"No, I'm not kidding," Kat assured him. "This is my point. The war your grandfather fought in is described in lots of history books, and hundreds of thousands of students your age have to learn all about the presidents, queens, and generals behind that war. But have any of those students ever had to study how important good latrines are in a war?"

Under the sudden burst of laughter from the class, Kat heard someone ask, "What's a latrine?" and someone else hiss back, "*Geez*—it's an *outhouse!*"

When they had settled back to listening again, Kat went on. "You think I'm joking, but tell me this. How can a general, no matter how many medals he has—how can a general win a war if his soldiers are all dying of dysentery and hepatitis?" As they pondered that point, Kat had the sense again that their ears were perked toward her, and she marvelled silently at how she enjoyed the sensation. "Wars aren't my specialty. I just use Adelmo's comment because it's a perfect example of what I mean—*everyone* is a part of history, whether they're digging a latrine or signing treaties. But when you study something like that war in school, who will you study? The soldier who saw the war as an endless series of latrines he dug over the course of three years? Or the general who remembers the same three years as being filled with tactical decisions and strategy meetings, and battles won or lost, territory gained or lost, and all the negotiations for terms of surrender? The books want you to study the story of the generals. I want you to study the story of the latrines. So we'll be covering both."

"We're gonna be studying outhouses?" moaned a girl with the longest fingernails Kat had seen on anything human. She thought perhaps the girl's name was India. "But I don't *need* to study outhouses—I've got one at my house!"

"Only figuratively," Kat assured her. "When you take your midterm and final exams, you'll be expected to know all about the version of history written in your books—all about the presidents, queens, and generals. But I wouldn't feel like I'd done my job if you didn't also learn about some of the unwritten versions of history, because they're just as important."

"Are you gonna give us latrine tests?" India snickered.

"No—no tests on the latrine version."

"Then how will you know if we've learned anything?"

"Oh," Kat rolled her eyes and gave them all a half-mouthed grin, "I'll know." She turned to the chalkboard and wrote in large letters PQGVH and KOLVH. "From this day forward, this class will study both the Presidents', Queens', and Generals' Version of History and Kat O'Malley's Latrine Version of History. There will be homework due in each category every time you come to class, and I don't want any of you neglecting one because you think the other is more important." She wrote page numbers next to the heading PQGVH, and next to KOLVH she wrote "Write a five-page historical account of the first day of school from your viewpoint."

"*Five pages!*" The feigned shriek came from Aaron. "But—but—"

"Not a word less. I want you to tell me all the details—what you did, what you wore, what you saw and heard. Everything."

"But what does that have to do with history?" Adelmo asked.

"You'll find out next week." Kat grinned. "Don't miss it."

As they were all tumbling out the door at the end of class, Kat saw Angelo wading his way upstream and into the room, stopping at each "Hi, Angelo!" to ask how history class was going. "Five pages!" she heard Aaron moaning to him. "How come you hired her?"

"I agree, Aaron." Angelo nodded seriously. "It's nowhere near enough. I'll have to speak with her about—" His audience was gone before the comment was complete. He grinned at Kat across the empty room. "So how's it going?"

"It's going—very well."

"You sound surprised."

"Well, I *am* surprised. I'm surprised by how comfortable I am in front of them. You know me—I *hate* talking in front of people. I don't even like talking *to* people."

"What? You mean you're not coming to dinner tonight and I've been marinating a chicken in vain since sunup?"

"No." She laughed. "You're different. I've known you forever. But I haven't known these kids forever, and yet here I am, having fun—"

Kat and Angelo were both startled into silence by Mu's voice in the doorway. "You've known each other forever! So *that's* how Angelo found our new history teacher. We've all been wondering."

Those damn slippers, Angelo cursed silently so only her cat-self would hear. *I can never hear him sneaking up.* Kat stifled a giggle by pretending to cough.

"What can I do for you, Mu?" Angelo asked.

"I came to extend an invitation to Kat—and to you, too," he added with just enough of a pause to tint his words with insincerity. "We're having a drumming at the pyramid on Sunday afternoon. Bring anything you'd like to beat on." He smiled his lizard smile at Kat. "As a history teacher, you'd love our drummings. They're so primitive."

"Thank you, but I don't live—" Kat stammered, unable to summon the poise she'd felt in front of her class moments earlier, "—I'm going out of town this weekend."

"Don't save a seat for me either," Angelo quickly covered for her. "I have a house to plaster before the weather changes."

"Ah well, we'll miss your company. Maybe some other time."

When Mu was gone, Angelo groaned silently, *I wish that guy would wear boots, or bells, or even high heels—something to give me some warning.* The way he rolled his eyes made Kat laugh. *I can't tell you how many times he's done that to me.* "So where were we?" he went on out loud.

"I was saying you're going to spoil me if you keep up with the marinated chickens."

"It's a standing invitation, and if you don't show up every week, Oso will be eating food that was never meant for a dog. And hey— my Italian grandfathers would boil in their graves if that happened."

Kat turned to erase the board. "Far be it from me to boil the dead. I'll be there."

"What's that you're erasing? K-O-L-V-what?"

"KOLVH. Kat O'Malley's Latrine Version of History."

"Latrine version?"

"Of course," she said lightly, retrieving her backpack from a peg on the wall. "Didn't you study latrines in history?"

"Uh, Ms. O'Malley," Angelo teased officiously, "perhaps it's time I sat in on one of your classes."

"Please do, Mr. diVita. Come next week. It'll be shocking."

With Angelo's help, the CatWoman had treats for the cats following that second trip to town. As he walked her out to her bicycle at the end of her last class, he handed her a half-dozen cans of tuna, saving her a trip into the heart of town. Since she had left the buggy on the mesa and her paniers were full of books and laundry, the tuna banged its way through the sage in the Cat-Woman's backpack, digging hard edges into her ribs with every bump on the trail. This week's cat sentry was only half as strong, but by the time she'd opened one can and the fishy aroma caught the breeze, every cat for miles was instantly upon her.

By opening the tuna, the CatWoman also broke the conversation ban that had been in effect since her less-than-triumphant homecoming the week before. Several cats asked her what life was like in town. A few who knew what a school was asked about school. The grey tiger and the apricot siamese asked in unison if she'd gone to live in a bookstore.

And do they need a cat? the grey tiger added.

People don't live in bookstores. The CatWoman laughed.

But the tortoise-shell said she got fat living in a bookstore, the apricot siamese complained.

Cats live in bookstores. People don't.

Why not? They could get fat there. Don't they want to get fat?

No—the CatWoman began, but paused as she recalled a time when people *had* wanted to get fat, and couldn't . . . and she knew then of a lesson to add to the latrine version of history. *No, people nowadays don't want to get fat. But even if a person lived in a bookstore, he wouldn't get fat like a bookstore cat gets fat.*

The grey tiger pronounced the concept too human to be understood.

∞

Kat didn't want to gamble on finding no firewood at the school the next week, so when she left the mirage for her third trip to town, she strapped a few sticks of kindling to the back of her bicycle. Likewise, she knew the only place to find willow switches along the way would be at the river, so she stopped at the footbridge to prune branches from a stand on the bank. But it was her need to bypass the shortcut road and trek halfway into town to find marshmallows that ate up the head start she'd given herself. By the time she arrived at school, she barely had a moment to stick her head into Angelo's office before running off to class.

"I'm building a fire in the fire pit today," she announced, out of breath from her ride. "Am I supposed to ask permission?"

Angelo scowled at her over the telephone he was dialing. "No, you're supposed to ask, 'How are you, Angelo? How was your weekend?' "

"How are you, Angelo?"

"Don't burn the place down, okay? I'll be sitting in today."

She offered no details when Belle and Leah caught up to her on the path and asked why she was carrying firewood into class. "Because we're going to study history's cruelest lesson today," was all she would say. By the time the day's session of book studies had come to an end, Kat had dodged at least a dozen more questions about her odd pile of props, including a silent one from Angelo, sitting at the back of the room.

History's cruelest lesson—with marshmallows?

To soften the blow, she replied obliquely.

"Enough books for today," Kat announced at last. "Meet me out at the fire pit with your historical accounts of the first day of school." As on that first day, the students didn't immediately jump into action, but looked at each other for a moment. By the time they did move and the last of them had scrambled across the yard with essays dug from out of notebooks and backpacks, flames were already beginning to crackle through twigs and kindling in the center of the fire pit used as a school meeting place.

"There," said Kat, standing back from the heat that contrasted comfortably with the cool, cloudy day. "Now we can start. What I'm going to show you is what happens to historical accounts as they're passed on through the years, before they ever get mentioned in a history book." She passed a small box to Beau, standing next to her, telling him to pull a slip of paper from inside and read it out loud.

Beau swung his head to the side to clear his face of black bangs before reading the message on the folded piece of paper: " 'Your historical account of the first day of school sits in your parents' closet in a pile of old notebooks. After thirty-two years, they do some serious housecleaning and throw it away. No one ever reads it. Toss your homework into the fire.' *What?!* Aren't you even going to read it?"

Kat nodded toward the fire. "Toss it in—and help yourself to a marshmallow. History's being cruel to you today."

"Aw, maaaaan," Beau moaned as the rest of the class laughed. "It took me all night to write that."

Zeke was next in line for the box while Beau squatted to roast a marshmallow over the fading remains of his homework. " 'You are illiterate and never learned to write. Your version of the first day of school is a story you tell to your children and grandchildren, but after three generations the story is forgotten. Toss your homework into the fire.' But mine is *cool!* I made the whole thing *rhyme!* That's not *fair!*"

"No." Kat shook her head, handing him a marshmallow and willow stick. "History's not fair. It's anything but."

Venus was next. " 'Your next door neighbor fails to clean his chimney for three years in a row and, in the fourth year, his house catches fire. Your historical account of the first day of school, hanging in a frame on your wall, is lost forever when your house and several others burn to the ground. Toss your homework into the fire.' " Venus' round cheeks nearly hid her eyes completely as she giggled. "Don't anybody tell my mom I ate a marshmallow. She thinks they're poisonous."

Aaron made theatre of his homework's similar fate. "But I got up at four this morning to write this! Angelo! Tell her she can't do this! This is a work of art! And I lost sleep over it!"

"No, Kat's right." Angelo laughed. "This is a critical lesson. I wish I'd thought of it years ago."

Aaron staggered dramatically toward the fire and held his essay aloft a moment. "Alas, poor homework—I knew it well."

"Not *that* well," Belle quipped, "if you didn't write it till four this morning."

Sheer coincidence led Shanti to pull the only slip of paper from the box that had a military theme to go with the military fatigues and boots he wore like religion. " 'Your country goes to war with another country and loses,' " he read. " 'The victorious army sweeps through the countryside destroying every book and man- uscript they find. Your historical account of the first day of school is officially declared a lie and burned. Toss your homework into the fire.' "

"It's not a lie!" Zephyr cried out indignantly. "Just because they lost the war doesn't mean they're all liars."

"No, of course it doesn't," Kat agreed. "But that very thing has happened over and over again. It's easy to find history written by those who win, those who hold power. It's difficult to find history written by the ones who lose."

Seventeen marshmallows had been roasted over seventeen flaming essays before one was finally spared. " 'Your historical account of the first day of school sits in a crate in a basement for nearly two hundred years,' " Pilar read to the group, practically hiding behind the tiny slip of paper. " 'Because the house is so old, it is declared a historical landmark and protected by the state. Anthropologists come upon your manuscript while searching the house and publish your essay in a professional journal, where it is read by historians worldwide. It is the only account they've seen of the first day of school, and they put it into all the history books from that day on. Give your homework to Kat.' "

In the ensuing moment of silence before the class roared in protest, Kat heard Angelo roaring with laughter.

"BUT SHE WAS ABSENT THAT DAY!" they all cried.

"Well, Pilar," she announced as the roar died down, "history is smiling on you today. Have a marshmallow to celebrate."

When the final three essays remaining in the group had met various historical ill fates, Kat read Pilar's piece to the group with the preface, "Now remember—this is the *only* surviving record of what happened on the first day of school. Future generations will point to this essay and say 'This is what happened.' " The essay described, in detail, a day spent sick in bed, punctuated by two trips outdoors to sit with her grandmother while she peeled "a green mountain of chiles. The mountain comes to my grandmother's table every year, and every year she says the same thing: 'Gracias a Dios, we'll eat well this winter.' But while she is thankful, I am sad, because I know the green mountain comes every year to tell me that summer is about to end."

"That's beautifully written, Pilar," Kat said as she handed it back to her. Pilar bit her lip and spoke volumes about herself in the silent blush she gave in reply. "Well, what do you think?" she asked the rest of the group, who seemed at a collective loss for words. It was Aaron who finally broke the silence, though he was obviously struggling to figure out just what he meant to say.

"It's not—it's not—*right*—"

"Not right?" Kat prompted. "Everything Pilar wrote is true, and it all happened on the first day of school. So what's not right about it?"

"It's not that it's not true," Zephyr interjected. "It's not right that it should be the only version to survive. People who read that would think we were all sick on the first day of school."

"She didn't even *mention* school, and that was the important thing that happened that day," Beau protested.

"It's *all* important," Kat reminded them. "It's *all* history."

"But it's not the whole story—"

"And neither is your history book."

Bravo, Kat heard Angelo call silently to her over the heads of a group that was silenced a moment by the thought. *You made your point. See you at dinner.* He climbed out of the group as inconspicuously as possible, his departure masked by a sudden flood of debate. When he reached the doorway to his office, he turned and called to her cat-self one last time. *Did you rig that, so Pilar would be the one?*

No. She smiled, trying not to show her distraction to the students who were nearly all talking at once. *I swear I didn't. But it was perfect, don't you think?*

From over the debate and across the yard, Kat could see Angelo wink at her before disappearing into the building.

By her third trip home from town and teaching, the CatWoman wished Angelo hadn't catered to the cats' tastes so magnanimously. "Oh come on," she remembered his words, "animals are for loving and spoiling." It's my mood that's being spoiled, she grumbled to herself, as the rain clouds of the day before opened their gates overnight, turning the path on the mirage into a bog she couldn't dry from in town. The last thing she wanted, as she slogged through miles of mud and drizzle, was the added weight of eight cans of tuna and four tins of sardines, edges hammering her bones. *No more treats till Angelo brings them himself,* she growled, peeling off pants that were muddy to the knees.

But you said you'd bring treats every week, came a cat-whine.

No, you said I would.

Well, when is he coming?

I don't know—sometime when he's got time. Till then, no more treats. Which of course didn't sit well with the majority population on the mirage, who coordinated a fifteen-day pout until the harvest moon brought Angelo back to the mesa.

With the harvest moon came a sudden golden chill that dripped slowly down the mountainsides, one aspen leaf at a time, igniting the very top leaves of the cottonwoods on either side of the gorge. The apples in the CatWoman's west orchard crisped and sweetened in the chill night air, and when she picked one off a tree on the morning before the harvest moon, her mouth over-flowed with the taste of autumn. By the time Angelo pedalled in that day, with an odd-shaped bundle strapped to his bike and Oso trotting along behind, the CatWoman had already gathered two bushels of fruit and was propped in the crook of a tree, watching the light shift on the aspen-robed mountains. A biting cedar smoke had drifted down from the kitchen chimney to spice the air and flare her senses, all of her wide open and savoring the turquoise morning.

"You've taken to living in trees?" he called up to her.

The CatWoman plucked an apple and tossed it to him. "They're worth the climb," she said between bites. "This is my second one already today."

Angelo held the apple out toward Oso. "I don't know, Oso. Should I eat this? The last time a man stood in a garden and took an apple from a woman, there were disastrous consequences for all of mankind."

"All of womankind, too," she chided. "But if ever there was an apple worth courting disaster, this is it." She tossed her core beyond the edge of the trees and climbed down. "What's that on your bike?"

"A chainsaw. I thought I'd add to your firewood collection and earn a bed in your sala tonight. The porch is going to be too cold."

"I don't need you to—"

"I *know* you don't need me to. I just *want* to. You must use a lot of firewood with that cookstove."

"I do, but there are dead trees all over this mesa. I just cut them up and haul them in."

"On your bike?"

"Or a sled, if there's snow."

"I don't know about you, Kat." Angelo sighed, shaking his head. "You're dangerously close to being a fanatic. Do you tan leather with your teeth?"

The CatWoman skipped ahead of him on the path to the house. "No." She laughed. "Go ahead—it's okay by me, but I can't speak for the cats after they hear that chainsaw."

The CatWoman could hardly speak for herself once Angelo set the chainsaw to work on a dead piñon a quarter mile away. The sound set her hair on end and made her twitch as if she were being nagged by a huge horsefly. As she carried baskets of apples through the courtyard, she found all her housemates wide-eyed and spike-haired, claws dug into whatever surface was underneath them. Angelo's work circled the house, the sound never growing faint with distance, never resting more than a moment or two. One by one, all fifty cats made their stiff-legged way into the kitchen to complain to her where she stood coring apples, and to each she replied through gritted teeth, *No, I'm not going to stop him. He's trying to do me a favor.*

Some favor, griped the tortoise-shell, who stayed in the kitchen long enough to see the noise-harried CatWoman cut herself and scrape her knuckles more than once on the pulper. When the cat snickered, the CatWoman glared over the knuckle in her mouth and marched outdoors. *Bribe him with food!*

Angelo left a trail of cut logs that would have been easy to follow if the horsefly's buzzing hadn't led the CatWoman straight to him. The closer she got, the harder she had to grit her teeth lest they rattle right out of her skull. Through five lifetimes she couldn't recall a worse sound, and couldn't imagine at all how he could stand it, being part cat himself. She found him in a small clearing, intently stripping branches from a long felled trunk, with Oso unfathomably asleep under a cedar nearby. The infernal buzzing masked her approach, so Angelo didn't see her stop in surprise at the sight of his bare back.

He's built like the iceman, she thought. I haven't seen a build like that since . . .

. . . since her fourth lifetime, when even then they were becoming less common. She had watched that same build carrying ice blocks up tenement stairs, day after day, week after week— the same build that tended a blacksmith's forge in earlier lifetimes, or shouldered a plow, or quarried stone. That kind of build was rare in this fifth lifetime when machines had taken over the brute tasks of lifting, carrying, pounding—rare in this lifetime when a man's build was more apt to be molded by recreational choice than by occupational demand. Angelo's thonged hair lay like a dark river in the canyon of his spine, deep between ridges of muscles barely moving under the minor weight of the chainsaw. The iceman in her fourth lifetime had looked just like that through his sweat-damp shirt, carrying the weight of four ripe pregnancies on one shoulder, up the stairs, a soft grunt after each landing . . .

The CatWoman blushed when she realized Angelo caught her staring at him. He shut off the chainsaw and reached to pull small plugs from his ears, his expression asking if anything was wrong.

"I was just—remembering something. It's happening to me a lot lately." She surveyed the proximate piles of wood. "You've done more in two hours than I could do in two weeks with my bow saw. Now I'll have to figure out what to do with all the time you've saved me."

"You'll think of something." Angelo made as if to put the plugs back into his ears, but the CatWoman interrupted the gesture.

"Why don't you stop for some lunch?" she suggested.

"Not yet. I'd rather finish first so I don't have to wash up twice. I thought I'd ride up to the hot spring when I'm done."

"This is enough wood—you don't have to do anymore—you can sleep in the sala anytime—"

"This won't last you a month."

"*Please,*" she nearly begged. "The cats sent me to bribe you with food to get you to stop." Angelo raised a dubious eyebrow at her. "Okay," she shrugged, "I'll admit it—I can't stand the sound of a chainsaw."

"I should have brought two sets of earplugs."

"Fifty-two," she corrected him.

Angelo and Oso disappeared to the hot spring after all the wood had been gathered in to the woodpile, leaving the cats to re-align their cowlicks and the CatWoman to tend the first huge pot of applesauce on the stove. Molten pops and gurgles soloed a muffled percussion into the otherwise sleepy afternoon. Through the hours of the sun's downward arc, the entire oasis catnapped until rudely awakened by the sudden explosion of a chainsaw just outside the courtyard arch. The CatWoman, who'd been drowsily keeping an ear on the applesauce from the porch banco, sprang up as a veritable covey of cats was flushed from every corner of the courtyard, straight up the porch posts to the roof and on into the towering cottonwoods. The chainsaw cut off after just an instant, leaving a silence of swaying cat-heavy branches and stifled laughter.

"Just checking the choke." Angelo grinned over the courtyard wall. "It was giving me a little trouble."

"Giving *you* trouble," the CatWoman scolded through her laughter. "I don't know about you. You're dangerously close to being—"

"A ten-year-old," he interrupted. "It's something a man never quite grows out of. And hey—I've been a ten-year-old boy five times."

"I doubt the cats will accept that as an excuse."

"Probably not." Angelo draped a wet towel over the wall in the last of the sunlight. "But they won't turn down tuna."

The cats did turn down tuna. As long as the CatWoman and Angelo sat under the butter-yellow moon listening to coyote tales, the cats sat a silent poltergeist overhead, afloat upon branches tethered on the breezy darkness. Angelo sang to the coyotes and even got Oso to join him in a throaty howl, much to the delight of his mesa cousins. The campfire in the courtyard had been restoked a half-dozen times before the coyotes finally sang good-night to the dark world and Angelo lay back on the autumn-dry grass, his head propped on Oso's belly.

"Enough coyote stories," he said, a tease in his eyes warmer than the firelight between them. "Tell me a story about Meghan Katlin O'Malley."

The CatWoman waved the request aside with the smoke curling toward her. "It's not nearly as interesting as a coyote story."

"Oh, now don't be so modest. There's got to be something to tell. Did you eat breakfast with a silver spoon every morning?"

"Yes, but—"

"Aha, Oso." He reached back to nudge the snoring mound of black fur. "I told you. The O'Malleys and the diVitas did not come from the same side of the tracks. You probably didn't even *have* tracks in your neighborhood, hm?"

"I don't remember any—"

"Just as I thought. While the diVitas' little boy was hopping rails to get to school every morning, the O'Malleys' little girl was eating a late breakfast on the terrace—"

"There wasn't a terrace—"

"—and being chauffeured to school in time for the bell." Angelo cocked a playful eyebrow at her silence. "So, am I right?"

She rolled her eyes. "Yes, there was a driver."

Angelo tugged on Oso's floppy ear. "Now this is getting interesting. Tell us more."

"Like what?"

"Like—ummm—did you take equestrian lessons?"

"No, but I wish I had. A horse would be a big help out here."

"No equestrian lessons, Oso. Take note of that. While the diVita boy was learning how to take care of a bicycle, the O'Malley girl was *not* learning how to take care of a horse. I suspected as much." The CatWoman groaned. "How about a debutante ball? Did you have one?"

Her sudden laughter startled the poltergeist overhead, setting the catted branches to swaying. "Only sort of." She giggled. "I didn't want one, and I told them if they tried to hold one for me, I wouldn't show up. They didn't believe me. So, they held a debutante ball, and the debutante didn't show up." Angelo's smile rivalled the moonlight as he watched her laughing at the memory. "Ohhhh, was I in *trouble!* But by that time, I didn't care. I was always in trouble."

"Were you ever in love?"

The CatWoman lost Angelo's green-gold eyes in the echo of his soft question—lost them with the slightest shift of the firelight on his face and saw, in their place, a pair of soft brown eyes mirroring streaks of orange from a setting winter sun. "Oh yes," she said wistfully, pulling herself reluctantly back through the centuries between the memory-eyes and those watching her now. "Feliciana was terribly in love." A flash of blue-grey shot across the green-gold, and she added, "And Regina was in love."

"And not Kat?"

Her gaze focussed on him again. "Kat?" she repeated, then busied herself with the fire that needed no tending, flushing a thousand sparks to nip at the butter moon. "Kat's in love with being left alone."

Oso protested sleepily when Angelo's hand stopped moving through his fur. "You give up a lot to take solitude for a lover."

"But look what I get." She shrugged. "Out here, no one's staring at my funny hair, wondering about me. I can go to sleep knowing there won't be a lynch mob at my door when I wake up."

"It still doesn't sound like a fair trade."

"Fair? No. It has nothing to do with fairness." The CatWoman was ready to end the topic. "Easy? Yes. It's been a blessed relief to be out here." Angelo's mildly dubious look made her prickly. "You don't understand, Angelo. If you'd been born Josefa and I'd been Julio—"

"That attitude's pretty popular this time around," he said dryly.

She looked at him sharply. "What attitude?"

He plucked at the grass and tossed the dry arrows at the fire. "That women are the only ones who've suffered through history."

"You should try it." She glared at him, then quickly regretted her tone, as a shadow not sent from a cloud swept over the green-gold eyes. She snatched at the grass herself and threw an impatient handful into the flames, and then another, and then several more, until the moonlight had softened her prickly temper. "You tell me a story," she said at length. "Tell me about Angelo diVita." When he didn't immediately reply, she prompted, "He grew up in a neighborhood with tracks—"

"He grew up in a neighborhood with tracks," Angelo echoed, measuring his words and holding her eyes, "in a family who taught him to know when life is being good to him. So you didn't eat last week? No matter—that's over—you got food now. *Enjoy it.* You got a strong back? *Use it.* You like to read? *Go to college.* Know when you've got it good, and do something with it."

"Did his strong back put him through school?"

"Every penny of it."

"And his family—were they proud of him?"

"Proud?" Angelo's voice softened as he gazed gently back through the years. "Operatic is more like it. There was a three-day feast. Angelo was the first one to finish school, much less go to college."

The CatWoman looked up at the moon, at the stars, at the sleek autumn clouds edged with silver and frost. "Was Angelo ever in love?"

His reply was so slow, she wasn't sure if she had really asked or if she just imagined asking. "Yes—" he said at last, more to the night than to her, "—but—"

She brought her gaze down from the heavens and saw him uncharacteristically at a loss for words. "But what?"

"But it was—ummm—hopelessly unrequited from the start. Isn't that right, Oso?" Oso barely moaned at the sound of his name. "Oso saw it all. How they met. How he tried to get her attention. How she was so wrapped up in her own world."

"What happened? Did he give up?"

Angelo stared unreadably across the fire at her. "No. He's a romantic Italian fool."

Oso heard the cats come down for the tuna, sneaking, creeping, down the tall trunks to the porch roof and posts and, finally, to the ground when they thought all were asleep. He heard the plates of tuna licked clean over the soft snores next to him in the sala and the incoherent sleep-talk wafting through the house from the direction of the bedroom. He even heard dozens of cat-yawns as the poltergeist disbanded and its constituent members draped themselves here and there all over the porch. But he didn't hear the tortoise-shell tiptoe through a cracked window into the sala and perch herself next to Angelo's head, so silently did she move.

Sheee's liiike a muuule, but don't give up on herrr, she called to Angelo's cat-self. *We neeed someone liiike yoouu in her liiife.*

Oso raised an eyelid when he heard the cat's soft, persuasive tone, then watched her make a silent path into the bedroom. *Stop being suuuch a muuule,* came the same persuasive tone through the dark doorway. *Liiife's beeing gooood to yoouu.*

When the tortoise-shell reappeared, she paused in her stealthy retreat to look at Angelo once again, then hopped noiselessly back up next to him to add, *Aaand don't briiing thaaat chainsaaww baack heere anyyymooorre.*

∞∞

With each weekly trip, Kat noticed the gelatin rumblings of life in town slightly less. A passing car that, originally, seemed to drown her with noise and threaten to capsize her bicycle, now seemed merely loud. The to-ings and fro-ings, flittings and goings of a valley full of people were filtered more and more by the mud walls of her house and the plum thicket surrounding it, leaving her to dream less often of earthquakes. She even sent Oso home from his Wednesday night sleep duty at her house; not to let himself be retired altogether, however, he thereafter stood on the stone ridgewall in Angelo's yard and watched for her on her days in town, barking when she pedalled into view. It was because of his welcoming bark and her ritual reply that Kat rolled all the way to the orchard gate soon after the harvest moon before noticing her squat little house had been thoroughly transformed. Angelo's weekend plastering work was finally complete, leaving a rounded, dusky rose casita tucked into the tangle of autumn-brilliant branches. But the greater surprise was finding Eli on a ladder in front of the house, paintbrush in hand and palette on lap, working on something just above the door.

"Hi." He greeted her in the same short, shy manner Kat knew from school. He climbed down from his perch and began to fold the ladder as she wheeled her bicycle through the gate.

"Don't go—I'll stay out of your way. What are you painting?" But she needn't have asked. Growing out of the ground on either side of the door, Eli was painting a tangled cluster of morning-glory vines onto the new plaster. Kat had interrupted him just as the tangle on the left met the tangle on the right, off center above the doorway, and meandered upward toward the low roof. The scrapwood palette in Eli's hand was thick with a collage of greens and yellows and blues, a batch of summertime now painted for all seasons onto the little house. "That's beautiful, Eli," she exclaimed. "I didn't realize you were an artist."

"Yeah, well, sort of," he said more to the ladder than to her, though Kat suspected the faint flush in his cheeks was as much from pride as from anything else. "It's for art class. I'll come back tomorrow—"

"No, please—finish what you're doing," she insisted. "I'll stay out of your way." To relieve him of further conversation, Kat went inside. She heard him set up the ladder again and, for about an hour, her cat ears followed the scratchings of his brush as the painted tangle climbed the last of the wall. The sun had nearly ducked below the horizon when there was a tentative knock on the door.

"You can get out your door now," Eli told her when she answered. "I'm taking the ladder."

Kat stepped out and away from the building to look back at his artwork in the late afternoon light. The mural was complete, just kissing the roof's edge with one final curling tendril intently heading off into the sky. On second glance, she realized the tendril was actually a chain of interlocking letters too tiny to read from the ground. "What does it say up top there?" she asked him.

"It's my name. I signed it."

"You should have signed it down here, in big letters," she

scolded him playfully, even as she could tell he was ambivalent about the praise. "You do beautiful work."

"Thanks." He packed up his paints and brushes without further comment as Kat stood enjoying the summery mural, imagining it greeting her on a grey winter day. *I wonder if Angelo told him I love morning-glories,* she was just thinking to herself, when Eli surprised her with a question. "Where do you live when you're not here?" Kat looked at him more sharply than she intended, making him hesitate before adding, "Mr. D said you live somewhere else—"

"Out of town," she said quickly, trying to think of an evasive answer that would still put the topic to rest. "Too far to ride on a bike, and I don't have a car. So I—uh—catch a ride into town for the days when I teach."

Eli nodded as if he'd been wondering on the question for awhile. "Are you gonna move here?"

"I hadn't really—thought about it," she replied warily, wondering why he was asking and why she hadn't already thought of answers to such obvious questions. *Someone was bound to ask sometime,* she chided herself.

Again Eli was nodding thoughtfully, not looking directly at her for more than just a glance. "I like your class," he said eventually. "You're a good teacher."

"Thank you—"

"See you tomorrow," he added quickly, and left the orchard, climbing the switchback trail to Angelo's house with the ladder under one arm and his paint box under the other. She saw him turn back when he reached the ridgewall, perhaps to view his work. When he saw she was watching him, he called down, "Are you—a nun?" touching his head to indicate her bandana.

Oh dear, she thought.

"A *nun?*" Angelo laughed when Kat retold the story over dinner that night.

"The bandana." She sighed. "He thought that's why I keep my hair covered."

"What did you say?"

"I was caught completely unprepared. I said I just like wearing a bandana."

Angelo looked at her sideways and shook his head. "Didn't I tell you at the beginning you're asking for trouble?" he admonished her. "You draw more attention to yourself by covering up like that than you would if you'd just take the damn thing off. Who's going to notice your hair in the same room with Meadow's, or Zephyr's—I mean, what color is Zephyr's hair this week, anyway?"

"Fuchsia."

"There, you see? Even the *name* of the color is more exotic than your hair will ever be to these kids. It's a different generation, Kat. You could be blending right in with them but, no, what do you do? You go and make yourself more mysterious." He waved his fork at her in warning. "And you can bet Eli's not the only one doing a lot of wondering about you. A nun!" He chuckled to himself. "Ha! You deserve that one."

"Eli's quite an artist," Kat said, steering the subject on an easier tangent. "And so are you. It's a sweet plastering job."

"Eli gets credit for plastering, too. Actually, he helped me on the whole house from day one."

"Training his strong back to balance an artistic nature?"

"Hey, there's nothing wrong with that. Like my uncle says: Chi ha quattro mani, mangia quattro pasti—gotta have more than one way to put food on your table. I'm proof of that. When I came to this town, all I had was a hammer and a teaching certificate. Nobody needed a teacher, so I swung a hammer for a couple years."

"Lucky Eli to have a Dutch uncle to teach him these things," she smiled.

"I'm the closest thing Eli's got to an uncle and I take the responsibility very seriously." Angelo nodded. "I want to make sure he doesn't starve when he goes off to college."

"He'll starve for company before he'll starve for food. He's so shy."

"Not with me. He's just shy around you cause you're new, and maybe cause you're a woman. I was shy around women when I was that age."

"You? *Shy*? No—"

"Yes, me," he countered, "seventeen and shy. And you may not believe it, but that's another thing a man never quite grows out of."

"Hmm," Kat said skeptically, slipping a potato off her plate to Oso, under the table. *Is that true, Oso?* she asked him silently, but he only gobbled the treat and went back to sleep.

Layira Moonfire, mother of Eli, member of the board of directors, was the first to bump up against Kat's closed-classroom rule. Mu was the second. She wished they were both as easy about it as the third visitor she turned away—Georgia, part-time art teacher and part-time school secretary, mother of Travis. But while Georgia only laughed her friendly, guttural laugh—"I hated having visitors in my first year too, honey. You let me know if you change your mind."—Layira and Mu would hear nothing of it.

"Now Kat, you're new," Layira twittered, her mother-hen voice accentuated on cue by tiny bells hidden in her shawl, "so you can't be expected to know what this school is like. But from the very start—and I was one of the people who helped get this school started—from the very start, this school has been a *community*. We *all* look after each other, and we *all* take care of the children. I make it a point to visit everyone's class a few times during the year so I can know what the children are learning and *help* them—"

"I understand," Kat said uncomfortably, wishing she were inside her classroom, where she knew the students were growing restless while she stood her ground on the issue for the first time.

"—even though I'm on the board, I'm not someone to be *afraid of.* I'm not *judging you.* Eli just tells me such wonderful things about your class, I'd like to see it for myself—"

"I understand," Kat repeated, knowing Layira would go on at least a bit longer before she would get a chance to put a period on the conversation and go to class.

"—had a teacher here a few years ago who was shy, too, and I put everything in my life aside that year to help her every day in class. I guess I could have been a teacher myself, if I hadn't been called to be a mother—"

Kat tuned her ears away from the singsong and bells, over her shoulders to where she could hear her gaggle of sixteen- and seventeen-year-olds. They were beginning to take advantage of her late arrival with some raucous laughter.

"—spent *so much* time with children, I really love them all, and the gods know I only sit on the board of directors because I want the *very best* for them—"

"So do I," Kat interjected as she heard her opportunity present itself, "and I give them the very best of me when I can concentrate completely on them, without distraction." She could think of no polite way to end the encounter without renewing Layira's singsong, so she simply added, "I'm late for class," and stepped through the door, closing it behind her. As she began her lessons for the day, she saw Layira's shawl, autumn-harmonized with golds and oranges, swinging elegantly left to right across the yard and through the door to Angelo's office.

A week later, as she stood in the same spot outside her classroom door, bucking the same issue with Mu, Kat suspected Layira had put him up to it.

"We're both teachers," he responded in that smooth way of his. "We're colleagues. We should be sharing ideas, Kat. You're welcome to come watch one of my classes. I've been at this for years, and you might learn some things that would help you."

"Thank you." She nodded, again with ears more attuned over her shoulders than toward Mu, as her restless afternoon class began taking matters into its own hands. "If I have the time and inclination, I'll do that. Right now, I have to get to class."

Mu was not as easily deterred as Layira had been. He took a step to follow her through the doorway, saying, "I'll just stay a few minutes." Kat stopped in midstride, reclosing the door as Mu inadvertently stepped on her heel. "Oh, excuse me, Kat—"

"I don't allow visitors—or any sort of distraction—in my room while I'm teaching," she repeated, resigning herself to let the chaos brew beyond the door while she stared Mu down.

Mu stepped back but in no way backed off. He leaned languidly against the wall, too close for Kat's taste, though she was determined not to move backward, not to give any sign that she might give ground. "What are you afraid of, Kat?" he started, in a tone that suggested he was willing, as the closest of friends, to donate the rest of his afternoon to the investigation. "I have a feeling you're running from something—"

"I'm late for class, Mu."

"—but you don't need to run from me. I don't *judge* you. I know first-year teachers have a lot to learn and I take that into account. So what are you afraid of? That I'll fire you? Angelo's the only one who can do that—and there's not much chance he's going to do that to an old friend, is there?" Kat didn't like the tone of that comment one bit, only wished she had kept more of a poker face while he let it slither out of his mouth. "We're a *community* here, Kat. We *help* each other—"

"I don't need help," she cut him off tightly, barely getting the words out over the breath she was holding. "I need to get to class." Rude though it may have seemed, she spun around, went indoors, and very pointedly locked the door behind her.

With these initial encounters so recently under her skin, Kat found herself unnecessarily loaded for bear when Georgia— diminutive, grey-haired Georgia of the friendly, gravelly voice— stopped by to ask if she might sit in sometime. Kat immediately marked her down as a friend when she accepted the visitor prohibition congenially. "I just used to hate it," Georgia went on in her chatty way. "There I was, the runaway mother with a toddler under one arm, trying to prove to the world I could chuck it all and survive. And then every time my boss would walk in the door, I'd get upside-down and tongue-tied." She patted Kat on the shoulder, adding, "It's smart of you to set your own rules like this."

"Thanks," Kat stammered, unspeakably grateful for the older woman's attitude.

"But there's something else I came to ask about, and don't tell me yes if you mean no. Eli turned in photos of his work on your house, but I'd like him to show it to me in person. I told him we'd better check with you to make sure there's no problem with us traipsing through your yard."

For a flash, Kat saw Eli on the ladder the day he was painting the mural—a surprise to find him there, but not an unpleasant one, and she had the same feeling about Georgia. "No, there's no problem." She smiled. "Thanks for asking."

The older woman must have heard more than Kat realized she put into her reply, for she leaned toward her and lowered her voice. "It gets a little loony around here, dear. But this is my fifth year and *I've* survived." She left a wry grin in the air as she walked out.

⬯⬯⬯

A first snow in the desert is a powdered-sugar snow, sweet and faint, dusting mountaintops and signalling an imminent end to the harvest season. Bring in the apples, hunt for piñon nuts, gather the seeds, turn the gardens, stack the firewood. The first snow chants its list into every waking and dreaming heart, reminding all of the chores to be done if winter is to be gently survived. The CatWoman heard the enumeration curling its whispery way through the cracked bedroom window, gliding into and around and through her vivid dreams of harvest—

. . . bring in the apples . . .

—as Oso held an apple in his teeth, whining for her to take it, nudging her hand until her fingers slipped around the shiny red skin and she bit into the teethmarks he left—

. . . hunt for piñon nuts . . .

—as the man with the soft brown eyes three hundred years old laid a lumpy bundle in Feliciana's palm, and she was so fascinated by the exotic nuts inside she almost missed the silk scarf he'd taken such care to wrap around them—

. . . gather the seeds . . .

—as Josefa crumbled handful after handful of flower pods and let them sprinkle through her tiny fingers into a basket at her feet, the breeze catching emptied husks and whisking them off to some unseen land—

. . . turn the gardens . . .

—as Regina sliced at the earth, bent under the weight of two children—one born, one unborn—sliced with a hoe dull and rounded, chopping dry stalks and turning them under in the tiny plot of sunlight wedged tight between fence and tenement wall—

. . . stack the firewood . . .

—as Angelo swung the splitting maul with his iceman's arms, the force of the driving arc lifting him to his toes before ending in the heart of the log before him, tumbling splits to left and right—

. . . *bring the tuna* . . .

—as the path through the sage rolled under her bicycle tires, each tiny bump magnifying itself a hundred times over in the jagged weight of a backpack full of—

Tuna? The CatWoman rolled over, half-asleep, bumping her nose into a shapeless furry mound on the pillow.

Good morning, said the tortoise-shell nonchalantly.

Is it morning?

Almost.

Why was I dreaming about tuna? A cat yawn was all the reply she received in the chilly darkness as the fur-shadow stood to stretch on the pillow. *Talk to Angelo about tuna.*

When is he coming back?

The CatWoman swung bare feet out from under the bedcovers to a slate floor no longer invitingly cool in contrast to summer but dull cold with the prologue of winter. I'll bet it snowed, she thought as she pulled on robe and sweater. And I still haven't cut any firewood. Where are the weeks going? She stepped out to the courtyard spring to draw the day's water and saw, as she knew she would, the season's first snowfall glowing on the eastern mountains, pearlescent in the setting moonlight.

Before the sun had cleared the sugared mountain silhouette, the CatWoman was already a half mile from her house, dragging the blade of her bowsaw back and forth across the trunk of a fallen cedar nearly too big for her arms to hug. Back and forth. Draw and push. Over and over like a dance, a pulse, a heartbeat progressing so minutely through the dense wood so as to seem sometimes *only* a dance and not a sawing at all. Back and forth, draw and push, and the CatWoman's coat was already off her shoulders and hanging from the bicycle's handlebars. Back and forth and draw and push, and the short curls under her knit cap were damp and sticky in the frosty sunrise. Back and forth and draw and push, and her arms were beginning to tell her it would be a long day of finding other things to think about besides the back and the forth and the draw and the push.

Load the buggy and pedal it to the house; unload the buggy and stack the wood. Think about splitting it all later, some other day, sometime when arms are fresh and shoulders aren't out of socket and feet aren't at war with each other. "This is why—I should have—taken—equestrian lessons," the CatWoman gulped as she pumped pedal over pedal. Fourteen times out and fourteen times back, fourteen loads on and then off again before she called it quits for the day and rode buggyless to the hot spring to soak her weary bones.

"Ten more days like today and I should be okay till spring," she said to no one, as the heat of the pool argued painfully with muscles too stubborn to relax easily. "Ugh." The steamy oasis lulled her into a phantom sleep, floating on the hot water and on the whoosh of the salt cedar marsh surrounding the pool, its infinite fingery branches humming in the cold wind like harpstrings.

Ten more days like today, they hummed.

Ten more sets of achy bones.

Ten more days working alone.

Why are you working alone? You could have help if you wanted. If you asked. If you'd just pay attention to what you've given up, taking solitude for a lover. Just ask Feliciana what you've given up. What you're missing. You could have it. If you'd pay attention. Life's being good to you.

Ten more sets of achy bones.

Ten more days working alone.

Why are you working alone?

It's hard working alone.

It's harder this year.

Why are you alone?

Why *are* you alone?

Because.

Because—

"—hell, I don't know," the CatWoman groaned out loud, upsetting her floated balance and rolling underwater. In one smooth mermaid stroke, she burst through the surface into the bracing autumn air and onto the rocks, where she dressed and rode straight home. Before the day's last sunlight faded to shadow, she had driven a splitting maul through each and every log cut that day, stacking the splits in a pile along the courtyard wall. When she threw doubly-achy bones into bed that night, she had to dodge the tortoise-shell who hadn't budged from the pillow since before dawn. Muscle by muscle, the CatWoman tried to imagine the heat of the hot spring back into her body—into her hands, her arms, her shoulders ohhhh her shoulders, her back ohhhh her back, her legs—

You didn't answer my question, she heard the cat pout somewhere beyond the primal groaning of her body. *When is he coming back?*

I haven't decided yet, she replied, or thought she replied, as she was too far gone over the edge of sleep to know for sure.

"*Okay*, did anybody cheat? I bet *you* did, Meadow—"

"I did *not!* Travis, tell him. You heard my stomach growling!"

"I heard it, Nanda—even louder than *my* stomach."

"But I bet *somebody* cheated—"

"Nanda, lay *off!* Nobody cheated, unless *you* did—"

"I didn't cheat, Travis—"

Obviously no one cheated, Kat thought, surveying the unprecedented crossfire in her morning class where twenty usually-well-fed teenagers were learning firsthand about hunger. Only a room full of empty stomachs could be so snarly with each other. "Settle down," she said, breaking into the fray and separating the bickerers with her voice. "It doesn't matter to me if anyone ate, Nanda. I said last week the fast was optional."

"But if someone's been eating and I haven't had a bite since Tuesday, it wouldn't be fair—"

"All together now—" Kat prompted the class.

"History's not fair, Nanda!" they all sang to him.

"*Geez!*"

"Nanda, believe me, no one here has eaten since Tuesday," Kat assured him. "I've never seen you snapping at each other."

"*Yeah,* Nanda—"

Kat sighed. Hope I make it through this one. "*Enough,*" she silenced them. "Get out your books—"

"Can't we do the Latrine Version *first?*" Sky moaned.

"Books—not another word."

In grumpy compliance, twenty very hungry teenagers pulled out history books to review homework from the Presidents', Queens', and Generals' Version of History. Their homework for the Latrine Version—a thirty-six hour water fast—was written all over their faces, their attitudes, their cross words to each other, leaving Kat convinced they had all stuck to the fast. She hadn't expected that to happen—had designed the lesson thinking, at best, she would be teaching it to a half-dozen truly empty stomachs. Yet there they were, twenty teenagers enduring a thirty-seventh hour without food on the promise they would get to eat again during the day's Latrine Version of History. They have such faith in me, she thought, touched. I wonder if they'll still be speaking to me by lunchtime.

The only one not to reveal any grumpiness through the homework review was Eli, and Kat could tell by the strained lines of his face that he had not only complied with the fast, he probably exceeded it. Probably started a day early, she suspected. That would be like him. Quiet though he was in class, his written work showed an intense sensitivity to the human condition in its most latrine-like forms, a precocious identification with the oppressed. Eli doesn't need this class, she had decided weeks earlier. Eli could have graduated with honors already. Rather than act bored, though, he threw himself wholeheartedly into everything she assigned, as he did today, coping with a stomach most likely emptier than the rest in the room. His intensity was mirrored in a lesser form by Travis and Meadow and, in her younger group, Zephyr and Pilar. Even if Kat reached no one else by the end of the year, these five made her feel she'd done what she set out to do.

It was with great groans of joy that the class ended their book studies and watched ravenously as Kat set up a table by her stuffed chair, announcing, "And now, the feast." All offers of help were refused as she carefully laid out steaming platters of food she had prepared before class under Angelo's skeptical eye.

"If I didn't already know how those kids hang on your every word, I'd say you're going to lose them with this one," he had warned.

"If I lose them," she had replied, "then you won't need to fire me cause I'll resign. How can they understand history without studying the politics of hunger?"

"Got me there," he had conceded. "Good luck—think I'll sit this one out."

Knowing there wasn't a full stomach in the room, Kat was ready to sit out herself, but pressed on nonetheless. "I'd like to tell you a story," she began, smacking her lips after snitching a raisin from the top of a baked apple and licking traces of syrup from her fingers with a flourish. There was more cinnamon in the syrup than she preferred but, as with all the food she set out, the spices had been intensified so as to make each nose describe in detail to each deprived stomach just exactly what sat out of reach.

"It's a story about a girl named Brigitte and her little brother—"
She lifted the lid from a pot of thick stew and took an extended
sniff of the mouth-watering steam. "—her little brother Marcel.
Brigitte was about your age." As twenty pairs of voracious eyes
watched her every move, Kat dished some stew into a bowl, tore
a chunk from a huge, honey-colored loaf of braided bread, and
sat down in the stuffed chair. "Marcel was four, I think," she said
with her mouth full. "No—no, I think he was five." Juice dribbled
down her chin and she ran her tongue as far around her lips as she
could to lick it off. "That's right—Marcel was five, and Brigitte
was just about to turn sixteen—or maybe he was six—"

"What does it matter?" Marta spoke up impatiently, eyes dart-
ing anxiously along the table-top from stewpot to bread to baked
apples to sliced cheeses, to Kat's fat cheeks as she stuffed herself.

"It matters," Kat went on, gesturing with the bread in her
hand. "He was six—now I remember because they were born ten
years apart, and that's because—" She smothered a delicate burp.
"—their mother had three other children born in the middle
there—" She dunked the bread into the stew. "—but the middle
ones all died of hunger. Even their parents were dead by the time
Marcel was six." The drippy bread made it only halfway to her
mouth before slipping out of her fingers onto the floor. "Oops.
Well, anyway, Brigitte was your age and Marcel was six." She
scraped the mess off the floor and dropped it into the stewpot,
then carried the pot to the trash can and dumped it. For the first
time all morning, the slouching, grumpy, empty stomachs sat up
straight, intent.

"You should have seen those two," Kat continued, spooning a
deliciously drippy baked apple onto a plate. "Brigitte was a gorgeous baby—but that was before they were thrown out on the
streets. No rent money." The apple gave in to the fork without
the least struggle, falling open and spilling raisins and nuts all
over the plate. Kat's nose twitched as she savored the sweet

steam wafting upward from the filling. "And by the time Marcel was born, none of them had seen a gorgeous baby in years. He was—" Kat nearly winced as the hungry faces tracked the forkful of apple from plate to lips, eyes falling with the drips of syrup plopping onto her lap. "Mmm—" She stopped her story long enough to enjoy the mouthful thoroughly, then scooped up the drips with fingers too sticky not to lick. "He was *scrawny*—there just isn't any other way to describe it. Brigitte started out fat and gorgeous, but by the time they were alone on the streets, she was scrawny, too. Come to think of it—" Kat picked through the raisins and nuts, popping them into her mouth one at a time. "—by the time this story starts, Brigitte was scrawnier than Marcel because she'd been giving him most of the food she found. You see, she always wanted a baby brother, and when all her other siblings died, she was bound and determined to keep Marcel alive, even though he was just a skinny little rat when he was born."

She pushed the half-eaten apple aside. "Brigitte was tough—as tough as they come. She had to be tough, because by the time this story starts, they weren't the only ones living in the streets." Kat picked leisurely through the plate of cheeses, bit into a piece, wrinkled her nose and tossed it into the trash to search for a morsel more to her liking. "The streets were full of kids like them, and adults too, sleeping in doorways and fighting with the rats for trash to eat. And I don't mean skinny-like-a-rat baby brothers—I mean *rats*." She picked and bit at a few more pieces of cheese, tossing them aside as well and, finally, emptying the whole platter into the trash with a disgusted grunt. She slouched sideways into the stuffed chair before a crowd of faces that had gone beyond hunger, blossoming indignation in its place.

"That's how the story begins. Marcel is scrawny and six, Brigitte is scrawny and your age, and they live on the streets at the edge of a big city, fighting with the rats for trash to eat. All her life, Brigitte had heard stories about the king and queen in the palace on the river—about how they took all morning just to get dressed and spent all afternoon sitting around in satin and nibbling on food and talking about sweet nothings. She already knew about all that. But the day this story begins is the day she heard about the lapdog." Half the class was watching Kat in her full-bellied slouch; the other half had their eyes trained on the trash can, considering the struggle of pride vs. hunger, of hope vs. a growing sense of betrayal.

"The queen had a lapdog, and the rumor on the streets was that this spoiled little thing would walk the length of the king's table every night at dinner—up on top of the table, mind you, not down on the floor—and nibble at the food left on the plates. Brigitte already knew the leftovers went to the pigs—everybody threw leftovers to the pigs, and Brigitte had sneaked into a few pigpens at night when she couldn't find trash on the streets. But a lapdog on the table? She even heard that the dog was getting too fat to sit on the queen's lap, it ate so well." Kat leaned over to the table to gather a sticky handful of baked apple and began to suck noisily on it. "Can you *imagine* what that sounded like to a starving sixteen-year-old with a baby brother to feed? No roof over their heads, barely any clothes on their backs, having to fight with rats and pigs for every crumb—and there's some fat little dog waddling from plate to plate—" She stuffed the apple chunk into her mouth and spoke around it, "Well, you can just *imagine* how Brigitte felt."

Oh boy, could they imagine. Kat could see in detail on their faces how tightly their imaginations had become glued to their stomachs.

"So she decided to take Marcel to the palace—crazy idea. I'm not even sure what she had in mind at first, except that she was desperate to find food for her brother. Luckily, it was autumn and the weather hadn't gotten too cold yet. If it had been winter, they might never have made it, because every time Brigitte asked for directions to the palace, they were sent down another blind alley.

Weeks—it took them weeks to get there, and with each new block of the city, Brigitte had to find new slop piles to scavenge and new doorways to sleep in. And all this time, the two of them dreamed of being the queen's lapdog."

Several baked apples were still steaming on the platter when Kat dumped it into the trash, then held the platter to her face to lick the syrup puddle left behind. All that remained on the table was the bread, round and golden, with only one chunk of its braid missing. "The queen's lapdog," she went on, tearing off half the loaf and peeling the crusty parts away to toss into the trash so she could mash the soft insides between her hands and fashion it into a dog. "All Brigitte wanted was to eat as well as the queen's lapdog. Is that too much to ask?" It was hard for her to go on, as indignation thickened the air and all eyes darted angrily between her face, the mutilated loaf of bread, and the trash can full of food-turned-to-slop. "By the time they got there, all Brigitte was really hoping for was to find the royal pigpen and sneak into it at night. But how was a scrawny street urchin supposed to know that palaces aren't like the rest of the city? They have walls and guards and gates, all so that people like Brigitte and Marcel can't bother the people inside, or touch their satin clothes with filthy hands, or ask for the leftovers from their plates." Kat bit the head off the bread-dog, then tossed it after its crust to land tail-up in the full trash can. "She never found the pigs. She and Marcel walked all the way around the palace—it took them two days, they were so weak with hunger—but all they saw were walls and guards and gates. And then, at one of the last gates, Brigitte saw an apple tree inside, just past the guards, full of apples perfectly ripe. She and Marcel had never had a ripe apple—they'd only ever had the rotten ones and half-eaten ones thrown out in the alleys. And that was when Brigitte forgot about the pigs and the queen's lapdog, and was overcome by an urge to run inside and grab an apple for herself and the scrawny little brother she loved."

Kat stood and began clearing the table, sweeping the last of the bread and its crumbs into the trash. "Have you ever been overcome like that? Wanted something so badly you couldn't think of anything else? Willing to do *anything* to get it?" She folded the table and set it against the wall. "Well, that's how Brigitte felt, so she told Marcel to stay put and she ran for the apple tree as fast as she could, which wasn't very fast." Kat sat down again in the stuffed chair and shrugged. "She was caught by the palace guards and sent to prison. And that's the end of the story."

In the midst of the class' angry silence, Meadow gasped. "What happened to Marcel?"

"I don't know what happened to Marcel, or to Brigitte after she went to prison. But I do know what happened to the king and queen."

"They were beheaded," Eli said quietly from the back.

Kat nodded. "They were beheaded by a mob of people who were tired of being hungry, just like you are *right now*—people who looked at the king and queen just the same way you're looking at me *right now*—people who had to eat pig-slop, just the same way you want to eat out of the trash can *right now*. *Remember that*," she said, walking around the room to hand each of them a ripe apple from her backpack, "the next time you see someone in an alley digging through the trash."

<hr/>

With her double life and all the shuttling back and forth, it was truly disorienting for Kat to show up for class the next week and find the school deserted. It *has* to be Wednesday, she thought. I didn't miss a day on the calendar, did I? Every building stood empty and not a single car sat in the parking lot, though the night's dusting of snow showed many tire tracks. It wasn't until Kat was stepping into her classroom that she heard a truck pull up and saw Georgia climb out.

"Kat! I'm glad I caught you!" Kat enjoyed the incongruity of tiny Georgia hopping out of a truck twice the size of Angelo's. "Everyone's out at Mu's place watching the eclipse. Angelo sent me to tell you they'll be a little late getting back." She laughed as she walked through the yard toward Kat's classroom. "It turned into more of a party than a science lesson—*everybody* showed up. We tried to call you, but Angelo said you don't have a phone."

Kat held the classroom door open for her, inviting her inside. "No, I don't."

"Well, dear," Georgia said as she shook off her jacket and sat down, "if you plan on being here very long, you better get one. Special events pop up all the time with this crowd. Mu wasn't inspired to do this till yesterday."

"Gee thanks, Mu." Kat groaned, sitting down as well. "I had something important planned for this afternoon's class."

"I know—it's not like eclipses happen by accident. But at least it was today and not tomorrow. Travis would be really upset if he had to miss your class. He *loves* your class."

"Even after I made a pig of myself while they were starving?" Kat asked, relieved to hear there would be at least one face eager to see her this week.

"*Especially* after you made a pig of yourself." Georgia shook her head. "Kat, I have to tell you what he did that night. We were sitting at the table and he wasn't eating—said his stomach hurt—"

"I'll *bet* it did—"

"—and then he just got up, put his plate into a box, asked me for the keys to the truck, and took off. Didn't tell me where he was going, just took off. I thought maybe he was being a teenager or something. But then, he was back an hour later with the box of food still under his arm, and he started going through the kitchen asking me 'Do we *really* need two cans of this stuff? Or two boxes of that stuff?' And he was getting impatient with me when I said yes. So finally, I asked him just what the hell kinda burr had gotten under his saddle, and he told me about your story, and said—get this, I'm not lying—he said he'd taken the box of food down to the grocery store and waited out back at the trash bins so he could give it away to anyone who showed up. And I think it was really frustrating for him that no one showed up."

"That's great." Kat grinned.

"This is *not* my boy, honey. I mean, Travis has complained ever since he hit his hormones that we never have enough food in the house. He's *never* been the type to give away food."

"Sounds like he is now."

"Layira's been calling you the Pied Piper, and after what Travis is doing, I think I'll start, too."

"Why is Layira talking about me at all?" Kat asked warily.

"Oh, I heard her complaining that she couldn't sit in on your class, that's all."

"No, I turned her and Mu away."

"To Layira, that's worse than death, being shut out." Georgia chuckled. "She has to have her nose in *everything*. Took me two years to get her to stop 'helping' me in my class. The whole rest of the loony crowd is fine by me, but just keep her clucking out of *my* earshot. And Mu, too—I could live without him."

"It's an odd crowd," Kat mused. "Angelo told me it would be, but I had no idea what he meant till I got here."

"Where are you from?" When Kat didn't answer, only shifted her eyes suddenly to look out the window, Georgia filled in diplomatically, "Another runaway? You and me and half of this town."

"Yeah." Kat sighed. "A runaway."

"You know, dear," Georgia went on, "they're not so bad. Except for Layira and Mu—those two would be on my nerves even *without* the bells on their toes. But the rest of them, they're just odd on the outside. Inside, they're nothing but a bunch of parents trying to do right by their kids, and I like that. I'd a whole lot rather be teaching in a school like this—have my son in a school where people have a little creative flamboyance to them—than anywhere else I've seen."

"They are wonderful kids," Kat agreed. "Not as flamboyant as their parents—except Zephyr." They both laughed. "You're the art teacher—what color are those bangs lately?"

"That's called nasturtium yellow. Now *there's* a free spirit if I ever saw one."

"And Meadow with her spikes. And Shanti—what's with the fatigues and boots?"

"Why honey, you must not have any children." Georgia chuckled.

"No, I don't."

"Mu ran away from a military father and he wears slippers— now he's raising a son who wears boots just like the father Mu ran away from. Grandparents' revenge, a classic case. Just you watch—Shanti will run away from the slippers and become a drill sergeant. I'd bet money on it."

As the two of them laughed, the parking lot outside suddenly filled with vehicle after vehicle, spilling students in a wave onto the schoolyard.

"Looks like the party's over," Georgia groaned, getting up. "Back to work. It's been nice laughing with you, dear. Let's do it again sometime."

Kat grinned after Georgia as she traipsed out through the tide of incoming students. "Anytime."

∞

In the routine of her weeks, Kat treasured her Wednesday night standing invitation to dinner and not just because Angelo was such a gifted, if not humble, cook. "You're going to make me fat," she complained one night as he heaped a monstrous portion of spaghetti into her bowl. "The cats will think I went to live in a bookstore."

"So what do cats know? I'm just teaching you how to eat. You needed to meet a good Italian boy with a spaghetti sauce that makes the angels sing."

"Oh, go *on*, you're insufferable with this Italian stuff. You're only Italian *this* time—"

"So I lucked out. I know when I've got it good—"

—and on and on they would banter, until Kat remembered the banterings better, even, than she remembered the food. She hopped from Wednesday dinner to Wednesday dinner as if they were stones in a creek, laid across the fall semester. But one week, long after the leaves fell and snow knit its cap over the mountaintops, the banterings never had a chance to begin. School followed Angelo home for the night and he barely touched his food.

"Oh, it's Shanti and Eli again." He sighed into his wineglass when Kat asked what was bothering him. "I thought Eli might get through his last year without trouble, but that was optimistic."

"What's the trouble?"

"Shanti's the trouble. He jumped him again yesterday. He's a bully, and Eli's an easy target because he won't fight back. He's always had it in for Eli."

"Why?"

Angelo leaned away from the table and his half-eaten food. "I don't know," he said wearily. "I've known those boys for ten years now and it's always been this way. I asked Eli a long time ago what was going on between them, and he just gave a typical Eli response—said that Shanti doesn't like him and he doesn't like Shanti. Period. If this were a Greek tragedy, we'd find out in the final act that Eli and Shanti are actually brothers—that Mu was Eli's father all along and never claimed him. But I don't know if that's true."

"He doesn't look like Mu," Kat said skeptically. "He doesn't really look a whole lot like Layira either."

"No, you know who Eli looks like? He looks like me, when I

was Christos—when I was his great-grandfather. He looks like the Papadimitrious. Watching him grow up is like living in two worlds." For a flash, Kat could see that other world, as Angelo stared it into focus for himself in the candlelight between them. "I tried to kick Shanti out of school for fighting last year, but the board of directors stopped me."

"*What?*"

"Yeah—I sent him packing after the third shiner he gave Eli and, by sundown, Mu had put together a board meeting and convinced them to override my decision."

"But Mu's not even on the board."

Angelo shrugged. "I told you before, Kat—this is one of the tightest communities anywhere on earth. Mu doesn't have to be on the board. He wields a *lot* of clout. So does Layira."

"What have *they* been doing about this problem?"

"Nothing. Ignoring it. They both think kids are inherently peaceful beings, so there must not be any *real* problem. Besides—" Angelo switched to the birdy singsong of Layira's voice. "—it's just a conflict of moon signs."

"Oh, come *on*—"

"I'm not kidding. Layira really said that. And hey—who am I to argue with a beautifully intangible explanation like that?"

"Layira won't even stand up for her own son?"

"No. She argued louder than Mu did to keep Shanti in school."

Kat was speechless for a moment. "*Poor Eli*," she exclaimed indignantly. "He should have had Regina for a mother. She'd have had Shanti by the back of the neck the very first time."

Angelo raised an eyebrow in the first hint of a grin all evening. "Regina was that type, huh?"

"Damn right, she was. Nobody messed with her babies."

"Well, Layira's not that type. And much as I've been tempted to take Shanti by the back of the neck myself—" He tapped the table with his fingertip, and Kat could see in the set of his jaw how very real the temptation was. "—I can't do it. It's not my fight, it's Eli's. Problem is, he won't fight."

"At all?"

"No. I offered to teach him how once, but he refused. And it's not that he's afraid to fight—I *know* he's not afraid to. It's just that he truly believes it's wrong to hurt someone." Oso stood up from under the table to sniff at the plate Angelo had been neglecting and to offer his services. "It's yours," Angelo said to him, setting it on the floor. "Eli wouldn't have lasted two weeks in the neighborhood I come from this time. It's a good thing he grew up out here."

"Good except for Shanti."

"Yeah, and I can't even kick the kid out of school. Big help I've been."

"Don't be so hard on yourself."

"I agree with Eli," Angelo admitted. "I've done my share of fighting in four-and-a-half lifetimes, and it's ugly. And it's wrong. But the rightness or wrongness of it *pales* when someone's fist is in your eye for absolutely no good reason. It takes a lot of willpower to go through that without swinging back." Kat watched as his green-gold eyes squinted through several unspoken memories of blackened eyes and bloodied noses, each memory printed forever on the set of his face, the peculiar line of his bones. "Or a good set of shackles," he added under his breath, still lost in the memories and quiet for so long that Kat wondered for the first time if he had a memory beast like she did.

"What are you remembering?" She nudged him under the table with her foot.

Angelo took a deep breath and shook himself free. "Cane fields." He sighed and emptied his wineglass in one long pull.

"Tell me about them. You haven't told me any stories since the girl in the red shawl."

"No." He shook his head. "Thaddeus in the cane fields isn't a story to tell. It's just a lot of sweat—and blood—and hating the guy on the other end of the whip. No—" He kept shaking his head until, with great effort, he was able to change the topic. "Now, Epifanio—*he* had stories to tell about. He had the girl in the red shawl, and six kids, and two dozen grandkids—but best of all, he had the pinto."

"The pinto was better than the girl in the red shawl?" Kat ribbed him, and saw him lighten up at last.

"Hate to admit it, Kat, but they were neck and neck. Epifanio spent his days with one and his nights with the other." He leaned back in his chair and stretched his legs. "Want to hear about the pinto?"

"Sure." She grinned. "I love stories."

Angelo grinned back in a way he couldn't have managed earlier in the evening, then his eyes glazed over as he began to pull the memory into focus. Before Kat knew it, she felt her breath suck in and stop, her chest swollen with the trapped breath as a great, screaming horse underneath her reared and lunged to a gallop—

—off and away, riding a thunderstorm, an earthquake without end, an arrow slicing the world to either side and carrying her breathlessly away from the world behind—

—an earthquake of a horse, a great pulsing flesh, a passion, a scream, a wildfire in flight—

—a wildfire of a ride, too hot to douse, too hot to breathe, too furiously hot for the world underfoot—

—a singe on the world, a rip in the air, a life in full streak from birth to death—

—from here to there—

—from now, to now, to now, to now—

—to a breath, at last—and a breath, again—and a world slowing finally to left and right—no longer a blur—no longer a streak—no longer—a—thunder—

—just a grand horse, snorting, prancing, ready to turn and do it again—

"You've been *practicing*," Kat whispered when the dry plains around her faded again to Angelo's house and the breath trapped in her chest flowed easily in and out.

"I thought I might want to tell you something important sometime."

Kat wasn't sure if he was still on the horse, or if he was really seeing her, but Angelo's eyes were grinning in that way he had—and it rushed through her in a wildfire as hot as the pinto's ride how very much she enjoyed seeing his eyes grin. "What are you doing—over the winter break?" she asked.

"Nothing."

"Ahhh—why don't you come out to the mesa?" The grin slid out of his eyes and onto his cheeks as she added, "You could tell me a few more stories."

"I'll think of some good ones."

A bonfire of breath, an earthquake of thunder, too hot, too hot — where is the horse? Where is the pinto? Where is the one to sweep me out of here? Stop these stones, cut these ropes, stop the sea flooding into my mouth. A horse, a horse, a galloping arrow, off and away from the world behind. Away, away, I need a horse. If only, if only *I had a*—

"Horse!" the CatWoman shouted, sitting straight up from a dream she couldn't remember. Within seconds, the dark bedroom was full of furry shadows asking her what was wrong.

I don't know. Her hands shook as she wiped sweaty palms onto the sheets. *What happened?*

You said 'horse', the tortoise-shell explained.

I don't have a horse. I don't know why I said 'horse.' Go back to sleep.

She lay back down, not admitting to the cats how her heart was racing and how it upset her to be screaming in her sleep. It's been months—

One by one, the cats left her alone in the dark, and one by one, the CatWoman slowed her heartbeats and calmed her nerves, trying to remember the dream, trying so hard she fell asleep with the effort.

She slept past the dawn and past the sunrise, and never stumbled sock-footed out into the sala until wintry daylight was glowing through the windows. It seemed every cat on the mesa was sleeping indoors, a sight that shouldn't have surprised her as they often did so in the winter. But for some reason, the CatWoman's eyes had been honed at a new angle overnight, and instead of fifty snoozing cats she saw a house overflowing with—

"Cat hair!" The cats jumped to attention and asked again what was wrong. *Look at all this cat hair!*

Since when do you care about cat hair? the tortoise-shell protested. *You're half cat.*

I'm half human, too. She snatched at piles on the pillows, on the windowsills, wrapped around the legs of furniture, muttering, "This is disgusting, and I've got guests coming—"

YOU DO? all cats asked in unison.

"—barely a week from now—"

Is it the man and the dog? squeaked one of the twin grey kittens.

"—it's going to take me a week just to get the sala clean—"

IS HE BRINGING TUNA? the rest of them chimed.

"—this is too much—one or two cats, maybe I could keep this place clean, but *fifty*—"

◯◯◯

Kat might have known something was afoot if she'd been paying attention to how closely her morning class watched her and how they sat in giggly anticipation only barely pretending to concentrate on their midterm exams. But her mind had drifted out the window and forward in time to the winter break set to begin the next day. She wandered obliviously around the quiet room, more aware of the angry clouds dancing on the horizon than of her students. Snow had already fallen overnight, prompting Angelo to insist that Kat ride to school with him rather than walk, as she'd been set to do. As they drove, he had wondered out loud if it might not be wise to postpone their trip to the mesa for a day and let the weather clear.

"The weather over here is always a lot worse than it is there," she assured him. "Once we cross the bridge we'll be fine."

"What if it's dark? I can't leave school till the end of the day."

"I've done it in the dark. It's not a problem."

Angelo had seemed a little skeptical, but mostly eager himself to get out of town. "I guess we can always turn back if it's bad. But you realize," he grinned, "this means we'll miss the Solstice Ball tonight."

"What Solstice Ball?"

He was surprised. "Layira didn't invite you to her big bash?"

"Layira hasn't come near me since I told her she couldn't sit in on my class."

"Well, no loss. It's just the high mass of the year for the commune crowd. She always leans on me to show up."

"Is tonight the solstice? I lost track."

"Boy." Angelo shook his head. "You send a girl to the big city a couple days a week, and look what happens—"

"Oh, come on—"

"—she loses track of the important things in life."

So it was while she stood staring at the western clouds, trying to reset her mental calendar, that the giggly anticipation brewed behind her back and finally boiled over.

"Kat?" She heard Nanda's voice break into the quiet imposed for the exam. "Aren't you tired of walking around? Why don't you sit down?" The comment wasn't as nonchalant as she knew he'd intended it to be. When she looked at her group of sixteen- and seventeen-year-olds, all with exams facedown before them, she finally noticed the conspiracy in their faces.

"Finished?" she asked, and they all nodded a bit too eagerly. "Okay—Nanda, would you gather up the exams, please?" She could tell by the way he jumped to the task that she must have played right into whatever game they'd concocted. He carried the papers to her where she stood, but instead of handing them over, he took her by the shoulders and led her to sit in the stuffed chair she hadn't once settled into all morning. Then he leaned over and kissed her as the class exploded with laughter.

"Surprise! Mistletoe!" he cried, pointing up at a sprig tacked to the ceiling directly above her chair.

"Oh, go on." She laughed. "I should have known."

If Kat had remembered the mistletoe, she might not have used that chair as she sat all afternoon grading the exams and waiting for Angelo's day to finish. But she forgot about it as she worked diligently to make sure she had no homework to take to the mesa. So, she was caught by even greater surprise when Mu's slippered feet got him all the way to her side to whisper, "Mistletoe!" and kiss her before she even realized he was in the room. She sprang to her feet and out from under the greenery.

"A little jumpy, Kat," he said smoothly. "You need a holiday."

"Don't sneak up on me, Mu," she said when her voice returned, wondering crossly how he could possibly get through the door without her cat ears hearing him. "What do you need?"

"I don't *need* anything," he said in his snake voice. "I came to invite you to the Solstice Ball tonight."

"Thank you, but I'm going out of town."

"In this weather? No."

"Yes."

"You won't make it a mile down the road," he assured her.

"Come to the ball. And wear something—*interesting.*" As soon as Mu's silent steps had carried him away again, Kat pushed her chair out from under the mistletoe and went back to grading the exams. As she reached for the last one in the pile, she heard the door open again and was surprised to see Eli walking in. Behind him, students were tumbling and laughing their way through the snowy yard, out toward the road and the beginning of their winter break.

"Hi, Eli," she greeted him.

"Uh—hi," he said in his shy way, and closed the door. His eyes darted quickly to the ceiling, noting that her chair was no longer under the mistletoe, and Kat wasn't sure if what she saw flash across his face was relief or disappointment. "I have something for you," he said, handing her a wrapped package.

"Can I open it now?"

"Sure."

What she found inside was a small watercolor painting of her house in the plum thicket, with the morning-glory mural splashing color through an otherwise snowy scene. "I thought you might want a picture of it for the days when you're not here."

"I have a budding famous artist in my class." She smiled. "*Thank you.* I hope you signed it."

"Yeah, well—" Under his grin, she saw a faint blush that made her heart melt for his teenage shyness. "Have a good vacation." As he left, he offered, "I can do another one in the spring—if you want—it would be different—"

Then he was gone, before she could say, "I'd love that."

∞

First, there were the half-dozen people who needed Angelo's attention after school, adding an hour to his day. Then, there was the patch of ice on the road just as they left, sending the truck into the ditch and eating up much of the stormy daylight left to them as they flagged down Georgia in her big truck and had her pull them out. It was undeniably dark when Kat raced through her little house, bundling up for what would be a cold trek even on the mirage. Finally, there were the few minutes they lost when Angelo flatly refused to load Kat's bicycle into the bed of his pickup truck.

"You gotta be kidding." He laughed.

"But I'm going to need it in two weeks to get back into town."

"No, you're *not* going to need it. Do you think I'm the kind of guy who would make you ride a bike while I drive?"

"You're staying for the whole two weeks?" she asked, surprised.

"Yeah," he said lightly, a grin flashing from his eyes and straight to her belly, making her tingle in a way she hadn't felt in lifetimes.

"Good," she said as lightly, wondering if her grin had anywhere near the same effect on him.

The first inkling Kat had that they might not make it to the mirage came when Angelo turned off the slippery main road and they found the road to the gorge rim beginning to drift over in the fierce wind. But she said nothing about turning back, only joked instead about a universal conspiracy against them as she helped put chains on the tires. It wasn't until she and Angelo and a snow-footed Oso stepped across the mirage-bridge to find the weather terrible there, too, that she let common sense rule.

"I've never seen it snow this hard over here," she said in amazement. "I don't think I'll be able to see the path."

"C'mon—" Angelo turned back to the east side of the river. "We'll wait out the storm at my house."

But even that was optimistic. After fighting their way back up the trail to where the truck was parked, they found that the furious north wind had thrown impassable drifts across the truck's recent track and blocked off their exit in that direction. "Hell of a wind." Angelo sighed. "But the shortcut road to the school might be okay. The wind won't be crossing it."

I hope not, Kat thought, wishing she had listened to all the day's earlier warnings and put off the trip till morning. She sat silently on pins and needles through the slow drive north, Angelo bulldozing their way through snow that nearly scraped the running boards. Under the ominous belly of the clouds, the town glowed in the distance with innocent warmth. A little closer and in their direct path, the sprawling communes dotted the snowscape with scattered speckles of light. Somewhere between them would be the school and the road they hoped would be plowed.

"See the biggest light out there?" Angelo nodded after nearly a half hour of focussed silence. "That's Layira's pyramid."

"Pyramid? So *that's* what I've been seeing out there."

"That's it. I worked on the crew that built it, when I first came to town. That's how I got involved with the school." He accelerated to plow through the first drift they encountered—not as bad as the ones blocking the other road, but enough to throw the truck a little sideways. Kat heard Angelo grunt softly and realized he was as concerned about the drive as she was. "A dumb design," he went on. "Too barny—all the heat gets stuck at the top. But it's the moon-chapel of Layira's dreams."

He fell silent again to concentrate on another drift, and then a few more as the road curved slightly east and across the wind's path. "This should be the worst of it right here," he said almost to himself, and Kat didn't reply as she didn't want to distract him from the monumental task of keeping the truck from being thrown off the road. She fixed her eyes and her thoughts on the town's innocent glow and clutched a handful of Oso's thick fur as the truck bounced left and right and finally, more than an hour after they stood on the mirage-bridge, reached the road they were looking for. Kat sighed in relief, knowing they were at last within walking distance of home should they get stuck.

Angelo gave a relieved sigh too, then quickly covered it by grinning at her. "That wasn't so bad, was it?" The words were barely out of his mouth, however, when the truck bucked them both out of their seats as it jumped over the frozen snowbank flung across their path by the day's plow truck. Neither of them saw the ice on the road beyond the bank, only felt the truck sneer at Angelo's attempts to turn the wheels and slide gracefully into the ditch.

Angelo turned off the engine and collapsed with laughter over the steering wheel. "It's the same ditch we were in this afternoon—" They both laughed till they cried, letting the tension of the drive shake off.

"Let's just walk," Kat suggested eventually.

"No, I don't want to leave the truck here. Someone else is going to hit that patch of ice and drive right into it." He looked through the back window to where Layira's pyramid glowed in the snowy dark. "Everyone who lives out here is at Layira's tonight. Someone's bound to have a truck that'll pull us out."

They left Oso curled on the driver's seat and set out straight across the snowy sage to the pyramid a mile away, the nasty wind trying to flatten them with every step. Kat was freezing and panting and sweaty all in one when they finally stumbled through parked cars and into the glow from the pyramid's porch lights. The muffled sound of a large crowd having a raucous time oozed through the walls. "You better—go in alone," Kat panted, stopping just out of sight of the front door. "Layira—didn't—invite me."

Angelo said nothing, but stepped over and pulled her jacket hood away from her face. He tilted her head back in his hands—back through centuries, back through lifetimes, back through a swirling blizzard of grinning, teasing, green-gold eyes—and kissed her warmly enough to melt her frozen lips. By the time he moved his mouth to her ear and whispered, *"I'm inviting you,"* Kat didn't feel anywhere near so frozen, only sweaty and panting and dazed. He climbed the porch steps and pulled a bell rope hanging by the door while she gathered at least enough of her wits to run her hands along her bandana, making sure her hair was all hidden. She hadn't yet stepped out of the shadows when the heavy door flew open.

"*Aaan*-gelo, we've been *waiting* for you," came the singsong voice, skating out into the night on the frozen rink of porch light. "Merry Solstice!"

Angelo's "Hello, Layira" was nearly drowned by a sweeping tinkle of bells as he was engulfed by a great shawl and pulled out of sight. By the time Kat reached the porch, the door was closed. In the moment it took to decide she'd rather go in than wait in the cold, the door flew open again. "*Ka*-at!" came the voice, adding a syllable to her name that landed somewhat flat on the threshold between them. "What a surprise! Come in!"

"Hello, Layira," she said, stepping past her into sudden, cheek-melting heat. Pungent incense and candle smoke burned her nose and watered her eyes, blurring the room beyond sense. The three of them stood in an entryway cluttered with mounds of damp coats; beyond the mounds, Kat's view of the pyramid's interior was blocked by perhaps a hundred people, dressed in all manner of masquerade, lit from above by a galaxy of candled chandeliers.

"Did you come *together*?" Layira cooed and, before either could reply, she slipped Angelo's coat off his shoulders and was helping Kat with hers. "*Aaan*-gelo, how did you get this little bird to come out of *hiding*? We've all been *dying* to get to know her—" The great shawl—black tonight, with gold-sequined zodiac signs and bells tied to every thread of fringe—shimmered and chimed as Layira swung between the two of them to slip an arm around Kat's waist. Bells jangled against the frozen flesh that was her thigh, slower to thaw than her cheeks had been.

"—and everyone, I'm sure, will be *so glad* you came—"

Kat's free hand reached surreptitiously behind to grab hold of Angelo, but the great black shawl and the rhythmic waves of tinkling bells swept her away from him into the sea of faces and general party chaos under the pyramid ceiling.

"—especially Eli—Eli just *adores* you, you know—"

"Angelo! Moon-brother! How's life treating you?" A voice penetrated the din, and Kat realized Angelo was surely being swept away behind her. She tried turning to catch his eye, but Layira's mandating embrace prevented her from doing anything but move farther into the crowd.

"—*there* he is—" she went on, and the shawled arm not holding Kat swept up to wave across the room. "*Eee*-li! Look who's *here!*" There was no chance the voice could have carried over the cacophony, but the glitter of sequins as she waved her arm would have caught a bat's eye at a thousand paces. Kat saw Eli dumping ice into a large bowl on a table. A quick half-smile was all he gave back across the crowd before Kat's view of him was obstructed by the upraised chiffon of a trio of belly dancers. "—so shy, but he just *adores* you. You're his first love, did you know that?" The arm gave a pseudo-conspiratorial squeeze and Kat realized she was expected to reply.

"No—no I didn't." She looked around for Angelo and saw him between Mountain Man and someone whose name she couldn't remember, invisible weblines of conversation pinning him into place for the moment. He caught her eye, and if his captors noticed his slight shrug to her, they paid no heed.

"—but mothers know these things, *especially* with sons, which is all I have in this lifetime. Maybe next time the gods will bless me with daughters. Do you have any children?" Before Kat could open her mouth to reply, another arm came around her waist from her free side and she found herself sandwiched between Layira and Mu. We'll never get out of here—

"A Merry Solstice!" called Mu, putting moist lips to her ear to whisper hoarsely, "I *knew* you would come!" Humid wine-breath betrayed him as one of the first guests to arrive and made Kat long for the biting wind she'd just been cursing. In fact, she realized uneasily, the whole room felt close and humid with wine and incense and candle smoke, and with clothing giving up its snow-fallen moisture to form a low-hanging haze.

Layira's shawled arm fell away with a glissando of bells. "Ahh, Mu—you're *just* the person—" With two hundred tiny bells to finish the thought for her, Layira swirled into a thick knot of conversation nearby and turned her back on them.

"What would you like? Wine? Tea? Layira brewed some of her solstice tea." Even the roar around them didn't camouflage the reptilian quality of Mu's voice.

"A truck. I need a truck."

"A what?" Mu's head leaned toward her with exaggerated interest until Kat thought his ear might get bitten with her reply.

"A *truck!*" she called. "We're stuck in the ditch."

"We who?"

We who, we who, what does it matter we who? she thought impatiently, wishing someone would turn down the piercing music. "Angelo's truck is in the ditch. We need to be pulled out."

"What's your hurry? Relax! Have some wine!" He wagged his finger at her. "If you don't toast the solstice, the sun may never come back."

Across the crowd, Kat saw Angelo was mostly obscured from her view by the great sequined shawl, shimmering with light as Layira offered him a glass of wine and obviously wouldn't take no for an answer when he tried to refuse. As he raised it to his lips, he caught Kat's eyes and she heard his cat-self say, *I guess we can't just walk in and walk out.*

"Would you get me some wine, Mu?" She sighed, not turning away from Angelo's gaze. *Just long enough not to be rude, promise?*

Promise.

The gold zodiac shimmered between them, blocking Kat's view, and she turned to find Mu gone. With a moment alone, she gazed over the crowd at the room itself, with its candlelit timberwork soaring right out of the ground to end in the four glowing panels of the glass peak. As pyramids went, she supposed, it was a stunning one, all black-stained timbers and red cedar walls. Not a chapel, Angelo, she thought. A cathedral.

"Why, it's the mystery history teacher!" Kat recognized neither the gravelly voice nor the face before her. The woman's voluminous skirts, many-layered so as to render the diaphanous opaque, were slow to settle at her belled toes, and her face was awash with paint and glitter. Kat thought there might be something familiar about her eyes and scanned the faces of her students for some connection. "We haven't met 'cause I missed the first day of school. I'm Willow Louise." Yes, but whose *mother* are you? Aspen's, perhaps— "How are my babies doing?" The woman pulled Kat's head forward with a heavily ringed hand until their brows met. "I never saw them get out of bed on time till they had you for a teacher." They? thought Kat, anxiously. "I want to know what you *do* to them."

Kat mustered a laugh and pulled gently away from the glittered brow. "I tell stories, that's all." *Angelo! Who are her babies?*

Figure it out, came a silent chuckle across the room.

Damn your sense of humor.

Relax, Kat. It's only a party.

A disembodied glass of wine came between Kat and both conversations as Mu reached around her from behind. "It's mulled. You look like you need something warm."

"Thanks," she said in truth, and let Willow Louise lure Mu's attention away with a compliment on his brightly embroidered shirt. The wine was cheap and too heavily spiced, but it was a warm diversion and an excuse not to talk. Her eyes were beginning to clear and the aureolas from the chandeliers overhead no longer overlapped from one candle to the next. With her next glance around the crowd, she noticed with some surprise a welcome face not far away. She excused herself and slid through the crowd to where Georgia sat alone halfway up the stairs to a mezzanine above.

"Welcome to the loony ball!" Georgia's laugh belied her demeanor. "I'm surprised you came."

"I didn't—Angelo and I are stuck in the ditch."

"*Again?*"

"Again." Kat nodded sheepishly. "We need someone to pull us out."

"I'll do it. I wasn't planning on staying much longer. Let me finish my wine." Kat noticed Georgia was, like herself, lacking in festoonery. Certainly the two of them, and Angelo as well, stood out in the crowd as outsiders. But while she and Georgia were being left to themselves, the chapel priests and priestesses seemed to be trying to recruit Angelo, closing him in with layers of conversation—Gulliver, tied by Lilliputians, still only a dozen paces in from the front door.

"I'm surprised *you* came," she said to Georgia over the din.

The older woman shook her head and Kat supposed she sighed, though the sound of it was lost in the auditory melee. "The loony ball is my yearly cheer-up ritual. It comes right at the time I put Travis on a plane to visit his father for the holidays. I come to watch, and I generally slip out before the finale."

"What's the finale?"

"Layira's solstice message from the spirits. Usually to the tune of love-one-another-in-the-new-year. It's her annual BIG MOMENT." Georgia chuckled, this time with more convincing humor. "Now, this is between you and me and the jackrabbits, but *look* at her." Kat had no trouble finding the glittering high priestess, hub of a whirling wheel of light, gliding from one knot of people to the next and commandeering all attention before gliding away. "Being that I used to be married into 'High So-ci-e-teee,' I can tell you from experience what you're looking at is your run-of-the-mill society party with the hostess in full regalia. And like any other grand dame, she makes sure the focal point of the party is herself."

Kat put the clothing she saw below her on the shoulders of the socialites who had raised her this fifth time and found the scene outrageous. "Yes," she laughed, "I see what you mean."

"Layira's loony ball always reminds me why I left, and how glad I am that I did, even while we're having to live payday to payday." Georgia lifted her wineglass in a toast unnoticed below and drained it. "I've had enough for this year—I can pull you out of the ditch anytime you're ready to go."

"Let me find Angelo." He had moved farther into the room now, still surrounded. *I found a truck,* she called to his cat-self.

Where are you?

On the stairs. Kat watched him turn to find her, his eyes wide and pleading.

Get me out of here!

Look who's talking, she laughed. "He's over there," she said out loud to Georgia. "I'll go pry him loo—"

Before she could finish the phrase, someone suddenly turned off the maddening music and, as if rehearsed, all voices in the room hushed. Georgia groaned. "Too late," she whispered. "Layira's on."

Kat's heart sank when she realized they were as far from the door as they could possibly be. "Maybe we could slip out along the edge," she whispered back.

Below them, Layira moved to the center of the room where the crowd had cleared a space for her directly under the pyramid's peak. Gold sequin-flames reflected in every eye in the room as she sent the shawl tinkling out the full length of her arms and turned in a slow circle, face upward to the glass peak. Just as Kat thought she might slip unnoticed down the stairs into the crowd, Layira's face came down and looked right at her. "Good evening, and good solstice to you all." Her voice had lost its usual singsonginess, filling the pyramid to its peak with the timbre of a long-bowed cello.

Kat, came Angelo's cat-voice, *there's a back door under the stairs.*

Meet me around front. She could see him inching his way backward through the crowd while Layira's voice bowed on about the spirits having blessed the gathering.

"There's a back door under us," she whispered to Georgia.

"My coat's by the front door," Georgia moaned.

"We'll get it somehow." The two of them stepped quietly to the bottom of the stairs as if to join the crowd.

"—and in special honor of the occasion—"

Kat squeezed between the bottom of the stair rail and the backside of a man dressed head to toe in black satin, looking for some sign of the back door.

"—the spirits will guide me in a past-life reading tonight—"

Georgia came up close behind just as Kat saw the door—and Mu, standing in their way.

"—that we, and they, might get to know one of our own new sisters—"

Mu's eyes looked blearily wine-sodden and Kat doubted they would focus on her before they slipped past.

"—Kat O'Malley."

Huh? she thought, as she simultaneously heard Angelo groan silently from across the room and Georgia hiss out loud right next to her. The crowd's attention turned in palpable waves toward her, as if they'd known her position in the room all along. *What's happening?* she asked an invisible Angelo.

She's going to do a past-life reading on you.

You've got to be kidding!

Mu's eyes were well-focussed on her by now, and he stepped forward to take her arm and lead her to Layira, waiting officiously for Kat to join her in the eye of the pyramid. "No—thank you—" She tried to stand put, but Mu quickly had her off balance and stumbling through the crowd.

Angelo!

There's no leaving now, Kat.

But Angelo! What if she—

She won't. Just go along with it. Then we'll leave.

The great black shawl swallowed her in greeting and for more moments than she cared to be, she was blinded and breathing the musty air of its woolen weight. When the shawl finally opened, Layira stood back at arm's length, her hands on Kat's shoulders. She lifted her face to the glass peak once again and stood frozen, fingers tight in Kat's collarbones for what seemed an eternity. Every candle seemed focussed upon them, as Kat knew every eye must surely be, and the over-stoked heat of the crowded room seemed intent on wilting her. Her bandana, still damp from their trek, dropped daggerlets of steam onto her scalp, and she had an overpowering nervous urge to scratch. But the solemn posture of the woman before her said: one does not scratch during such a moment.

One does not scratch.

One does not giggle . . .

. . . like that time in her first life, when she and Julio had knelt for hours in the village chapel, drowsy and knee-sore under a pall of incense and priestly incantation that seemed to drone on till they would surely turn grey. Out of the shadows of that solemnity had appeared a mouse, nose twitching and body waddling the length of the altar in search of food, not a hand's breadth from the obliviously chanting priest—until it skittered irreverently up inside the cloth skirt of a carved madonna. She and Julio had both been beset by laughter of the sort that can never be laughed in such a solemn moment and had to be ushered outdoors until the fit passed. The memory was so vivid for Kat, it pulled now at the edges of her mouth and made her catch the breath that would have been a giggle.

Kat, are you all right? she heard Angelo ask.

Do you remember that mouse, Angelo—the mouse on the altar, that first time—

The mouse on the—for christ's SAKE, Kat, don't think about that now!
I can't help it—it's too late—

She could hear Angelo coughing in the crowd, trying to cover his own simmering laughter. *Kat, don't—*Even his silent voice was choking.

Just then, Layira dropped her arms and lowered her face to gaze around the room. "Kat O'Malley, she is called now," the cello began, "but she has not always been so—"

If she calls me Josefa—
She won't.

"—she was Anandizha," the cello bowed long and lovingly over the syllables, "third of the lesser pharaoh queens—"

Queen? I scrubbed floors!
Hold on, Kat—

"—fertile mother to her people—"

Thirteen people. All girls.

"—great pharaoh madonna—"

At least I never had a mouse run up my skirt—
No! Kat! Don't think about the mouse!

But it was too late, for Kat's eyes squeezed shut with stinging tears of laughter and the hand she clapped over her mouth served only to convulse her more. By the time Angelo reached her, she was bent over and wheezing, wiping her eyes and very obviously shaking with laughter at the wrong moment. No matter how she tried to tell herself how very wrong the moment was, she was no more able to stop her fit than five-year-old Josefa had been.

"I'm sorry—" she choked to the stunned high priestess before her, "—I was thinking of something else—"

Angelo fairly lifted her off her feet and toward the door. "She's exhausted—we got stuck—had to walk—" No one moved to block their exit, only glowered at them through the candlelight, blurred again now in Kat's laughter-filled eyes. The last thing she saw before Angelo pulled her and their coats out the door was the glow from ten thousand gold sequins—still, not shimmering—fringed with two hundred silent bells.

The bitter cold slowed their laughter eventually by making icicles of their tears and burning their lungs with each gasping breath. "Kat," Angelo scolded between after-chuckles, "I didn't know you had it in you to be so bad."

"Laughing at high mass—it just isn't done." Kat giggled into a kerchief in an attempt to blow her laughing nose. *"Now* how will we get out of the ditch?"

"I'll pull you out," came Georgia's voice and crunching footsteps from the direction of the back door. She stepped into the light, wearing Eli's jacket and a face as red as their own from laughter. "Finally, someone livened up the party. But I can't say I envy your position in society right now, honey."

"What?" asked Angelo. "Kat's off the guest list for next year?"

"No, she's the first one to laugh at Layira." She led them out into the darkness toward the cluster of parked vehicles. "I don't think she's ever been laughed at before."

The words sent a windy chill up Kat's spine. She'll think I was making a fool of *her,* she thought, instead of making an ass of myself. As she settled into the cold truck cab between Georgia and Angelo, she wondered what Eli would think.

<hr />

With just minutes to go before midnight, Angelo's truck finally pulled up to the orchard gate. The peripheral light from the headlamps cast a yellowy glow on snow-sleeved branches bent over the path to the house, barely visible through the curtain of falling snow. The scene might have been magical, had Kat any energy left to think magically. But whatever fueled her during the long drive and hike and fiasco in the pyramid had flared and spent itself, leaving her exhausted. She would have slept through the drive following the truck rescue but for a swelling tide of dread inside her. For the first time in months, Kat felt the memory beast sharpening its claws on her stomach.

"Your house is going to be an icebox." It was the first either had spoken since they pulled the truck out of the ditch, and Angelo's voice sounded as tired as Kat felt. "C'mon and stay up at my place. It's bound to be warmer than yours."

Kat shook her head stiffly, her voice a croaky whisper when she tried to speak. "No—thanks—I'll be fine." She pushed Oso's big head off her lap and climbed out to the snowy roadside, reaching into the truckbed to gather her pack.

"Let me get that for you," Angelo offered, but she stopped him as he stepped out his door.

"Stay in the truck—it's cold out here—goodnight."

"Try again tomorrow?" he called to her back as she walked to the dark house.

"Sure," she said, but Angelo couldn't possibly have heard her deflated whisper.

"Kat, wait—" She heard him walking to catch up with her. "You're not thinking about the mouse, are you?"

His attempt to joke made her turn to look at him, a dark shape in the snowy night. "Why did she do that to me?" she asked hoarsely.

Angelo shrugged uneasily. "Who knows why Layira does anything? You're an enigma to her. To everyone. You make her uncomfortable."

"*I* make *her* uncomfortable?" she hissed.

"She wanted to name you—"

"I have a name."

"—make you—one of her flock—" His voice drifted off.

Kat shook her head at the dark figure on the path, silhouetted by the lights on the still-rumbling truck. In the silence of a thousand snowflakes, Angelo kicked at the path impatiently. "*C'mon,* Kat. Can't you see? She was trying to embarrass you in front of *me.*"

"Why?"

Angelo threw his hands in the air in speechless exasperation and spun around to pace down to the gate and back. "I don't know—she's been after me for years. I think she hates it that I never fell under her spell."

"How could you resist?" she retorted. "She could drown a whale with that cloak of hers."

"*Kat. She was my granddaughter.*"

"And I was your sister." Kat heard her words reverberate some-how, rippling the night air and rocking the boat the memory beast was preparing for sail. As the last ripple faded, dogs woke to bark in the distance and Oso scratched on the truck window.

"You know me, Kat." Angelo forced a steadiness to his voice. "She's not my type."

"And I can't afford to be," she said, reining in a wobble she wished weren't creeping up her throat, "if that's the kind of trou-ble I'd be stirring up."

"Layira can't make trouble for you—"

"*She will.*" Kat cut him off. "I *know* it." She turned toward the house but Angelo's terse words tripped her first step.

"You're making a big thing out of nothing."

"A big thing out of *nothing?*" she choked as her head sud-denly throbbed with a heat that left even her fingertips dizzy. She threw her pack against a tree, showering the both of them with snow. "Damn it Angelo, *you know nothing about these things!*" She yanked off her snow-topped cap and bandana, throwing them onto the trodden snow at her feet. "*Nothing!*" Her shout was exciting all the dogs in the valley to a barking frenzy. "You have *never* had a town turn on you because— overnight!—someone declares you a bit odd—overnight!— someone needs to blame you for their own stupidity." The barking ricocheted through her throbbing skull making the snow and shadows swim before her eyes. "You have *never* been trapped in a town and had to watch them come for you with their pockets full of stones! Do you have *any idea* what that's *like*—"

"For christ's *sake,* Kat, no one's stoning you!"

"—no, you couldn't possibly know what it's like. You've always been a *man,* you always had a *horse,* you could always *leave!*"

Angelo sucked in his breath and held even the wind frozen still around them before he spoke, his voice low and hoarse and furious. *"That's not true*—damn it, Kat, you're *not* the only person who's ever been trapped! You should ask *me* about traps—ask me why Thaddeus didn't just hop on a horse every time there was a whip on his back! He was a *man*—why didn't he have a *horse,* Kat? *Because they never let people like Thaddeus have a horse.* They *needed* him to be trapped. Nobody—*nobody*—would ever work a cane field unless they were trapped. So you come ask *me* sometime— I'll tell you about traps, and not the kind that kill you in a day. Let me tell you about the kind that kill you for *fifty years* and then go after your *kids,* and your *grandkids,* till you dream at night about strangling your own family—*anything,* just so they won't have to live through what you've lived through! You come ask *me* about traps, Kat—sometime when you're not so wrapped up in your own goddamned world you can't even see when you've got it good!"

Kat was having trouble thinking through Angelo's furious tirade, knowing she wanted to say something but being too distracted by a pounding heat in her head that was almost unbearably nauseating. She reached for a branch to steady herself, but missed, and found instead she was being pulled down the path and through the door of the dark house. Dizzy and already shaky on her feet, she tried unsuccessfully to dig her heels into the snow. "What are you *doing?*" she hissed.

"I'm going to show you something." Angelo planted her in

front of a tin-framed mirror by the door, holding her there while he flipped on the light.

Kat half-shrieked when she saw why her head hurt so badly. Nearly every autumn-colored hair was standing half-up and out like the fur on a hissing cat. She frantically tried to smooth it all with her hands, only adding bruise to the throbbing by forcing it down.

"I thought you'd want to know," said Angelo curtly, and he stalked out, leaving the door open behind himself. He reappeared a moment later with her snowy pack and cap, flinging them onto the floor. Kat hardly noticed him as she stood staring at her reflection in the mirror, but he caught her attention when he hit the doorframe with his open palm, making her jump. "You had better not be teaching anyone at *my school* that men have never been trapped," he growled in a voice low enough to rumble through the very bricks of the house. "That's something *you* know nothing about." With that, he slammed the door and crunched off through the snow.

Moments later, Kat heard the thump of something soft hitting the door, followed by the sound of Angelo's truck driving away. When she looked outside, she found her damp bandana lying limp in the snow.

∞

As the solstice twirled the year on its spindle of marathon darkness, its most glacial pirouette before coming to rest on the sunlight side of the calendar, only one dog in the east valley took any notice at all. And even this dog would have slept soundly through the event had he not spent the first half of the night huddled on the frigid vinyl seat of a stranded pickup truck, and the second half of the night jolting awake with each groan and cry of the nightmared man beside him, reliving a distant hell. And had he

slept soundly, the dog would have been awake at dawn and outdoors tasting the wind for a menu of the day's weather, just in
time to see a bundled figure struggle to push a bicycle through a
snowy orchard below. He'd have seen how the orchard gate preferred to snap off its hinge rather than plow a knee-high drift out
of its path, and he'd have seen how an entire plum tree plopped its
snow onto the frustrated traveller when the bicycle was lifted
clumsily over the broken gate, catching its handlebars on a low
branch. The dog would have been too far above the scene to hear
the traveller mumble a curse into her woolen scarf at the snow,
the bicycle, and the plum tree all in one—would merely have seen
how a heavily booted foot reared back to kick at the gate only to
rebound in obvious pain.

And had the dog slept soundly rather than fret through the
night over a man who had never before been known to talk in his
sleep, he'd have been awake to see the bundled traveller, covered
with snow, limping slightly, pushing an uncooperative bicycle
westward down an unplowed road, the dawn light too faint to
highlight her tracks in the snow.

And he would have barked.

But the big black dog snored through the year's slowest dawn,
as did the man whose nightmares kept sleep out of reach for most
of the night. And when at last the two of them stumbled outside
to a grey morning sky ice-welded to a grey morning earth, there
was nothing left of the dawn's scene in the orchard but a gate
hanging off its upper hinge and parallel tracks from skinny tires
and fat boots.

"Ohhhh, damn it, Oso," came the man's hoarse, sleep-shy
voice as he stooped to gather an armload of firewood. "Don't ever
fall in love with a cat."

And later, as the dog settled into his favorite spot by the morning's fire, he let himself fall back into that dawn sleep, for when he

saw the man spill open the large pack by the door and stuff its contents into closet and drawers, he knew they wouldn't be going anywhere soon.

∞∞

The longest night of the year didn't escape the notice of any of the fifty cat tails on the mirage-mesa, curled tightly around fifty cold noses. None of the one hundred pointed ears, tracking the shifty wind, were unaware of the marathon darkness spinning around them. Not a single feline dream masked the glacial pace of the solstice's crawl as every cat forsook the comfort of the sala to sit in frozen sentry around the porch, waiting, thinking of only one thing: tuna.

With no tuna by nightfall, they assured themselves it had been optimistic to expect delivery ahead of the year's earliest sundown, and such an unusually stormy sundown at that. By midnight, half were convinced the tuna wouldn't arrive till morning but preferred to continue their vigil rather than risk missing out on a late-night feast. All through the long hours before the year's laziest dawn, fifty huddled and hopeful felines fooled themselves out of catnapping—*It'll be any minute now, any minute now—is that them I hear out there?* But when the first and third and even fifth hour of steely daylight passed over the mesa with no tuna on the horizon, the frozen sentries abandoned post en masse to thaw themselves in the relative warmth of the sala, feeling a bit crabby.

And a bit vocal with their crabbiness.

And they were nearly all griping at once when a bedraggled mound of snow-on-wool sneezed her way into the house on a sled of icy wind and collapsed against the heavy door in an effort to close it. The crabby concerto cut off as the choir stared at the snow-woman for a moment, then stared expectantly at the closed door for a few more moments, then leapt all as one furry river through the cracked window to the porch. The mound of snow-on-wool hardly noticed the exodus, caught as she was in a fit of sneezing, and likewise hardly noticed the reverse exodus as two hundred cat paws pranced back through the window and parked in front of her.

Where's Angelo? they sang in fifty-part disharmony. *Where's the tuna?*

Only a sneeze answered them. Only the strained blowing of a nose competed with the whistle of the wind outdoors. A thousand cat claws tapped a metronomic beat as they counted to whatever number cats count to, until they at last turned away, crabby cats stomping off to all corners of the house to catch up on lost sleep. For awhile, the snow-woman leaning against the door didn't budge or melt in any way, just sat frozen in a red-nosed stupor until there was a crabby comment, sotto voce, from the direction of the couch.

You'd think a woman who's half cat would remember tuna.

At that, the mound of snow-on-wool melted—flared and exploded, in fact, in a scream that was decidedly unhuman, throwing her cap at the nearest cat cluster and scattering them in every direction, including skyward. "I'M SICK AND DAMNED TIRED OF BEING HALF CAT!!"

winter/spring

Unlike history, the cycle of a year is not cruel with surprises, does not turn kings to beggars in the wake of an unforeseen sunrise. Nor is it capricious like the weather, bringing green mountains of chiles on one day and killing whole orchards of fruit on another. Sunrises cycle on, ever on, humming the year's steady basso profundo, unaffected by historical rumblings or syncopations of weather. Behind the thickest winter storm, each day brings slightly more sunlight; in summer's worst scalding heat, each day brings slightly less. Animals know this cycle with their bodies, and the rhythms of their coats mark the rhythms of the sun. But humans try to know the cycle with their minds, which are already distracted by a symphony of human activities. When life's trumpets and cellos weave a fugue to mask the year's basso profundo, humans cry foul in this mind game of theirs, accusing time of racing by. And when the basso sings solo—no oboes, no violas—humans cry foul again, wailing that time holds them captive in doldrums. In truth, the year cycles on, never varying its beat, making each day shorter or longer than the last, leaving humans to compose their own melodramas above.

And so it was that the CatWoman, being part cat, knew with her body that each day following the solstice was ever so slightly longer, leaning toward the idea of spring even while caught in the fact of winter's worst storms. But being part human, her mind listened only to the whine of the wind, saw grey clouds upon grey clouds masking the sunlight and freezing time to a standstill. The human in her, still humming the melody from violins she had only barely admitted were playing in her heart, began the new year thoroughly depressed.

It didn't help matters, either, that she was sick as a dog.

One hundred and eighty-six sneezes, and only nine words out of you since you got back.

The CatWoman didn't need eyes to know who kept count above her poulticed head and chest. The heat from mounds of wet towels piled high upon her had long since faded to the semi-warm of the sala, and she was drowsily thinking about dragging herself upright to re-stoke both sources of warmth. But the tortoise-shell's voice set her eyes to shut even tighter in the pretense of sleep, hoping the cat would leave her to her misery.

Come on, I know you're awake. Not even a human who's half cat would stay in bed for eight days straight.

Her one hundred eighty-seventh sneeze struck a flint deep inside her nose and, try though she might to ignore it out of existence, it jolted the CatWoman ungracefully out of her act, knocking wet towels to the floor.

Hundred and eighty-seven. I knew you were awake.

There wasn't a fresh handkerchief within miles of where she lay on the couch by the fireplace, only dozens of faded limp ones draped like downed doves half-on and half-off the nearby table. In her blind gropings for a moderately reusable one, the Cat-

Woman's hand came upon her teacup and the medicinal brew she had only half finished. It, too, had lost its heat, was in need of re-stoking. But the thought of standing up, much less stoking a fire and brewing more of a tea that seemed to benefit her not one whit, was exhausting. A few more minutes, she told herself, set-tling back under the towel mounds. Then, I'll get up . . .

Where's Angelo? We thought he was coming with you.

Angelo's never coming, she thought as she'd thought over and over in the last week. Angelo thinks I'm a freak. I think I'm a freak. I *am* a freak.

She replayed in her mind the sight of herself in the mirror, and shuddered. The tortoise-shell mistook her shudder for a chill and climbed onto her chest to push the tepid towels aside. With two quick turns she had settled in, paws tucked under, purring a warmer poultice into the CatWoman's chest than the whole mound of tow-els had done when they were fresh. Eventually, the old calico joined them, perching herself on the CatWoman's belly and purring her ripe ninth-life purr, deep as a ship's engine. Before long, she was piled entirely with purring cats, buzzing head to toe with a heat she could never have coaxed from a fire, or from a tea, or from a whole mountain of steaming towels. When the purring finally reached into the very center of her bones—the very coldest, iciest thread inside her, numb for centuries it seemed—she began to cry.

And for hours, as that icy thread melted into tears, the cats purred on.

◯◯◯

I'm a freak.

So's he. You were made for each other.

No, the CatWoman sighed into the frosty darkness, *I mean really a freak.* Steam from the warm spring was freezing onto the bare olive branches over her head, chrome edging under a moon finally visible after two weeks of hiding. *I have a lot more cat in me than he does. My hair stands up—when I—um—*

Fight? the tortoise-shell finished for her. *That's good. You need that before a fight.*

Not that kind of a fight. I'm not trying to scratch anyone's eyes out.

But if you ever wanted to, that's the first step.

I'll remember that. Now that the sun was down, the air was really too cold for the CatWoman to be sitting in the spring, but it was a relief to be out of the house and away from the smell of a sickbed, even if it was her own. *That must be what happened last summer, when I thought I had a hangover and he swore I didn't. It felt like someone pulled my hair out.*

If you were all cat, it wouldn't have hurt. You'd have known what to do next.

What's that?

Put it in your claws, of course. The hair is just for openers. Once you've done your screaming and the real fighting starts, you put all that muscle in your claws where you can use it. That's how you win in a cat fight.

Another good one to remember, the CatWoman said dryly. *Just put it in my claws.* She splashed water over her eyes and rubbed them wearily. *Do you realize this hair trick of mine has probably been going on all my life and I never knew it?*

Now you do, said the cat matter-of-factly. *You'll know what to do next time.*

But I don't want *there to be a next time. I don't* want *to be fighting with Angelo. I had something entirely—else—in mind.*

What were you fighting about?

For a moment, the CatWoman's memory was as foggy as the air above the pool. *What were we fighting about?* she wondered, backtracking past the image of herself in the mirror to the sight of him standing in the snow, silhouetted by the truck lights. *Traps,* she said eventually. *I need to go ask him about traps.*

∞

Drying a trail for herself from the house to the gorge was no problem, as the storm soon abated on the mirage-mesa. But Kat needed much more than the small mud trick her first mother taught her to clear a bicycle trail on the east side of the river, where two weeks of snow, wind, and ice stood obstinately between her and town. She parked her bicycle on the mirage rim and left for school a day early, knowing this would be her routine until the worst of winter had passed—at least a month of a lot of walking. It would have been a great help if her cold had cleared up before she returned to school, but it hadn't. She was still muddle-headed from too much sneezing, and teas were only calming her cough during the daytime. In spite of all this, Kat was ready for school to start up again and ready to ask Angelo about traps—ready, she thought, to hear what he had to say. She carried in her pack, wrapped in wads of clean clothes, a peace offering of dried tomatoes from her pantry.

She begged off telling a story that first day back, partly due to her scratchy voice but mostly because she couldn't think of one to tell. Her train of thought and momentum had snapped over the winter break, and she convinced herself she would just need a few days to get rolling again. If her students objected to reading for nearly the entire classtime, they kept quiet about it, not yet rolling again themselves after two weeks of vacation in the snow.

Angelo was sequestered in his office all day, so Kat didn't get a chance at school to begin building a peace between them. Of the several cars that stopped to offer her a ride as she walked home, none was his truck. When darkness fell, however, she could see there were lights on in his house, so she gathered her peace offering and climbed what she could find of the trail cut into the hillside. As she cleared the top and stepped through the cut in the stone ridgewall, she stopped short at the sight of a second dark shape in the driveway—a van, melting into the twilight but for a fluorescent moon on the driver's door. Through the uncurtained window a few steps to her left, Kat could see a table set for two and the tail end of a glittering sky-blue shawl swirling out of sight through the kitchen doorway.

"Silly me," she choked quietly into the windless night. On her way back down the dark path, she dumped the dried tomatoes into a snowbank.

∞

"*If* you're thinking of snatching that man, you better just do it. There are at least a half-dozen women in this town who'd walk barefoot in a blizzard for the chance to darn his socks."

Georgia's husky voice blended seamlessly into Kat's view out her classroom window, where husky mammoth clouds were trampling the western horizon, stampeding the latest snowstorm toward town. She had been watching for Angelo's truck to leave the parking lot before starting home herself. Georgia interrupted the vigil just as Angelo could be seen across the yard, locking his office door.

Kat moved quickly from her post to feign a need to fuss with her backpack. "I—uh—I'm not good with a needle." Her voice was nearly as husky as Georgia's from coughing late into too many nights.

"Neither are they, I'm sure." Georgia smiled a worried, maternal smile at her. "Are you all right, Kat? Travis told me you haven't been yourself in class these last few weeks. Did something happen over the break?"

"No—I've been sick, that's all. I must have picked up a cold that night you pulled us out of the ditch." In the face of Georgia's skeptical nod, she added, "I haven't—gotten my voice back yet."

"Hmm—well, whatever bug bit you, it must have bitten Angelo. He won't talk either."

"Maybe it's the weather," Kat evaded. "I just need the weather to clear and I'll be fine." She glanced out at the snowy mammoths again, with a cloud of white steam in the foreground where Angelo's truck was pulling away. "Maybe I should have gone to teach in a school farther south."

"Here, here," Georgia agreed. "I'll be thinking the same thing a month from now when the mud gets bad. That's when I start dreaming of all those lucky kids in the canyon."

"What canyon?"

"Vermilion Canyon—it's a school about a day's drive west of here. There isn't a more beautiful spot on earth, I guarandamntee you that. They get half the winter we get here. But the *best* part?" She chuckled. "The whole canyon floor is sand. *No mud in the spring.* Now *that's* prime real estate if you ask me."

"Why don't you move there?"

"They've got an art teacher already, and she's not moving. Can't blame her either."

"If you ever hear that they're looking for a history teacher, let me—"

When Kat couldn't finish without sneezing, Georgia asked, "Have you seen a doctor yet?"

"No, I'm fine. Really I am. A change in the weather is all I need."

"A warm body to hold you at night is what *you* need, dear." Georgia winked, turning to leave. "Hope you find a remedy soon. Travis is afraid you're turning into just any old teacher."

Just any old teacher, Kat thought miserably, walking home with the gathering dark of a mammoth stampede nipping at her heels. Just any old teacher. She hadn't told any stories in class since before the winter break—had neglected the latrine versions of history and slid into a rut of having the kids read in class because it took no effort from her. The part of her that had enchanted her students all through the fall semester felt numb now, numb and fading, leaving only the part of her that was just any old teacher.

"How depressing," she mumbled as she stepped off the road into the ditch at the sound of a car coming up from behind. The car was actually a beat-up old van, which pulled up next to her rather than pass by. When the driver leaned over to open the door on her side, she realized it was Eli on the inside of the frosty window.

"Hop in—it's gonna start snowing any minute," he called. Over her shoulder and barely a mile behind, the ridge where the school sat was already shrouded by snow, and Kat still had two miles to walk before she'd be under a roof. For the first time since the schoolyear began, Kat swallowed the reflex inside her to refuse and climbed aboard. The door had no intention of latching shut behind her until Eli walked around to slam it from the outside, and she noticed it wasn't measurably warmer inside than it had been out in the snowy ditch. But it had wheels and it was rolling, and when tiny snow-bullets soon began bouncing off the cracked windshield, she was relieved they weren't bouncing off her cheeks.

"Well, what do you think?" Eli asked in less than his usual shy manner.

"Of—?"

"Of my van. I just finished it this weekend. I've been rebuilding the engine and I finally got it running."

"Well—" Kat searched for a compliment. "—I'm impressed. It runs. And the doors open and close—almost. It looks like a van that'll—uh—get you there."

"Where?" Eli grinned at her obvious struggle.

"Wherever." She shrugged, and they both laughed clouds of warm breath into the cab of the rattletrap.

"It's not much to look at," he said. "I haven't done any of the body work yet. But it'll all be done by summer, and then—" His hand mimicked a jet taking flight from the dashboard.

Kat wondered at how talkative Eli was being and at how her depression was shedding next to his light mood. "Where are you headed?"

"Wherever," he replied, an unusual dash of braggadocio in his voice. "Just anywhere but here."

"College?"

"Maybe. Maybe not. Mostly, I just want to get away from here." I can well imagine, Kat thought to herself, as Eli steered the van slowly around curves on the semi-icy road. Away from Shanti. "Next, I need new tires," he went on. "And maybe the heater, but I can live without the heater if I have to. I could just go park on a beach."

"And eat bananas all day?" Kat's laugh was hoarse and started her coughing for a moment. "I did that once."

"You *did?*"

"Uh-huh. And I left when I got sick and tired of bananas."

"Did you ever go to college?"

"Oh yes. I couldn't be your teacher if I hadn't done that."

Eli was quiet then, guiding the van across the highway and onto the neglected end of the road for the last mile to Kat's house. "Mr. D's really on my case about going to college," he said after a bit. "He threw a fit when he found out what I'm gonna do with this van—just like my mom did." So that's why you're talking to me, Kat thought. You've lost a friend over this van. "He says it would be a waste."

Kat sighed a steam-sigh into the frigid cab, thinking of the operatic family who held a three-day feast for Angelo, the first of them ever to go to college. What a contrast they were to the O'Malleys, for whom college was just a matter of course, a change of address. "I agree with Angelo," she said slowly. "But there's more than one kind of waste. There's the waste that would happen if you didn't go, because you've got the kind of mind colleges were made for. And then, there's the waste that happens when someone goes to school but just goes through the motions, just takes up space." Which is what I've been doing lately, she scolded herself silently. The van slid to the left as Eli stopped in front of the orchard gate. "I'm sorry to hear you and Angelo aren't getting along. I know he cares an awful lot about you."

"Yeah, well," Eli said uncomfortably, looking away from her and up the hillside toward Angelo's house, "he just needs to get off my case is all." As Kat stepped out of the van, he called, "Wait—I brought you something for your cold." He dug around in a ratty box between the front seats to pull out a small muslin pouch, tied with a leather thong. As on the thong Angelo wore in his hair, there were tiny buffalo bird feathers stitched to each end. "It's full of—stuff—to make your cold go away." He was back to the shy Eli she'd known all year. "You have to soak the bag till it makes a tea—and drink it—and then tie it around your neck so it sits on your—" He put his hand to his chest in a gesture of teenage speechlessness. "—right here—while you're asleep. My mom uses it on me when I'm sick."

Kat twirled a feather between cold fingers. "That's so sweet of you," she said softly. As the van skidded its way down the road, she shook her head in its vapory wake. "They're going to be standing in line for *you*, Eli."

Odds were, the remedy would work, Kat decided, judging by how wretched the tea tasted and how fumes from the moist bag on her chest drove a buzz saw right up her nose. It was the first feeling she'd had in her head at all in a month, and for that alone she was willing to get up at midnight to re-steep the bag for a second round. She woke from a dream of Angelo standing in the falling snow, whispering, "You come talk to *me*," and his words made clouds that hovered near his cheeks before floating toward her . . .

Or was it Eli?

She couldn't sort it out in the fog of fumes from the bag boiling on the stove. The second round of tea sent her head over heels into a dream of the tortoise-shell cooing over her, "Pobrecita mijita, brillarás como estrellita . . ."

Or was it her first mother?

Or was it the daughter who taught her to sign her name like a queen?

Or was it Layira—"Queen Anandizha, Anan-*di*-zha"—bowing a cello nestled between the folds of a skirt made all of sequins . . .

Or were they stars?

A queen made of stars, and coyotes singing to the moon over her head, "Angelo! Moon-brother!"

And Angelo standing in the starry snow . . .

. . . or standing in snowy stars? . . .

. . . with the moon over his head— "Moon-brother!"—and the moonlight in his eyes— "Moon-brother!"—and the moonglow on his cheeks, and her lips falling toward those cheeks, and her lips melting on those grinning cheeks . . .

Or were they grinning eyes, in the starry snow, or the snowy stars?

"You come talk to *me* about cheeks . . ."

Or was it traps?

Or was it socks?

Or was it tea?

Or was it time to get up?

Get up.

Get up, Kat.

Layer by layer, she peeled off the dream to find a dark house on a dark morning, where the clock told her she had better start hiking soon if she didn't want to miss her morning class. The clammy muslin bag stuck to her chest as she sat up with the first clear head she'd had since the solstice.

"That's a wicked tea, Eli," she groaned, her voice still hoarse but her throat no longer raw. "Your mother taught you well."

And later that day, so did Kat, for the first time in weeks.

∞∞∞

"I'd like to tell you a story about hysteria and redheads."

"Me!" called Zephyr proudly, shaking a mop of newly fox-red curls.

"No." Kat grinned. "People who were *born* redheads."

"Not me." Zephyr shrugged, and the whole afternoon class laughed. It was a welcome sound for Kat. She had finally shed her cold and cough, finally gotten back into the familiar routine of enchanting her students. Never mind that winter was nasty outside, or that her trips to town were three days long rather than two, or that her Wednesday night standing invitation to dinner had lost its legs and lapsed entirely. She was enjoying her classes once again and they were enjoying her, and Kat told herself that was what mattered most.

"No, these were born redheads, and before the story can start, you need to know about the blondes and the brunettes, too. In the beginning, there were just blondes and brunettes living in the land where this story takes place. It's hard to say if they were living together peacefully or not—it was more like a wary coexistence. And since no one was ever sure if there were more brunettes than blondes, or the other way round, both groups put on a show of friendliness *just in case*, if you know what I mean."

After five months with them, Kat had a pretty good idea whom she was reaching with her latrine versions of history and which facets of a story would hold the interest of which students. Pilar and Zeke would hear the poetic and philosophical themes in everything she told. Zephyr, Adelmo and Venus would be incensed if any characters lacked shoes or adequate clothing. Beau didn't like any situation where people were being bossed around. Shanti thought every problem could be solved if there were just someone in charge, giving orders. If Kat had walked into her teaching job with a single outcome in mind for her students, she wasn't getting it. What she was getting, however, was a lot of lively debate.

"For generations and generations, the blondes and brunettes lived in this way. People were born and grew up and grew old, spending their whole lives living on one side or the other of this tenuous balance. And then one day, that balance was nudged by the great fingertip called Fate. The whole blonde and brunette world was flipped upside down when—*the redheads moved in*."

Soukishna giggled her squeaky, mousy giggle. "What's wrong with redheads next door?"

Kat could have predicted the question the same way a speech writer predicts applause. Her stories had taken on the rhythm of a call-and-response lately, much the same as her banterings with Angelo had been before their ballet of mutual avoidance began. The only regular, non-feline conversations she was having now were with students, and she was beginning to treasure her classtimes for that reason, if for no other.

"Ask the redheads, and they would have said there was no problem at all," Kat answered. "They were a wandering tribe—it wasn't in their nature to stay in one place for more than a generation or two, so they had seen many places before they got to the valley of the blondes and brunettes. They thought they were just moving into a new place like they'd done so many times before. But if you asked a blonde or a brunette? *They're* the ones who had a problem. None of them had ever left the valley, and none of them had ever seen a redhead before. Unfortunately for the redheads, it wasn't in the blonde or brunette nature to look at their new neighbors as interesting and refreshingly unique. They looked at them as freaks."

"Good thing you never lived there, Zephyr," Adelmo teased.

"They're jealous, it's obvious to me," she quipped.

"Could be," Kat continued, "but there was no way they were ever going to admit it. They just sat back and made comments like, 'Look how *odd* their hair is,' or 'Look how *red* their faces get in the sun.' Eventually, the more outspoken ones started saying things like, 'I'm so glad *my* kids weren't born with those blotchy freckle-things all over them. *Yuck.*' The blondes and brunettes chattered among themselves constantly and, mysteriously enough, became closer allies than they had ever been before they had the redheads in the valley. They may have had their differences before, but now the blondes and brunettes became an US while the redheads became a THEM.

"Some years went by, with the redheads building their own little community nearby, separate from the blondes and brunettes since they were never invited to move in among them. With everything the redheads did, the comments grew louder. 'Look at those *houses!* What kind of people would live in dumb houses like *that?*' 'Did you *hear* them? They can barely talk! They talk some kind of jibber-jabber. I think they're half-wits.' By the time this story starts, the blondes and brunettes had forged a gossip alliance against the redheads, watching everything they did. All this time, the redheads were just going about their lives, building houses, planting vegetables, having babies. And, by the way, they *weren't* speaking jibber-jabber and they *weren't* half-wits. They spoke an entirely different language from the blondes and brunettes and, like anyone else who learns a second language, they had a bit of an accent. If the blondes and brunettes had taken the trouble to learn the redheads' language, they'd have had an accent, too. But they never did. They thought any language other than their own was just jibber-jabber.

"So that was the situation at the time this story starts, which was the summer of the drought. It was the first drought the blondes and brunettes could remember in their lifetimes, and it came in the third year after the redheads arrived, the second year after the extra-cold winter, and just a few months after a two-headed calf was born. It was the summer when the snide whispers about the redheads being half-wits turned to angry whispers that they might be devils. It was the summer when the blondes and brunettes began to spy on the redheads."

"My grandpa does that," Shanti threw in. "He has binoculars and he watches what everybody does all day."

"That's creepy," India muttered.

"He's not a creep," Shanti countered hotly. "He's retired. What else is he gonna do?"

"That's precisely why the blondes and brunettes were spying," Kat intervened. "They didn't really have much else to do. Their crops were dying and their livestock were wasting away. When they otherwise would have been tending fields, they spent their days staring at the redheads' settlement across the valley, wondering. So with all this idle time, the spying began and, of course, it happened at night. And, *of course,* the first thing the blonde and brunette spies saw were the full-moon fires, because that's just how Fate works.

"You see, the redheads were fond of singing and fond of full moons. Each month the whole settlement would sit around small campfires outside their houses and sing the moon from east to west, all night long. It was just something they loved to do. The spies were immediately suspicious when they saw this because blondes and brunettes had never been comfortable with the night, had never been fond of the moon, would much rather go to sleep with the sundown and ignore the spooky darkness. They scurried back to their village and confirmed everyone's worst fear—yes, the redheads were devils. They saw it with their own eyes. Only a devil would sit up all night singing jibber-jabber to the moon, with fires to boot.

"For the rest of the summer, any time redheads ventured into town for whatever reason, they were watched *very closely*. The townspeople even made their children hide indoors when redheads came near, just in case they had come to weave their evil deviltry on people now instead of on crops and hapless calves. There were full-time spies stationed out near the redhead settlement, waiting in the dark for something—*anything*—they didn't know what, but they were convinced they'd know it if they saw it."

"What 'it' ?" Beau interrupted.

"No one knew." Kat shrugged. "The big IT that haunted their dreams ever since the blondes and brunettes decided the redheads were devils. Once they heard about the fires and the moon-singing, there wasn't a brunette or a blonde in the whole town who wasn't convinced the redheads caused the drought, and the extra-cold winter, and the two-headed calf."

"It was their own fault." Shanti snickered. "That's dumb to sing to the moon."

"There's nothing wrong with singing to the moon," Zephyr scolded. "They're not hurting anybody. They're just *singing*."

"Yeah, but it looks suspicious."

"Then my mom better watch out for people like *you*, Shanti," India spoke up. "She sings to her garden every day in the summer. Does that make her a devil?"

"But they should have *known*—" Andrew said in Shanti's defense.

"How are they gonna know?" Aaron argued. "They just moved there."

"But it's dumb," Shanti grumbled. "*Nobody* sings to the moon."

"The redheads did," Kat said simply, "and they'd been doing it all their lives, and so had their ancestors. It was part of their culture, just like avoiding the nighttime was part of the culture of the blondes and brunettes."

"But what happened?" Soukishna asked, wanting to get back to the story.

"Well, the big IT happened," Kat went on. "The sign they were all looking for. The great terrible thing. What happened was, a blonde man missed his dinner."

"*That's* the big IT?" Beau asked impatiently. "So what?"

"Well, *you* might not think it sounds very big, but the whole town was in an uproar. This blonde man had been walking down a back street that day when a young redhead man and a young redhead woman came walking toward him. They were both about your age—"

"They're *always* our age." Zephyr laughed.

Kat grinned. "It's a good age for stories. So anyway, the blonde man was the type who liked to bully people around, even his own kind, so he stood in their path until they were forced to go around him. But when they tried to step past, he moved so they couldn't. Then he asked them where they were going and just exactly what their business was. The young woman could understand him better than her companion could, so she tried to answer him with her broken speech. But the blonde man didn't *really* want to hear what they had to say—"

"I *hate* people like that," Venus said vehemently.

"—he just wanted to scare them. So while the redhead girl was speaking, he threw his hands out at them, shook his head, and yelled jibber-jabber at them till they turned and ran back out of the town. And while they ran, what did the blonde man do? He *laughed*. He *roared*. It made his day to see those two teenagers run scared. The only thing that would have made it better would be if some of his fellow blondes and brunettes had seen it happen, but no one had. All his neighbors were hiding indoors, avoiding the chance of meeting a redhead somewhere. So the blonde man decided to go to the nearest tavern and brag on himself, tell everyone what a great devil-tamer he was."

"What a *jerk*," Venus muttered.

"He went to a tavern, ordered a beer, and started to tell the story. When he finished the tale, he told it again, and again, each time ordering another beer and adding a new exaggeration. The redheads weren't teenagers, they were adults, *big* adults. They weren't just carrying empty packs for buying supplies, they were *armed to the teeth*. They weren't just sunburned and freckled, they had *fire* in their eyes, just like devils would have. After five tellings and five rounds of applause, the man was so drunk with the beer and his own bragging that he could barely walk. When he left the tavern it was dark, and he took a wrong turn, ending up in a cornfield instead of at his house where dinner had long been cold."

"That's not a big IT," Beau protested. "There's gotta be more to it."

"Well, Beau, the problem was that there *wasn't* any more to it," Kat told him. "The man was too drunk to find his way home. Period. But do you think he was going to admit that after claiming to be a devil-tamer?"

"No way." Adelmo snickered.

"No. He got home around midnight and swore to his family that the redhead girl had put a spell on him and that's why he got lost. By noon the next day, the entire town of blondes and brunettes was up in arms over this latest incident. It was obviously the big IT they'd been expecting."

"Big deal," said Aaron.

"They made it a big deal, Aaron. When people are primed for hysteria, a tiny thing like this can become a wildfire, because that's what hysteria is. It's a wildfire of people who aren't thinking—just reacting. By nightfall, a mob of blondes and brunettes stormed the redheads' settlement, went door to door searching for the girl, tied stones to her waist when they found her, and threw her into the river."

"*What?!*" Zephyr cried.

"And that's the end of the story," Kat finished.

"No!" protested most of the rest of the class.

"How come your stories always end like that?" Zeke complained.

"Because it's the Latrine Version, not the rose-garden version," Kat said over her shoulder as she wrote on the chalkboard. "Here's your Latrine Version homework." She wrote: Think of all the people you ever thought were strange or different from you. Choose one of them and talk with that person until you find at least three things you have in common.

"*That's* the homework?" Andrew asked skeptically.

"That's the homework," Kat nodded.

"The only weird person *I* know is Eli." Shanti snickered under his breath, and Andrew and Sean snickered with him. Kat bristled with the insult, for they were talking about someone who was rapidly becoming a dear friend.

It had been rapid, this transformation in Eli from shy student to talkative friend. The process was aided by his van; he casually managed to drive down the road Kat walked on her way home each Wednesday and gave her a ride through the worst of winter. It wasn't lost on her that he was never in a hurry to reach her house or that he found a new topic to discuss each time they arrived at the orchard gate. It also wasn't lost on her that she didn't cut off the conversations, either. Her mood and health were improving with each ride, and she was almost reluctant to see the weather clear enough for bicycling again.

Mostly, Eli wanted to hear about the places she'd been, the travelling she'd done. "Have you ever seen a jungle?" he asked her once. Kat remembered the tortoise-shell's panther story so vividly she said yes, she had. "What are the colors like?"

"Uh—I don't know—" she stumbled. "It was too dark." She told him how very dark the jungle is, so unlike the desert where night is night and day is day. She told him how, in the jungle, daytime is only a lightening of night, and the creatures don't see their world so much as they taste it. "Even a cat needs more than just eyes to see in the jungle."

"I want to paint the jungle," Eli had said. "I'll drive south till I find one. I've painted enough deserts."

. . . and Kat dreamed that night of walking south—walking and walking over the dry desert until it became damp, and then wet, and finally thick with a darkness she could taste. With each step she changed, until she was no longer a woman but a panther, and then no longer a panther but a panther's eyes and breath . . .

On another ride, Eli had asked her where she learned all her stories. Did they come from college? he wanted to know.

"Ha!" She laughed. "No, they came from living."

"Where have you lived?"

"Oh," she said evasively, "here and there. Stories happen everywhere. It's just a matter of keeping your eyes and ears open. Maybe it's like you, being an artist. You see things others don't see because you've got an artist's heart. I see and hear things that others miss because I've got a storyteller's heart."

"I could tell a few stories," he had said under his breath. "But I'd rather paint."

. . . and Kat dreamed that night of Layira and Mu and Shanti dancing in a circle around Eli, who was pointedly ignoring them. Eli at an easel, Eli with his paints, Eli biding his time until their game would be choked dead by the exhaust from his van as he drove south to find a jungle . . .

On the last Wednesday before the weather cleared, Eli wanted to know how Kat knew Angelo. "Mr. D said he knew you a long time ago."

"When we were growing up," she said carefully.

"Was he—your boyfriend?"

"No—just someone I knew."

"How come you never talk to him anymore?"

Ahh, Eli, she thought, you have a storyteller's heart, too. You don't miss a thing. "How come *you* never talk to him anymore?" she countered.

"He's still pissed about this van." He waved his hand as if to dismiss Angelo's opinion. "I don't see why college is such a big deal to him."

"It was a big deal for his whole family," Kat told him, as if she'd been an eyewitness to the event. "No one in his family had ever been to college."

"But I want to *do* stuff, not just learn about it. Like you."

"Like me? But I went to college."

"You said your stories come from living. I want to *live*—"

"But you wouldn't be hearing my stories if I hadn't also gone to college. I've done both and, frankly, I think it would be a waste if you didn't do both, too. *And*—" she interrupted him when he opened his mouth to speak, "—I know Angelo well enough to know he feels the same way. He wants you to do both. *He's* done both. He's just not as loose in thinking about the time schedule as I am, I guess."

"Yeah, well," Eli mumbled, and then stared quietly up the hillside long enough for shadows to visibly lengthen in the plum orchard around Kat's little house. The colors in the morning-glory mural framing the front door fell flat in the low light, and Eli's tone matched them when he said softly, "Y'know, I was only gonna travel for a year. I really was planning to go to college. But Mr. D got so upset, I didn't get around to telling him that part."

"So tell him now," Kat nudged him.

Eli shook his head shortly. "He's been so grumpy lately. You'd think he was my father, the way he's been acting."

It was Kat's turn to shake her head. "You don't have to be someone's father—or mother—to want to see them do well with all their talents."

"Yeah, well," Eli repeated, staring again up the hill. Though the driveway was hidden from their view, they could see through the window on the ridge side of Angelo's house that someone had just turned on a light in the sala. Eli chewed on his lip and thought awhile longer, then sighed, "Well, I guess I better get up there before my mom shows up. Can I leave my van down here?"

"Sure." Kat nodded, wishing he hadn't reminded her what had become of her Wednesday night standing invitation to dinner.

"Thanks." He climbed out onto the road and up the slippery, snowy switchback trail.

Kat watched out the window of her little house until it was too dark to see, and Eli's van was still parked at the gate. Soon after dark, she heard him drive away and knew, if she'd climbed the hill herself, she would see another van with a moon on its door in the driveway at the top of the ridge.

. . . and Kat dreamed that night of Angelo's cheeks, with her lips melting like ice cream upon them. Again.

⬭⬭

If you stare at that moon much longer, you'll burn holes in your eyes.

The CatWoman stroked the old calico's fur without moving her gaze from the ice-colored full moon overhead or turning her ears from the wolf-song floating toward it for the second time since the solstice. *Is that what cats tell their kittens?* she asked thoughtfully.

It's what I always told mine.

The CatWoman watched her breath make frosty lace to curtain the moon. *In my first two lives they used to say if you looked at the moon too much, you'd become a lunatic. Maybe that's what's happening to me—I'm turning into a loony.*

A coyote voice joined the wolf's for a few measures, then dropped out. It was too cold for coyote tales, but the wolf's cry kept renewing itself somewhere out in the dark. The CatWoman knew if she sat up to look at her campfire, she would see the wolf singing in the flames. But she didn't. She preferred to lie on the frozen ground and stare at the ice-moon, inviting it to ice over the human inside her who was feeling less comforted, and more lonely, with each passing week on the mirage.

"I don't think I want to be here anymore," she said to the moon, but it was the cat who replied.

Really? I thought you didn't like being in town.

I don't—that's what's so loony. She turned her face away from the moon at last and rubbed cold hands over her eyes. *I don't like being there, and I like being here less and less, and I really don't like going back and forth all the time. That's probably what's getting to me,* she added, knowing it was only half the story. *The only thing I really like lately is the teaching.*

At least there's something, the calico grunted.

Yeah, sighed the CatWoman, warming her fingers in the cat's fur again. *But I don't know if it's enough to keep me there.*

Where would you go?

The CatWoman shook her head slowly under the ice-moon, under the wolf's song. *I have no idea,* she said. *A year ago, I thought I'd be staying on this mirage the rest of this lifetime. If Angelo hadn't ever showed up, I probably would have, too.*

Well, damn that man, the cat said dryly.

It's not his fault. I didn't mean it that way. It's just that some days I wish my cocoon had never been burst. It would have been easier.

To be dumb and happy?

No. The CatWoman set her eyes back on the ice-moon and began her silent ice invitations again. *To be dumb and not lonely.*

⟨⟨○⟩⟩

It was a whip.

She was sure it was a whip.

Right outside the window, *right outside.*

The crack of its snake-tongue, the hiss as it wraps, the snap of its tail slapping bloody flesh.

Crackssssnap! Cracksssssnap!

Right outside, right there, she was sure it was a whip. She didn't need cat ears to tell her—

—but her cat ears told her in detail, and her cat body sprang her out of bed, out the door, and her cat claws buried themselves in the man with the whip—

—the hated man at the other end of the whip—

"*Don't you touch him!*" she screamed in her panther voice. "*I won't let you touch him!*"

And her great paw swung to knock the man out of her way, out of her dream, out of whip's reach of—

"—a plum tree," Kat panted. "It's a plum tree—wake up—" She wrapped her arms around the dark trunk before her and stood in the pre-dawn, barefoot and freezing and panting too hard to move. Her body was wracked by a shiver so violent she sank to the ground and leaned against the tree for support. "It's a nightmare—it was a nightmare—" The dream and the cracksssssnaps were still echoing through the valley of old orchards, receding slowly as the cold ground reminded Kat she was awake now. "A nightmare—a fifty-year nightmare—*fifty* years—oh *god*—"

Fifty years was unmercifully long.

Horridly long.

Much longer than she'd ever been alive.

A nightmare to live fifty years with a whip on your back. On your legs. On your face.

On your grinning cheeks—

"*I'd have killed him!*" Kat hissed with steamy breath lit by the stars. "I'd have *slit his throat*—I'd have *spit on his children*—I'd have *pulled his hair out one by one*—"

And he'd have killed me, she thought.

Killed you.

Kat stared through tangled branches at the house on the ridge above, nearly overcome by despair when she saw that no lights were on, that she couldn't walk barefoot up the hill at that very moment and tell Angelo she suddenly understood what he meant about traps. She pulled herself up the tree's trunk and walked barefoot across the orchard anyway, then across the road, then up the switchback trail to stand at the ridge wall.

Angelo, she called to a sleeping cat-self she wasn't sure could hear her, *I—uh—*

Her night-eyes saw it clearly—a curtain moving in a shadow so dark it was nearly swallowed by the night. She held her breath, held her shivers, lost the bravado of her dream, wondering how to go on now that she had an audience and her words wouldn't fall merely on the deaf ears of night. Then she heard the very faintest of whines and the click of dog toenails batting at the windowpane where the curtain now moved in jerky, eager, canine movements.

Kat mouthed a hello to Oso and listened for other sounds behind him. But Angelo was obviously sleeping too deeply to be bothered by the sound of a dog whining in the night or the sound of someone being chased by a nightmare. The house stayed dark and silent as she let out her breath and shivered her way back down the hill, biting her finger to keep from crying out at the cold path underfoot.

Officially, it would still be winter for two weeks. Signs of spring would be sparse for even longer, and the interim season would have little of the charm of either of its neighbors. It would, for all the world between the eastern and western mountains, just be the mud season—something to endure, something to test one's sense of humor.

Angelo's description, flip though it may have been last fall, manifested itself in perfect detail. The heating system *did* die out, as if on cue. The yard *did* turn to a huge mudpie, refusing to bake dry in the sporadic sunshine. The students *were* cabin-crazy and, with nowhere to venture but into the mudpie yard, they brought piles of the muck indoors. Kat discovered the ultimate insult of the season when she began requiring that all shoes be left at the door, only to be faced with an unwinnable choice: she could either teach class in a room full of teenage-sweaty socks or open the windows and lose what little heat the heaters struggled to produce. She seriously considered using her mud trick on the schoolyard when the smell of sweaty socks became too much, but restrained herself at the last minute. She had been trying to lie very low ever since the fiasco in Layira's pyramid. But no matter how low her profile, she had a persistently uneasy feeling that, as with the redheads in her story, anything odd at the school would focus all eyes accusingly upon her.

Angelo's other prediction came true, too. Tempers on the teaching staff veered sharply toward crabby with the first sign of mud in the yard and stayed that way. Even Mu, whose snake voice never spiked beyond a slither, bordered on shrill when he tried sneaking up on Kat in her classroom only to have his mud-sticky footsteps alert her cat ears for the first time. She was so pleased her ears had at last saved her from one of his unpleasant surprises that she grinned ungraciously while declining his latest invitation, this time to celebrate the upcoming equinox.

Mu was shrilly manning the yard during lunch when Kat arrived early for class one especially muddy day. She was no longer having to come to town a day early now that the ice had cleared from the roads and she could ride her bicycle. But the ride along the shortcut road from the gorge splattered her so thoroughly, she always arrived early enough to shed muddy clothes for fresh ones. As she swung herself off the bike and into the mud of the parking lot, she could hear Mu's shrill naggings in the distance and Georgia's griping nearby.

"I said *no*—" She and Travis were slogging toward Kat from across the yard.

"But *Mom*—"

"I *need* the truck this afternoon—you go find another ride if you think your legs won't carry you—"

"But—"

"Now Travis, you just get on out of here before I start spitting snakes and toads."

Travis spun and would have stomped away, but for the blobs of mud clinging to his soaked sneakers.

"I hate it, I hate it, I hate it," Georgia grumbled when she reached Kat, trying to kick the mud lumps from her own boots. "Spend my days with fifteen pounds on one boot and twenty on the other."

"I know what you mean," Kat agreed, grumbling herself at the clammy cling of mud-splattered pants.

"Time to move to the canyons." Georgia handed Kat an opened envelope. "I don't know if you were serious, but if you were, this is for you."

"For *me*? Who's writing to me?"

"It's that school out in the canyons—it's your lucky day, dear."

Kat read the letter inside, addressed to Georgia. No, it said, they would not be needing a new art teacher in the fall, but they would need a history teacher for the upper grades. Interviews would be held in the summer, and if she knew of anyone who might be interested, please pass the information along. Kat had just barely scanned the last sentence when she heard someone driving into the lot near them. She looked up to see Angelo and Eli climbing out of the beat-up van, laughing at something until they stepped into the mud and then griping in a harmonized duet.

"No one else has seen the letter," Georgia went on, nodding toward Angelo. "I thought you might want to pursue this—discreetly. I know how touchy things can get with a boss if they find out you're scheduling interviews."

"Thanks," Kat said, slipping the letter into her pocket. "I'll—think about it."

Georgia headed away toward her classroom, muttering, "Send me postcards—tell me what it's like to enjoy this time of year — ahhh *yuck*—" She sent a wad of mud flying ahead of herself with the flick of a boot. "Hate this stuff—"

When Kat looked back at Angelo and Eli, she heard Angelo demonstrating mud curses in several languages as they labored to scrape goo from their boots at the door to his office. They must have worked out their problem, she thought, enjoying vicariously the sound of Angelo's laugh and thinking she would miss it if she took a job at another school. But then he looked up at her as he held the door for Eli and the laughter died. He nodded to her in the awkward way they had managed to acknowledge each other's presence all winter and Kat thought, I already miss it. What would be the difference if I left?

∝∝∝

Signs precede events; official dates and pronouncements be damned. By the time the equinox balanced day with night, crocuses were already blooming in mud and snow, lambs were already taking their first steps in frosty fields. The signs came as a great relief to Kat as a teacher beleaguered by mud season, even though one of those signs only aggravated her growing discontent. Romances began blooming among her students, and the crossfire of Cupid's arrows in the classroom turned it into a minefield. Heaven forbid she should pair Victoria with Sky on any five-minute project, for Nanda would fall into an immovable sulk. Woe be upon her if she separated the class into two sides for debate and neglected to put Andrew and Belle on the same side, for they would both lose all mental capacity and stare moon-eyed at each other across the gulf. May hell open wide and swallow her up if she held her afternoon class one minute over schedule, for Travis would be pacing the yard waiting to escort Zephyr home.

"He must have gotten his mama's eye for color," Georgia chuckled one afternoon as she and Kat watched the two of them elbowing each other toward the parking lot and into Eli's van. Zephyr's china-blue locks shot a delightful streak of color through an otherwise drab, mud-colored day.

"He's got good taste." Kat smiled.

"He thinks I'm standing in the way of their romance by not letting him use the truck every day to drive her home. BIG BAD MOM," she groaned. "She doesn't even live a mile from here. They could *walk*—hold hands—do all that stuff we old folks used to do."

"In this mud? Come on, Mom." Kat nodded out toward the van as it left. "Is that Eli taking up the slack there?"

"Chauffeur to the Frustrated Chivalrous." Georgia laughed. "All Travis wants in the world right now is to fix up a van like Eli did. He's been palling around with Eli a *lot* since that van started rolling."

"He's got good taste there, too." Kat nodded. "Eli's one in a million."

Though Eli was no longer giving her rides home, he invariably returned to school after delivering Zephyr and Travis on the pretext of helping Kat load her bicycle. They often stood talking in the parking lot as they had sat a month earlier at her orchard gate. While the rest of her world was turning to gripy, goopy mud season, Eli's excitement about the end of school and the beginning of LIFE was as upbeat and infectious as the first springtime breezes. Kat spent her Wednesday evenings buzzing with Eli's dreams of leaving, of setting out into the world as if it were a feast for the taking, something she had never considered before. In a world of mud, the two crocuses in her landscape were Zephyr's unpredictable hair and the crush that led Eli to tell his history teacher all about his plans.

According to Eli, those plans now had Angelo's support, though not his mother's. Kat studiously avoided Layira when she made her appearances at the school, but she couldn't help noticing from a distance that the shawls were swinging less elegantly side to side, her gait was losing its camel-trek luxury. She carried herself less like a pharaoh queen now and more like a mother in the midst of a feud with a teenage son. Or, maybe she doesn't like Italian food, Kat thought dryly, listening to a strained singsong outside her classroom one morning arguing with Eli before he walked into class. When he finally stepped indoors and Kat heard the door surreptitiously locked behind him, she suspected Layira had been trying to come in to observe. Seconds later, Kat saw her traipsing angrily across the yard to Angelo's office, mud clinging to skirts and fringes.

If this mud season doesn't end soon, Kat sighed silently as she watched Layira slip and catch herself on a bench, something's going to explode.

⚭

Spring break can mean very little to a dog, not at all the great sigh of relief it is for humans living under the same roof. Dogs don't count the minutes until its arrival, don't see it as a heavenly oasis afloat in the mud season. For a dog, nothing really changes except that the humans sleep in, don't drive away after breakfast, and offer competition for napping space on the couch. Spring break isn't a break for a dog. It just means the humans will be home a lot for a little while and notice more keenly how much mud they track in on their paws.

So the big black dog in the house on the ridge was sleeping by the woodstove as spring break began for humans, barely noticing when the man with the dark thonged hair plopped himself onto the couch nearby with a groan of relief. The man was groaning a lot lately—groaning when the telephone rang, groaning when the weather was bad, groaning each time the lady in the shawl drove her moon-van into the driveway. The dog didn't bother paying attention to this latest groan or to the man's pacing all evening, interspersed with long gazes out the window at the empty house in the orchard below. He didn't even stop snoring when the man shot out of bed before dawn, saying, "Oso, let's get the hell out of here." In fact, it wasn't until he saw the big camping pack that the dog sat up and took note of what was going on, and not until he saw hiking boots being laced that he danced in ecstasy the way students and teachers had danced the day before.

The big black dog practically took hold of the steering wheel himself as the man drove them to the gorge, then pranced impatiently behind him down the steep trail to the river and up the other side. Once at the top, the dog took off at a gallop down the thin strip of dry ground bisecting the muddy mesa.

The man's sharp whistle brought him up short. "Oso!" The dog spun to look at the man, who wasn't following him but was instead heading off through the sage well to the north. The dog whined at him, reluctant to follow when there was such a conveniently dry route available. "This way, Oso," the man called, but the dog only sat where he was, refusing to budge. The man groaned, as was his habit lately. "My own dog, for christ's sake," he muttered, then waved him away. "Go ahead, go ahead. It's me she doesn't want to see." He set off alone through a mesa well-muddied now that the sun was an hour above the eastern mountains.

The dog sat watching until the sage swallowed the man and his large pack, and then finally, reluctantly, stepped off the dry path to follow him in his quest for a spring break. But it's not really a break for a dog. It's just another week of mud.

Under a third-quarter moon and some clear weather, the mirage-mesa came into estrus. The oasis around the little house and its towering cottonwoods cried for its earth to be turned, cried for seed, cried for the touch of a farmer's hand to usher in the growing season. The smell of soil no longer freezing overnight had always wakened the CatWoman in the past, sending her straight to the gardens at dawn with shovel in hand, eagerly ending winter's hibernation and forced inactivity. But this year, the smell of spring taking hold of the earth sent her to the orchards with a set of pruning shears. The gardens would not be turned, the earth would not be sown. The great task before her was to prune the orchards into a slumber so that when she left the mirage, as she'd decided to do in the summer, the trees would survive without her there to irrigate them.

The tortoise-shell scoffed at her talk of leaving. *But you said this is the most wonderful place you've found in five lifetimes.*

I wasn't lying. The CatWoman shrugged, carrying a bundle of pruned branches to the edge of the orchard and then starting on the next tree. *But it's only wonderful if it's where you want to be.*

Well, why don't you like it anymore? You're half cat. Cats love places like this.

The CatWoman climbed the hefty lower limbs of an apricot tree and set the shears to work overhead. *I'm half human. I'm ready to go.*

Did Angelo talk you into it? the cat asked slyly.

Angelo has nothing to do with this. He doesn't know I'm going.

So he's not going with you?

No.

Good. Then he can keep bringing us tuna.

The CatWoman threw a twig at her. *A steady supply of tuna and you'll forget I was ever here.*

It took three days to finish the pruning and a fourth to cut and stack all the debris. A year from now it'll be wonderful firewood, the CatWoman thought. I should tell Angelo it's here in case he wants it. But she wouldn't tell him anytime soon. She had decided to make her resignation formal at the end of the year for the sake of her students. Angelo's reaction wouldn't be a problem; he'd be glad to see her go, she was sure, and if it meant he would come to the mirage more often, the cats would be glad to see her go, too. Her students were another story, however, and there was no merit in modesty if it blinded her to how they felt. She was undeniably a favorite teacher for them, and those who weren't graduating would be disappointed by her decision to leave. Better to finish the year without breaking the news to anyone until the last minute. Mud and romance are hard enough, she thought. Disappointment would be too much.

The question of where she would go remained unanswered. With Georgia's complicity, she had sent off a letter requesting an interview in the canyons, but there had been no reply yet. If she were scheduled for an interview, there would be a whole host of other considerations, not the least of which was her nervousness about interviewing. "Wish I could skip that part," she said to her naked west orchard, even though she knew she had better get used to the idea, as she would never again be handed a job simply because the boss was her former brother.

With the pruning done and the smell of eager earth filling the air, it was all the CatWoman could do to keep herself from grabbing a shovel and tossing out a few seeds in the remaining days of her spring break. It was unnatural to be so idle at the dawn of the growing season, and the cats complained several times when she woke them with her unconscious pacing.

Humans! grumbled the apricot siamese after it got to be too much. *You're all alike. All you ever do is walk, walk, walk. I wish you'd just go do your pacing at the hot spring with Angelo.*

The CatWoman's path detoured abruptly with the cat's comment. *What do you mean?*

Go pace with Angelo. Let us get some sleep.

Angelo's at the hot spring? Since when?

Since a few days ago.

Why didn't anyone tell me?

The courtyard assembly shrugged in unison. *We thought you knew.*

No—The CatWoman sat heavily down onto the porch banco, nearly squashing the grey tiger as a million thoughts sang through her at once. *I didn't know. Why hasn't he come by here?*

He started to, the tortoise-shell piped up.

What happened?

He turned around and went back.

The CatWoman nodded stiffly in the twilight as the last thought faded and the apricot siamese chortled into the silence it left. *Go pace with him—that ought to make the dog dizzy.*

No, the CatWoman said quietly, *if he's been here that long and hasn't come by, then he doesn't want to see me. He just came to soak in the hot spring. Fine,* she added with a forced casual air. *It'll all be his in a few months.*

She went into the house and straight to a fidgety bed. When dream-curtains finally rose for her that night, they rose mercilessly on an opera of laughing eyes and kissable cheeks.

⚬⚬⚬

"Either my bandana's too small or my hair's too long," Kat muttered to her empty house. The tin-framed mirror reflected her frustrated efforts to stuff all her hair under one single square of cotton. No matter how she poked and tugged, the faded black of the bandana stretched lumpily over buried curls, giving her head the appearance of an aging eggplant too long in the bushel basket. She pulled the rag off the wild hair and began again, this

time trying to twist it all into a bun before cinching the cloth over it. Again the hair rebuked her efforts, laughing out of her fingers while she tried to gather the bun with one hand and drape the bandana over it all with the other. "This—damn—pissy—snow—" A half-glance out the window confirmed what her hair had already told her; the surprise spring snowstorm that forced her into town a day early was still falling outside, fat pinwheels of warm, wet flakes landing with audible splats on puddles of never-frozen snow. Kat's hair was soaking up the humidity like a rose soaking up sunshine, opening wide until each petal stands separate from all others. "Good for roses, bad for bandanas." She sighed as she realized she had no scissors except on the mesa and would have to wait until the weekend to trim her curls. "What I need—" She twisted the hair anew. "—is a second pair—" Her mind's eye tracked her other hand, backward and upside down, trying to tie a knot. "—of hands—"

The beginnings of a knot in one hand and a precariously wrapped bun in the other both slipped from Kat's fingers at a sudden sharp knock on the front door at her elbow. Who on earth? she thought as her heart startled right up into her mouth.

"Kat," called a strained and familiar voice. "Are you home?"

Kat held her breath as the bandana parachuted silently to the floor.

"Kat—we need to talk."

She set herself to open the door to a grin she knew wouldn't be there and dropped a mask over her eyes to hide her disappointment. Angelo's dark hair was wet and snowflecked as he stood in the moist splatterings, and drips from his wet nose and chin blended into his sopping coat. Kat wondered how long he stood outside before knocking, to get so wet. He's too wet for just a walk down the hill, she thought.

"I'll give you a ride to school," Angelo said, stomping snow and mud off his boots and shaking flakes from his head. "But I need to talk with you, and I'd rather do it here than there." His words had the rhythm of a cup scooping flour—measured, weighed, precise. Rehearsed, Kat thought. He stood in the snow and rehearsed this. She was glad of her mask as she nodded.

"Have a seat." She went to sit at the kitchen table and he joined her, leaning his chair against the wall and looking quietly out the window at the soggy plum thicket. Last fall, she thought, he'd have filled this moment with a joke about the snow. He'd have teased a grin into his eyes and his cheeks would have—she bit her lip to keep her mind off the image she knew would surely follow that thought. "What do we need to talk about?" Her voice, through bitten lips, sounded as measured as his.

"There was a board meeting last night," Angelo said slowly, "and you were the main topic." He looked at her with too many unspokens in his eyes for her to decipher, and she thought, He only came here because he was forced. "I know I said Layira couldn't make trouble for you, but I was wrong. She's doing it. She's convinced the board there's something shady going on in your classes, and that's why you won't let any parents in."

Kat breathed the entire damp morning in and back out again before asking steadily, "What kind of 'something'?"

"She didn't get specific." Kat knew by the way he looked down at the table that Angelo was lying, and her mind was suddenly filled with a sickening array of the types of somethings Layira would freely toss out about her. "She knows just how to work an audience to her advantage. She made it sound suspicious that the kids like you so much as a teacher."

And that Eli has a crush on me, she thought.

"I stood up for you, Kat," Angelo said wearily. "I told them it was a deal we made when you were hired and I wouldn't go back on it. But as your—former brother—I'm telling you, you'd save yourself a lot of grief if you'd let the board sit in on one of your classes."

Or they'll believe the worst about me. Kat was mute with the thought, setting her eyes on a sagging plum branch out the window. Like they believed about Josefa . . . and Feliciana . . . and Ivy . . . but not Kat, oh please, not Kat . . .

She stood stiffly and stepped back to the mirror, twisting her hair into a bun so tight her eyes teared and hearing the bandana rip slightly as she tied it over her head. The green-gold eyes in the mirror were having a hard time staying masked. "Tell them to be there tomorrow."

"Good," came a relieved whisper from the table behind her.

"On time," she added.

"Do you want me there?"

Kat pulled on her heavy coat and paid closer attention than necessary to the zipping and buttoning. "My classes have always been open to you."

That's not what I asked, Kat.

The silent comment surprised her, as no one but cats had spoken to her cat-self in months. When she looked up at Angelo, she had to forcibly rein her gaze from his cheeks to his eyes. "No, it's not what you asked," she replied out loud. "I'm not sure I want my boss watching when he's seen better." Angelo's only response was a barely perceptible squint at the word "boss," and Kat wished she could unsay it. With the squint came a mask as deliberate as her own. "Yes," she conceded, turning away to pull on her boots, "I guess you'd better be there."

"The boss will be there," Angelo said flatly to her back, and for all Kat regretted ever using the word, she couldn't bring herself to change it for something she wished were closer to the truth.

They drove slowly and silently out to the school, wiper blades swishing a soggy beat unadorned by conversation. Kat felt as sodden as the low-hung sky, with the beginnings of a headache fraying her peripheral vision. When a passing car splattered the truck and momentarily blocked view of the road, Angelo downshifted impatiently, grumbling, "I don't know why it pretends to be snow. It's just mud falling from the sky." The school's lot was a rutted ocean; the incessant snowfall wasn't cold enough to build on itself over the brown sea the way it had on the sage beyond, where branches sagged heavily to the ground under the weight of spring's nasty sense of humor. Angelo pulled up to a spot where Kat might have a shallow, if not dry, path to her classroom. He protested as loudly when she went to unload her bicycle as he had when she'd insisted upon taking it in the first place. "Would you just leave it where it is, Kat? I said I'd give you a ride home. You can't ride in this stuff."

"I've done it before," she said stiffly.

"Well, don't do it today, all right? Your boss can't afford to have any more teachers out sick." He drove the truck beyond her grasp before she could open the tailgate and parked it in the very muddiest spot available. With the slam of a door and a dozen splashy steps, Angelo was across the lot and gone into his office.

"To hell with the bike." Kat kicked a clod of snow and mud as she turned toward her classroom. "To hell with this weather," she muttered into the bulk of her coat. "To hell with the board, to hell with people—" She stomped into slushy puddles for emphasis. "To hell with stupid—" Splash! "—small-minded—" Squish! "—ignorant—" Splash! "—malicious—"

Kat's chant was drowned by a sudden burst of laughter she thought for an instant came from her own head, an auditory brush-stroke dipped in hues from mobs past, painting in the colors of her mounting dread. But as the hues sizzled with a second round of laughter, she realized the voices came from the far end of the yard, not the far end of her memories. Mob laughter, her ears told her, though all she could see was a cluster of backs.

"Wee willie winkie," sneered Shanti's voice across the wet

yard, "couldn't find his—" A volley of snowballs ended the rhyme in a spatter of thuds, as the two others with Shanti all cocked their arms and threw a unified barrage at some unseen target. The third round of laughter sent a ripple of nausea through Kat, so sickeningly familiar was the tone. "Winkie dinkie Eli, couldn't zip his own—" Another barrage of snowballs, another round of wicked laughter, and Kat's head swam with a distant chant,

> Lousy, lousy Ivy
> Doesn't go to church,
> Eats with the rats and
> Sleeps in the dirt!

Lousy, lousy Ivy, winkie dinkie Eli, to hell with the board, to hell with this weather, to hell with people who do this over and over again—*Eli?*

Kat jerked herself out of the memories and ran across the yard to find Eli held spread-eagled by Diego and Sean, while Shanti, Andrew, and Cheyenne packed stones into snowballs with their bare hands. Eli was covered head to toe with slush tinted pink from a cut on his cheek. She saw in the silent glare he gave his tormentors the fury of Ivy and Feliciana and Josefa, the same fury she felt swelling in herself now. The scene froze to a breathless photograph when Kat stalked into the path of what would have been the next attack. Cheyenne, Andrew, Diego, and Sean all looked suddenly embarrassed; Shanti looked mostly irritated by the interruption. Kat didn't look at Eli as she pulled all eyes toward her, holding them short-reined and taut with the fury of her own glare. She knew by the tingling of her scalp that her hair was trying to stand under the bandana, that if she didn't do something to break the tension her bandana would rip right open and lay her bare. She wanted to spit. But people don't spit in this lifetime, she told herself. Josefa spat when they lit the kindling at her feet. Feliciana spat when they tied the stones to her waist. Ivy cursed them all to hell when they came to her door.

To hell with this weather. To hell with the board. To hell with stupid, malicious people who do this over and over again.

Never again. No more burnings. Never again. No more stonings. *Never. No one. Ever.*

Kat threw her pack onto the ground with enough force to splash all of them with frigid slush to the knees. Her reins snapped and they all, including Shanti, looked uncomfortably at their feet. "This is *exactly* why I'm a teacher," she hissed at them. "Have you learned *nothing* all year?" If any had tried to reply, she would never have heard them over the electric crackling in her ears, her cat-self in a roar. *"Get in the classroom."* The five from her afternoon class dropped their snowballs, dropped Eli's arms, and slunk toward the building. Kat didn't remember Eli until she reached the door herself; when she glanced back at the soggy yard, he was gone.

No more burnings. No more stonings. *No one. Ever.*

The cooped-up chatter of an indoor lunchtime ground quickly down when Kat herded the five into the classroom and locked the door behind herself.

To hell with the board.

She stunned the group into frozen silence as she strode from window to window, yanking the curtains closed.

No one. Ever again. *This is why I'm a teacher.*

When she felt the bandana strain and begin to tear, Kat flipped the lights off and stood in the semi-darkness, willing her hair back down, slowly down, pulling the tension of every strand back into her body and down her arms like the tortoise-shell told her. Her fingers clutched the back of the stuffed chair, nails straining to bite the cloth. The bandana eased, the pounding in her head became a rhythmic flexing in her hands and fingers.

She glared at the attackers, huddled together as far from her as they could get in the small room. "You want to know what that's like?" she whispered furiously. When they looked down at the floor, she hissed, *"Look at me! All of you!"* She turned to the whole wide-eyed group, where no one blinked, no one breathed, and sent out an ivory claw in her voice. "I have a story to tell you— about a girl named Ivy. *Look at my eyes—*" And with her ivory-claw voice, she breathed into each and every one of them the breath Ivy drew when she saw the crowd coming for her—

—the crowd who turned her out to live with the cats, then damned her for a witch when the cats loved her—

—the crowd who taught their children to run away from her, lest she turn them into mice and eat them—

—the crowd who believed they must rid their souls of hate, but saw nothing hateful in stoning a fifteen-year-old girl who was too well-liked by cats—

—the mob of *good people*, gathering outside her shack to do whatever the devils of their imaginations would goad them into doing.

Good people.

Stupid people.

Ignorant, fearful, narrow-minded people.

"To hell with the lot of you!" came the curse from twenty-one Ivys, as Kat breathed into the room the pulsing tension of the armed mob.

"Do you renounce your witch life?" called a voice.

"To hell with you all!" cried every Ivy in the room. "I've done nothing but live quietly here. May you all rot in your own hells!"

"Kill her before she curses us!" someone shouted with the first stone, landing at her feet. As twenty-one Ivys stooped to pick it up and hurl it back, the breath was knocked out of them all with a wave of stones shattering ribs from every direction. Stones from here to shatter a wrist. Stones from there to crush a cheek. Stones to send each Ivy to her knees, gasping to find a breath—

—a breath—

The stones.

—a gasp—

More stones.

"Do you renounce your witch life?"

—a gasp—

"To—hell—with—you—"

More stones. Stones to smash the feet, stones to snap the knees. Stones from everywhere, one at a time, over and over. Stones to rattle the brain and black the eye. Stones—nowhere to run—stones—nowhere to crawl. A mob with stones, and not yet the stone that would end it all and stop the breath—

—the grating breath—

—the raspy, bloody, bubbly breath of twenty-one dying Ivys—

"Do you renounce?"

—but the voice rippled and wobbled and made no sense in a world filled with a gasping breath—the only thing left of a fifteen-year-old girl who frightened a whole town by being too well-liked by cats . . .

Kat had no idea how much time had gone by when she opened her eyes and pulled cramped, aching fingers from deep within the ripped stuffing of the chair before her. Her students slowly opened their eyes as well, no longer Ivys but not yet free of the images. Kat could think of nothing to say, could think of nothing but the seasickness of the memory beast stomping around in its boat. "Class dismissed," she whispered, and stumbled out of the room, out into the pissy snow, where she leaned over a bench and retched.

She was just getting to her feet, just wondering which direction to point herself, when Angelo came trotting through the slush from his office. "Kat, what's wrong?"

Kat sat down on the bench to calm the memory beast and anchored herself with the dampness soaking through to her from the seat. "I think I just taught my last lesson," she whispered. "I dismissed them early, but I don't know if they can walk yet—"

"*What?*"

"Maybe you better go in there—" Kat felt faint and retchy again. "You're right, boss," she said, wobbling to her feet, slowly uncurling her cramped fingers from the bench boards, "I can't ride in this stuff. I'll wait in your truck."

"Kat, *what happened?*" Angelo held her from falling as she stumbled toward the parking lot.

"Get the class to tell you," she croaked, having a hard time judging the distance between each foot and footstep. "I think I went too far."

"What did you do?"

"Go check on them." Kat climbed into the cab of the truck and crawled across the seat. "I went too far." She collapsed into a faint or a sleep, she didn't know which, and didn't notice how tenderly Angelo tucked his coat around her and touched her ashen face before hurrying off to her classroom.

"*No,* no one said a thing about you. They just spent the rest of the classtime giving Shanti and his buddies holy hell, and I didn't interfere." Angelo steered the truck very slowly over the rutted road in deference to Kat's dizzy head.

"For beating up on Eli. I caught them at it."

"So I gathered. Why didn't you come get me?"

Kat shrugged, exhausted even after sleeping the afternoon away in the truck. "It never occurred to me to go get you. All I could think of was Ivy." The muscles in her hands still throbbed; her nails felt as if she'd been hung by them. "So I—turned them all into little Ivys—to give them a taste of what it's like, being beaten up on."

"You didn't—"

"I did."

Angelo groaned softly and, in its current capricious fashion, Kat's mind pulled her eyes across the cab of the truck to his cheeks, which weren't glowing, weren't laughing. At best, they looked tight with frustration. "Next year, I swear, I'm sending everyone home for mud season." He pulled the truck off the road and shut off the engine. A sunset was trying to break through the clouds over the mirage-mesa, even while the snow kept falling on them in the east valley. Angelo stared at the orange and yellow glow for awhile, then leaned his head against the back window-pane. "Well, you certainly got your point across. If those five had had tails, they'd have been between their legs. I've never seen them intimidated before, especially not Shanti." The glow was melting the clouds from behind, slowly, surely, inching its way toward them and making instant waterfalls of the snow clustered on the sagebrush. "I don't know—maybe they heard you and didn't notice how you did it."

"Maybe." Kat's head wasn't so dizzy now that the truck was stopped.

"Tell me what you told the kids."

"No—I can't tell it again."

"How can I stand up for you if the parents start—"

"I'm not asking you to stand up for me," she cut him off quietly. "I'm just asking you for a ride home."

"Josefa-Feliciana-Ivy-Regina-*Kat*," he said slowly, looking out over the orange-glowing sage that promised a break in the storm, "in four hundred years there's never been anyone as mule-headed stubborn as you."

"I know." Kat laughed feebly. "And Ivy tried to throw that first stone back. I never remembered that part till today." She shook her head in wonder. "Can you imagine that? She tried to throw the first stone *back*."

The orange glow took on an edge at last, slicing through the clouds and bathing the truck in a brief, blinding ray of gold while meandering snow still danced all around, faint prisms of sunset sparkling in each flake. Magical, Kat thought to herself, and was just about to lose her awful day in the fairy prisms when Angelo slipped his hand over hers.

Good for Ivy, he said to her cat-self when she looked at him.

She nodded and turned back to the sunset, squeezing his hand softly. *Good for Ivy.*

∞∞

Kat expected the bells, was only surprised by how early they arrived, sweeping into her room a half hour before class was due to start. *The least she could have done was give me a few moments to gather myself,* she thought, resolutely setting out chairs for the board members without turning to greet her visitor. But the slippered footsteps behind the bells *were* a surprise, as was the closing of the door and the click of the lock. Kat turned to find Layira and Mu smiling at her in patronizing triumph from across the room.

"Good morning, Kat," cooed the bird voice. "I'm so excited we're *finally* going to visit your class. The kids all talk about you *so much*—"

I don't believe this woman, Kat thought. *She's got my neck in a noose and now she's choking me with sugar.*

"—can practically quote your lessons word-for-word. Unbelievable! Does Shanti do that, Mu?"

"Word-for-word," slithered the reply.

What was his word for yesterday's lesson? Kat wondered dryly. *Ouch?*

"—so now we'll *all* get to hear you. Where would you like us to sit?"

Outside, Kat wanted to say, though she answered steadily, "It's a little early yet. There's a pot of coffee in Angelo's office."

"Oh, I know, I'm in there every day," Layira sang. "Mu and I wanted to come early so we could talk to you about what happened yesterday."

Kat nodded, reminding herself of what Angelo said as he dropped her off the evening before: "Don't make any assumptions about what the kids might have told their parents. If anyone asks, get *them* to tell *you* what they heard." By letting Layira open the topic, Kat realized to her relief that "what happened yesterday" was the scene in the yard, not the scene in the classroom.

"—both *very good* boys, you know. They've been together since they were in diapers, and I *know* there's nothing to be concerned about. But then, Mu and I can't expect you to know that since you've never raised any children—"

The hell I haven't.

"—just have to work things out by themselves. I suppose they'd have gotten it all settled by now if their moon signs weren't in such conflict—"

"That's been the problem all along," Mu interjected smoothly.

"—and there just isn't anything to be done about *that*. If they weren't both such dear sweet boys, maybe I'd be worried, but Kat—" She put her hand on Kat's arm and tinkles bounced off every wall. "—I *am* Eli's mother. If there were anything to be worried about, I'd *know* it. He's my *baby*."

Kat removed Layira's hand from her arm so calmly and deliberately the bells barely murmured. "What I saw didn't look like a conflict between moon signs. It looked like a blood feud."

"It's nothing like that, Kat," Mu crooned, "and you don't need to get in the middle of it. You really came down awfully hard on Shanti. He wouldn't even eat supper, and that's not like my boy, is it, Layira?"

What did Shanti tell you? Kat wanted to know.

"—not like *my* boy either," Layira twittered. "I think Eli was so *embarrassed* to have you step in like that, Kat, he just wouldn't touch his food. He needs to learn to stand up for himself, you know, and the gods know how hard it's been for me to let my baby learn this lesson, but he'll never learn it if he doesn't get tested every now and then—"

Someone turned the doorknob, found it locked, and then knocked.

"We're having a conference," Mu called before Kat could move.

Kat, it's me, Angelo called silently from beyond the door. *Is that Layira and Mu in there?*

"—don't want you coming down so hard on Shanti, he's really a very dear boy, and so sensitive—"

This is worse than a Greek tragedy, Angelo, she called back to his cat-self. *They're scolding me for breaking up the fight. It wasn't even a fight—it was an ambush.*

"—just needs to learn to stand up for himself—"

They've tried that line on me. Don't give them an inch. I'll talk to the two of them later.

"—hate to see him so *embarrassed* he won't eat." Layira's singsong flitted over the sound of Angelo's retreating footsteps. "So, as his mother, I'm going to have to ask you to stay out of the matter. I know it's hard to watch, *especially* for us women, but it's all part of how boys grow and learn. And Eli needs to grow and learn."

Kat turned to Mu. "And what does Shanti learn from all this? What did he tell you he learned yesterday in school?"

The question must have startled Mu, for he missed several beats before replying. "Shanti came home so traumatized he wouldn't eat, he wouldn't talk about it at all. I had to call India to find out what happened. He's a very sensitive boy—"

Kat lost the last of her patience and interrupted him. "What I saw yesterday was your *sensitive boy* and his buddies attacking

Layira's *sensitive boy*. And I stopped it." She turned to Layira. "And if I see it again, I'll stop it again." She pointed at the chairs at the back of the room. "Those are the seats for the board. I'm going to get a cup of coffee." As she walked outside, she thought what she'd thought all through her restless night: to hell with the board. Ivy threw the first stone back.

⟨◯◯◯⟩

"It can't be," Kat groaned. "That's not—"

But it was. It was unmistakably Eli's van, splashing toward the gorge rim on the muddy shortcut road direct from school, and he was too close not to have seen her getting off her bike at the head of the trail. As if I haven't been through enough already, she thought, wanting nothing in five lifetimes more than to fade onto the mirage and soak the last twenty-four hours out of her mind. The morning's class, crammed with board members, plus Angelo and Mu and even Georgia, had not been the stellar lesson of the year. The only ones with anything to compare it to, of course, were the students, but that was small consolation, since they were the audience Kat cared about. She hadn't gotten tongue-tied, and that was good. Nobody brought up the topic of yesterday's Ivy lesson, and that was even better. But the two-and-a-half-hour session was singularly uninspired and flat-out dull, to the point that she saw even her most enthusiastic students studying straw flecks in the plastered walls. Without a glance at Angelo, she left school immediately after the last bewildered visitor struggled to phrase a compliment, and she pedalled straight for the mirage. Her one comforting thought, as her tires splashed her with muddy slush, was knowing she wouldn't be around to be offended when the board voted not to re-hire such an ungifted teacher. Georgia had slipped a letter to her after class; her interview in the canyons was scheduled for late June.

But she wasn't in the canyons yet. She was still six weeks from finishing a year that was souring daily. And to top it all off, here came Eli, skipping class to follow her to the mirage on a day when the board of directors was ready to believe she was doing shady things with her students.

He parked the van but didn't get out. "You're playing hookey," she joked, trying to sound jovial.

"It won't kill me—I'm ahead anyway. My mom had you locked up this morning, so I couldn't talk to you." Kat hated that the past two days now made her edgy around him as she waited for him to get to the point. "Thanks for what you did," he said simply, looking not at her but out across the wet mesa, where springtime drove winter's swan song off the sagebrush and into tiny rivulets in the sand. Everywhere around them was the soft trickling of water heading for the gorge. "I'm going to miss you—when I leave," he added, shy again with her like he hadn't been in months. "If I write to you, will you write back?"

I'm leaving, too, she said to a cat-self she knew he didn't have. *I'm getting out of this town just like you are. I'm going to live in a place where I'm not sneaking back and forth, hoping no one will discover me. I'm going to leave—and I'm going to miss you, too . . .*

"You can count on it," she said out loud.

"Good." He smiled at the view and let another few moments of winter-melt flow between them before asking, "Why do you come out here?" The phrasing told Kat this wasn't the first time he had seen which road she took when she left school.

"It's a quiet place," she said. "I do my best thinking in quiet places."

"So do I." He nodded. "I'll let you get back to thinking."

As soon as the van was out of sight, Kat wasted no time being relieved, but wheeled her bicycle quickly down the muddy path to the river. In her haste to get across the mirage-bridge, she didn't notice how the water was already beginning to rise, a sure sign that spring was hard at work making winter into history.

⌒⌒⌒

"I should count my blessings," the CatWoman said to herself, pacing her sixty-fourth circle around the courtyard under a first-quarter moon that was making sweet springtime dew all over the mirage-mesa.

No, you should sit still, the apricot siamese grumbled from a perch that would have been a cozy napping spot if the pacing human below would just settle down.

"It could have been a disaster—"

Why don't you sit down and tell us the blessings? yawned the tortoise-shell.

"—but I guess they just heard what I said—"

Sit down and tell us the blessings, begged the grey tiger.

"—not how I said it. I got off easy this time." She detoured across the courtyard grass, feathery with springtime, and made a figure eight that set her pacing in the opposite direction. "That was an awful thing to do. How could I do that to my students?"

What's her problem? asked the old calico as she walked out of the house where the pacing had wakened her, too.

She put her students through her third lifetime last week, the tortoise-shell groaned.

"—and just when they've gotten over this, I'll be resigning—"

Maybe I shouldn't have shown her how to tell a good story. A year ago, all she did was mumble in her sleep.

That I could live with, complained the apricot siamese.

"—why did I ever think I'd just be walking out? I have to say good-bye to them. How many lifetimes has it been since I didn't want to say good-bye to someone—" The pacing carried the CatWoman indoors for a moment, during which the cats scurried to try to close the door behind her and lock her in. But she was out again seconds later, oblivious to the furry maneuverings. "—a hundred and three. A hundred and three years since I said good-bye to someone I might miss. I'll miss them—how could I get so attached in just a year? I'm a *hermit*—I'm half *cat*—"

I'm starting to doubt her lineage, the calico said dryly. *If she were really half cat, she'd be asleep right now.*

"—and Angelo—I don't know *what* I'm going to do about Angelo." She plopped onto the porch banco, scattering the twin grey yearlings. "He thinks I'm a freak, and I keep dreaming about his cheeks. How do you say good-bye to someone like that? 'Good-bye, and get out of my dreams'," she said to the moon. "How about that? 'Good-bye, and give me my dreams back. Let me get a good night's sleep again—' "

Precisely! cried fifty feline voices, but she never heard them.

"This damn hair," she was griping with her next turn around the moonlit grass. "It could have been perfect—this could have been the lifetime of my dreams, and what happens? I get born with cat hair, and then I fall in love with someone who knows I'm a freak, and—"

To the cats' great collective relief, the CatWoman muttered her way out the archway and into the darkness beyond.

Into the house! cried the tortoise-shell. *We'll lock her out!*

They flooded into the sala from every corner of the night and massed themselves against the heavy wooden door until it swung closed. They could hear the CatWoman returning outside, still muttering as she circled the now-empty courtyard.

"—but if it weren't for the hair, I'd never have been hiding out here, and I'd never have met him—I should count my blessings—ha!"

Lean against the door in case she heads this way, the apricot siamese instructed, and they arranged themselves into dogpiles of cat bodies against her entry.

"—can't live this way anymore. I need to leave—start fresh—like Eli—"

As the CatWoman continued to make her mumbly circles under the first-quarter moon, the door muffled her footsteps and the cats eventually got some sleep, even though she herself did not.

◯◯◯

It was the week when plum blossoms began to flower all around her little house in town that Kat missed her first class all year. Springtime's nasty sense of humor was gone for the moment, leaving the entire east valley to throw open its doors and windows to the scent of lilacs beginning to flower. The roads were dry, the sun was warm; there was nothing to slow Kat down as she left that morning for one of her final weeks at the school. It was because of the very lovely weather, however, that she never made it to town until school was over, for when she got to the mirage rim, she saw Eli's van parked at the trailhead on the opposite side. Far below, he was sitting near the bank of the swollen river, painting. Like a caged panther hidden on the mirage, she paced the day away as Eli shifted from spot to spot, painting different views of the river and gorge. A safe half hour after his van disappeared toward town, Kat rode straight to Angelo's house, sat with Oso by the front door, and waited for him to show up.

He was surprised to see her—that was obvious even before he got out of his truck—and Kat thought maybe it was even a pleasant surprise by the way his face softened. But he didn't grin, or laugh with his eyes, and she pretended yet again that it didn't matter to her if he did.

"You could have gone in," he said casually, pushing the door open. "It's not locked." Not until they were inside and Kat had sunk onto the couch in the sala did he ask, "So what happened?"

"Eli was in the gorge."

"Uh-oh." His mild response in no way matched the unreasoned panic she'd been fighting down since pacing the rim.

"He was painting. He followed me there a few weeks ago and caught up to me on the rim. He asked why I go there."

"What did you tell him?"

"That it's a quiet place where I go to think. And then there he was again today, skipping class."

"He wasn't skipping. He's working on something for Georgia's class. She let him out."

So, no problem, she thought. He wasn't skipping, and I just missed one class, and Angelo probably covered it easily, and why did I come over here in a panic? Why did I come over here at all? "Well," she said, trying to match his irritatingly casual manner, "would you tell her to keep him at school—at least on the days when I'm coming and going?"

"That's tricky—those are the days she teaches. But I guess it looks like I'll have to. At least the year's almost over."

"Yeah, not long now." She pictured the letter of resignation sitting in her backpack and the date of her interview in the canyons circled in red on the calendar out on the mirage. Right now, she thought. Give him the letter.

"Would you like some dinner?" he asked, interrupting her thoughts with what sounded like an afterthought. There was nothing of their former bantering in the air, none of the comfort of his ribbing humor, nothing to show her that he cared one way or another if she stayed for dinner—

—until his cover was blown seconds later at the sight of Layira's moon-van turning into the driveway outside the window. With his groan, Kat realized Angelo's nonchalance was as forced as hers, that he really did want her to stay and knew now that she wouldn't. "Gimme a break, already," he muttered under his breath, then mimicked Layira's singsong voice, "*Aaan*-gelo, we need to talk about *Eee*-li—" He sighed an apology to Kat with his green-gold eyes, then said quickly, "Come to town a day early next week—I'll make dinner for you." It was the old Angelo who rolled his eyes at the knock on the door. "She only ever barges in here on Wednesdays."

"I'll be here." Kat nodded. "I have something to give you." She cut ahead of Angelo to open the door. "Hello, Layira."

"Why, *Ka*-at! Hello—" she began, but said no more for her audience was already carrying her bicycle down the hillside, thinking, Only on Wednesdays? Interesting timing.

◯◯◯

Spring is fickle, a lover to avoid, purring one moment and hissing the next. It teases the world with signs of life after winter's hibernation, makes green where there was brown and blue where there was grey. It melts icecaps into irrigation water, warms breezes to tease the shirts off foolish youth, dares the fruit trees to blossom in warm afternoons. But spring's heart is a cyclone, spinning loose when the shirts are off and the blossoms are open. The snowmelt becomes a flood, the seductive breeze becomes a fury. Spring is a half-breed, well-versed in seduction, and every year, a winter-weary world quickens with its flirtations.

On the day Eli was painting in the gorge, spring was at its sweetest, its flirtiest. For the next five days, however, it threw a petulant snit of wind and rain. The CatWoman had been watching the river rising slowly with each trip to town, reaching for the rickety footbridge sagging from bank to bank, and was especially glad the mirage-bridge floated safely above it. But when the latest rains brought the snowcaps down in a torrent, its thunder rumbling through the mirage to wake the CatWoman miles away, she wondered if the mirage-bridge was really immune to flood. She left for town and her dinner with Angelo thinking she could very well be trapped, in spite of spring's sudden, coquettish turn to sunshine and gentle breezes. If she didn't show up for dinner, Angelo wouldn't be the only one disappointed; she was anxious to give him the letter of resignation and be done with it. Last week's momentary glimpse of the old Angelo had given her pause, a moment when she thought she might tear up the letter. But she didn't. Her leaving was only partly because of her awkward relationship with him and mostly because she was ready to move on and start over. No, there was no question in her mind that she was leaving. The only questions left were: Will you laugh for me with your eyes, one last time before I go? and, If I write to you, will you write back? There had been a third question—Will you come away with me?—that slipped uninvited into her dreams, but the CatWoman had sent it packing at dawn. Not a snowball's chance in hell, she thought, pedalling through the sage that afternoon. Don't even think about it.

But she did think about *avoiding* the thought with such great effort that she was halfway down the trail to the river before she realized she wasn't alone in the gorge. Three hikers could be seen on the opposite side, and even from this distance, the CatWoman could tell one of them was Zephyr. No one else in the world, this week, had hair that particular shade of orange. She was certain another was Eli, but the third? It wasn't until they were at the bottom of the trail that the CatWoman saw for sure it was Travis. She leaned her bike against the cliff wall and took off her pack with a frustrated sigh. I just can't live this way anymore, she thought. So much for dinner with Angelo.

The pantomime below was easy to narrate—three teenagers, one of them about to graduate, all seduced by springtime's flirty weather to chase after wild oats on the breeze. Eli's mood was nothing short of ebullient, a young man on the verge of realizing his dreams of escape, a racehorse at the gate just before the bell.

The CatWoman had never seen him capable of such lightness, such laughter as the three of them clowned so close to the river's edge she caught her breath watching them tease at throwing one another in. It's only fun, she told herself, beginning to pace back and forth on the trail and trying to fight down the same unnamed panic she'd felt the week before.

The clowning adjourned for awhile and the CatWoman watched as Zephyr led the others to investigate something on the tumbled, rocky bank. Then in a flash, they were at it again, as she splashed water onto Travis from a puddle and a water fight erupted among all three. By the time they were all soaked, the game had moved downstream to where the decrepit swinging bridge met the bank.

The CatWoman never knew just what it was that finally named her unnamed panic. It wasn't merely something she felt, like the gust of breeze that came out of the south just at that moment to turn her face away from the scene of innocent play—or something she heard, like the hawk's sharp cry as it rode that breeze down to the river in one long, seamless line, carrying her attention with it—or something she saw, like the sunlight glinting off the geyser molded by a tangled mass of uprooted trees, dipping and bobbing as the muddy torrent pushed it downstream. It was something mysteriously more than these, in sum or in part, that finally whispered the name of her panic into her ears and showed her its face as well.

"That'll catch on the bridge," she gasped, then screamed in horror when she spun around to see Eli obviously daring the other two to venture out onto the footbridge. But as their pantomime was muted to her ears by the rushing water, so was hers muted to them, and the mirage hid her from their sight as she shot down the trail, racing the logjam and Eli's foolhardiness. The water was licking at the bridge where it sagged lowest in the center—dangerous, but not deadly-looking to a young man about to conquer the world. Eli was already halfway to the center when Zephyr saw the logjam and yelled to him, though the CatWoman could see the warning was blurred to him even at that close range, and her own breathless screams were as if to the deaf as she ran downhill. He was just at the lowest point of the bridge, still unaware of the approaching logjam, when the floating trees rammed the old timbers and knocked him into the flood, where he disappeared. Zephyr and Travis both screamed and ran along the bank looking for some sign of him, as the CatWoman reached the mirage-bridge at last and raced across it.

Kat had seen Eli surface, riding the rapids with a death-grip on the tangled branches. She scrambled right past the other two where they yelled in blind panic for him—right to the spot where the trees jammed again between the rocky bank and a boulder out in the current. Eli was pinned between the boulder and the trees, scrambling with one hand to scale the slippery stone while holding his head above water with the other. Kat saw that his hand bled with the effort of trying to pull himself free, and in that instant she knew—knew in the same way Regina knew she wouldn't live to name her thirteenth daughter—that Eli was about to die.

Kat threw herself to her knees on the jagged, rocky bank and scraped her palms violently across the stones until a film of blood appeared. Then she leaned out over the logjam, only to feel Travis and Zephyr trying to drag her back away from the water. "Don't pull!" she screamed. "Just hold my legs!" They each grabbed an ankle as she crawled onto the logjam, crawled over the muddy spray, stretched much farther than she'd ever reached before to grab Eli's fingertips. With his desperate eyes locked on hers, the words came out of her in a flood—

—the words of her nightmares—

—the words she'd taken for a curse for four hundred years—

"Te doy el gato, las vidas del gato, la oreja, el ojo, el corazón del

gato—lo que te doy, NADIE TE LO PUEDE QUITAAAARR—" The jam shifted suddenly and Kat slipped, losing his fingertips as her head and arms ducked underwater. Travis and Zephyr yanked her back, dragging her over the rocks and well away from the water's edge as Eli was swept away again and the jam rolled him underwater. She lay panting in a muddy puddle slowly staining itself red, listening to Zephyr and Travis run downstream, their frantic cries soon lost to the river's roar.

Kat pulled herself up to crawl out of the puddle on all fours and looked downriver in a daze where two teenagers ran in mute slow motion, up and over rocks next to a roiling, boiling, slow-motion flood. *"Oh-my-god-what-have-I-done?"* she choked. She leaned against a rock and sat staring numbly at the sky, losing all track of time, all track of feeling, all track of everything except the silly, innocent blue overhead, full of foppishly white spring-time clouds—

—until Zephyr collapsed in tears next to her. "Kat!" she wailed. "We can't find him!" Kat only barely felt Zephyr in her arms as she soothed her, overcome by a numb timelessness she couldn't shake.

"He's gone, Zephyr," she whispered into the wild orange hair, her eyes still trying to make sense of the silly, innocent blue above. "We tried." She rocked the sobbing girl over and over as Regina had done with her daughters, over and over, then did the same with Travis when he appeared, choking and sobbing as well.

When a hundred silly white clouds had floated by and they were finally quiet enough to walk, Kat led them up the trail to the gorge rim. Halfway up, as they stopped to catch their breath, she finally noticed that the fronts of her thin pants were shredded from scrambling over too many rocks and being dragged back from the river's edge. What was left of the cloth had glued itself to her mud-crusted, bloody legs. That looks like it should hurt, she thought dully. I should be screaming.

They bypassed Eli's van where it sat, as none of them knew

how to hot-wire it, and instead hiked through the sage to the highway. When an elderly farmer pulled over and Kat numbly explained to him what the bedraggled crew had just been through, he gave them a ride straight to Angelo's door. She didn't hesitate to walk indoors even as she found the driveway empty, and made Travis and Zephyr trade their wet clothes for dry ones scavenged from Angelo's closet. Once she had re-dressed herself as well, she called the school where Angelo was just about to end his day.

"Angelo—" she began.

"Kat?" he asked, surprised to hear her on a telephone for the first time.

"Angelo, I'm at your house. There's been an accident. Eli's been killed." Then she hung up, forgetting to wait for his reply.

Of course Kat couldn't explain how she got to the river; she'd left her bicycle and pack on the mirage side. Of course Travis and Zephyr couldn't explain how she got there either; they never saw her until she ran past them and never saw the bike hidden on the mirage. And, of course, the board of directors never believed her for one minute when she quietly denied Layira's hysterical accusation that she'd led the kids to the gorge on a Pied Piper joyride. The skeptical tribunal only barely listened to Travis' and Zephyr's adamant protests, not swayed in the least by their description of a heroic Kat crawling toward Eli over the logjam, nor by Georgia's heated admonishment, "I know my boy—he's not a liar, and that's what you're calling him."

Nor, Kat supposed, would they have listened to Angelo if he had spoken. But he hadn't. He sat in heavy silence through the board meeting called immediately following the recovery of Eli's body. When Kat, Georgia, Travis, and Zephyr were told to leave so the board could confer in private, Angelo barely managed to walk outside with them and ask Georgia to give Kat a ride to his house. Kat let the third-person request glide over her without comment and obediently walked through Angelo's door under Georgia's watchful eye. She couldn't bear the thought of another night like the last, though—sitting awake in Angelo's sala as he sat awake in the bedroom, a stunned silence between them. As soon as Georgia's trucklights were headed away again, Kat set out for the mirage in the dark.

When she got to the mirage-bridge near midnight, she couldn't bring herself to set foot upon it, even though it floated safely above the high river. She sat on the bank and stared at the dark water rushing by, her face growing heavy with a sorrow finally reaching her through the numb timelessness of the past two days. The sorrow pulled on her cheeks, her eyes, her mouth, down down down until there was nothing left of Kat on the bank except her thoughts as the river roared by.

No trace, she thought. Nothing left. The river doesn't care that Eli was so talented, so sensitive—that he would have done great things with his life. The river closes in as if he'd never been there at all, as if Angelo and I had never loved him as much as we did. It doesn't care that we'll miss him—

—that Layira will miss him—

Kat saw Layira then, huddled on the floor under the pyramid's glass peak, rocking and sobbing. A mother like Regina. A mother like all five of her own. A mother who, even with all her faults, would mourn this loss desperately and never be comforted, as Kat tried to be, knowing Eli would get another chance.

Another chance.

Another chance, Josefa, came a whisper from nowhere and everywhere, skimming the froth of the river's midnight roaring.

Just like you wanted for your Eli, I wanted another chance for my Josefita.

Josefita dulceciiii-taaaaaa . . .

A shriek of pain from Kat's raw, skinless thighs shot through her at last with the fading whisper, and she screamed into the river's roar until she had no voice left. When her scream finally shrank to a hoarse gasp, she hobbled across the mirage-bridge to begin the long, excruciating trek back to the little house under the cottonwoods.

⟨∞⟩

The river doesn't care.

So what if she'd miss him? So what if there were things she hadn't said to him? So what if his eyes hadn't laughed for her in months, that she'd never kissed those grinning cheeks?

The river doesn't care.

That swirling life-river. That cyclone with spring in its heart one day and winter the next. He was slipping away, his fingertips barely touching hers, something pulling her back as she stretched toward him—

Don't pull—don't pull—

The river doesn't care, just sweeps along, closing around the holes left by questions unasked and chances not taken.

Will you come away with me?

But the river doesn't care, just closes in around the fingertips slipping from hers, and the eyes not laughing, and the cheeks too far away to kiss into laughter.

Don't pull—if I could just reach that much farther—

I love you, Angelo.

Come away with me, Angelo.

I'd miss you desperately, Angelo.

Come with me.

"Come with me." The CatWoman half-woke to her own whisper, and mouthed the words again until she knew what she'd been dreaming. "Come with me," she said into the springtime darkness. "I love you, Angelo." She slipped out of bed to walk barefoot outside and stood by the stone cairn. "I love you, Angelo," she said to the moon, wondering dreamily if he was looking at it, too, and if it would pass on her message. "The next time I see you, I'll ask you to come with me."

Go ahead, grunted the old calico from somewhere in the shadows of the porch. *He's camped at the pond.*

The half-sleep fell abruptly from the CatWoman. *Angelo's here?* she asked, as anxious now as she'd been dreamy a moment earlier.

Uh-huh, came the tortoise-shell's voice. *And he's still awake.*

When did he get here?

Just after dark.

He'll need to sleep, the CatWoman fretted, taking a step as if to pace the courtyard. *I'll wait till morning—*

Noooooo, came a unified chorus from all around her, and in a flurry of leaping shadows, all her housemates ran to block her path. When she stepped toward them, they all arched their backs and began to hiss.

All right, all right. The CatWoman backed off. *At least let me get some shoes.* The feline entourage surrounded her as she gathered shoes and warmer clothes, then escorted her forcefully to the courtyard arch. They were still there, blocking any possible return, as she disappeared into the piñons.

She couldn't creep silently like a cat, for her legs hurt too much from hours of painful scrubbing and ointments that burned too feverishly not to be doing her some good. If she'd known in town how bad the scrapes were, she'd have cleaned them at Angelo's house. But she merely covered them up with a borrowed pair of pants and numbly forgot them in the rush of people and interrogations and accusations that followed. She couldn't forget them now, however, after hours of singing her first mother's lullaby—"Pobreciiiiii—yeow—ita mijita, brillarás como esssssss—ouch-ouch-ouch—trellita"—as she picked stones and shreds of cloth from well underneath her skin. She could neither forget them nor command them to carry her silently, so she walked to Angelo's camp knowing his cat ears were probably tracking her every step.

Whether he heard her or not, he didn't look at the CatWoman until she was standing fully lit by his campfire, and even then he was slow to pull his eyes from the flames' hypnosis.

"Hi," she said self-consciously, her heart beginning to flutter as she dared herself anew to keep her promise to the moon.

"Hi," he said slowly. "I didn't mean to wake you—"

"You didn't—"

"—I couldn't stay in town."

The CatWoman nodded and bent as if to sit down next to him, but the scream of young scabs beginning to tear overpowered her attempt to be graceful. She fell against him with a pained hiss, then rolled aside to arrange her legs straight out toward the fire, gritting her teeth until the scream faded.

Angelo looked at her sharply. "Are you okay?"

"It's just a scrape," she said quickly over a heartbeat now doubly agitated. "How did it go—with the board?"

"Not well." Angelo ran his hands through his loose hair with a sigh. "Not well." His strained face went back to the campfire, and the CatWoman saw even more lost sleep in his eyes than she felt in her own.

"Am I out of a job?"

"I don't know. I—uh—left before they got to that part." A cool spring breeze shimmied through olive branches along the pond's shore, a fidgety sound to match fidgety fingers, as the CatWoman ran her hands through the sand, teetering on the brink of blurting out the question she'd come to ask him. But as she opened her mouth to speak, Angelo said softly, "No, I'm out of a job."

"*You?* Why?"

Angelo looked off into the darkness toward a lone coyote voice bouncing between crisp springtime stars and the dark mesa.

"They ordered me to fire you, and I—uh—told them to go to hell. Said I'd quit myself before I'd fire an excellent teacher."

"You don't have to," she said. "I've decided to leave."

Angelo didn't look surprised, only sad. "I don't blame you at all." The CatWoman could hear him measuring his words. "Your mirage treats you a lot better than the school did."

She shook her head, trying to keep her voice steady. "No, I'm leaving here, too."

Angelo looked at her sharply for a second time, now quite obviously surprised. She saw a faint wash of color drain from his face in the flickering light. "Where—?" was all he could say.

"West of here—out in the canyons—there's a place Georgia told me about." Swallowing had become nearly impossible for the CatWoman, and while her heart raced, her head seemed slow and thick, distracted by every flicker from the campfire, every bounce of the coyote's song. "They're looking for a history teacher." Angelo nodded but said nothing, staring into the flames again and letting night and starlight settle between them. "I wish you would come with me," she croaked into the silence, and for a maddening eternity equal to her entire second lifetime, the CatWoman thought he might not have heard her, that she might have to say it again and wasn't at all sure she could. Finally, a slow grin began to creep into his eyes and, just as she feared and hoped it would, the faintest echo of that grin caught his cheeks, making her lips fairly melt with a trembling desire to kiss them.

"Kat," Angelo said hoarsely, and she could see he, too, was having a hard time swallowing, "do you have *any idea* how I've loved you since we met?"

The CatWoman could neither close her mouth nor open it to speak, could only sit dumbly shaking her head, tears welling in her eyes to make a blurry surf of the firelight, breaking all around her. "No," she barely whispered. "Maybe you'd better tell me."

"Let me tell you," he said, taking her hand and putting it gently to his lips. "Let me tell you," he breathed warmly into her open palm—

—and with his warm breath on her skin and the green-gold of his eyes caressing the green-gold of hers, the evening's cool darkness melted and slid away, replaced by the shimmering heat of early summer. The CatWoman saw her east orchard and felt herself leaning against a branch, watching a woman with a shovel wade and splash her way through the trees. The woman's legs were bare and sun-browned below a blousy pair of pants rolled up to the knees, and a faded gold shirt draped gracefully over shoulders familiar with work. But what caught the CatWoman's eye, and her breath, was the woman's hair—a tumbling, wavy jungle of color, on fire with sunlight, setting the air around her to glowing. The CatWoman felt herself holding back an urge to walk forward and touch that hair, to warm her fingers between strands of black and gold and red and cream. She wanted to see the woman's face, wanted very much to see her face, to have the woman's eyes fall upon her familiarly, warmly. She felt herself saying something to get the woman's attention, and then those eyes were on her, green and gold and deep as the ocean she'd seen long ago. "Is it that late?" came the woman's voice, and the CatWoman recognized her own, and recognized her own eyes, but not the face. The face was beautiful and soft in the shade of her floppy hat, softer than hers looked in the mirror. The face was young and proud—and wary—and the CatWoman felt rising in her the words, "Don't be afraid of me," but felt them die somewhere short of her lips—

—and in the dying, the afternoon faded to a late-summer's morning. The CatWoman stepped into the house to find a terribly comical figure scurrying around the corner from the bedroom, one slipper on and one off, nightshirt worried with wrinkles, and a head of wildly uneven hair leaping overboard in every direction. The CatWoman felt silent laughter teasing her eyes, though she fought it down, and heard a voice from her own mouth asking, "Am I allowed to laugh?" when all she could think was, "Are you trying to make me fall in love with you?"—

—and fall, and fall, out of the summer morning into the Fall, where she walked under a turquoise sky with a woman who seemed to hold the very season itself in her face, in her hair, in her laugh, in the way she bit into an apple from a tree she had climbed. The apple was her cheeks, her cheeks were the apple; the woman was autumn itself, with the last of the green left on earth in her eyes—

—and those eyes kept the earth's green and held out promises of spring into the grey winter wind, until they closed, and looked away—

—and the CatWoman found herself looking away, down from the ridge above her house in town, looking down and feeling chilled and seeing no smoke from the chimney below, afraid there might never be smoke from that chimney again. Beyond the cold chimney, she saw a cold lifetime spreading out before her, spreading to the farthest winter-grey horizon and beyond, dipping over the edge into dark sadness. And there were no words inside her—

—until the green eyes returned, but held no promise of spring, no memory of autumn. Silent words welled up in her again and again, saying, "I miss the springtime in your eyes—look at me that way again! I miss the autumn in your hair—show me your hair again! Let me run my fingers through your hair. I miss you. I miss you . . ."

"*I miss you,*" she felt Angelo whisper to each of her fingers, each whisper a comet shooting through her to explode into the springtime stars.

"You saw me—that way?" she asked, her voice catching on yet another comet as Angelo slid his lips slowly up her little finger to land in a long kiss on the very tip.

"I still do," he said to her fingertip, then slid his lips along her ring finger so slowly the CatWoman thought she would forget how to breathe, waiting for him to kiss that fingertip too, and the next.

She took one of his hands to place it gently in her hair, and when he raised an eyebrow to look at her over the fingertip he was kissing, she said, "Laugh for me—with your eyes—"

His fingers moved as slowly through her hair as his lips did along the miles of her last finger. "Give me something to laugh about," he whispered, his eyes catching flames from the comets inside her.

"*I want you to come away with me.*"

Angelo's lips moved side to side along her palm as he shook his head. "Any dog could be a travelling companion."

"But I don't want—just a—travelling companion," she stammered as he ran his lips down to the soft underside of her wrist where they hovered like a bee's wings.

"What *do* you want?"

"I want *you*—"

"To keep you warm?" He kissed the pulse of her wrist. "Any cat could keep you warm."

"*Angelo!*" she said, exasperated, and when he looked up from over her wrist, she saw the laughter from her dreams had flooded his eyes at last. "I love you, Angelo," she whispered. "*I love you*— and I couldn't bear it if your eyes never laughed for me again." She brushed her kissed fingertips ever so softly over the cheeks that had wakened her at night and driven her to distraction during the day. "There—" And she leaned forward to kiss those cheeks, those eyes, the grin that was his very soul. "*—that's* what I want."

◯◯◯

Not even Angelo's arms around her and his sleepy breath in her hair could keep the CatWoman from waking somewhere between midnight and dawn, her hands clenched and sweating, her breath and heart in panicked syncopation. She snuggled further backward into the warm curve of him, willing her breath to slow like his and the image of a drowning Eli to stop reverberating through her with each heartbeat. She draped herself on the breeze in the cottonwoods outside and rode it across the mesa, rippling over sage and piñons and rocking her very nearly back to sleep, but not completely.

Angelo, she called softly to his cat-self.

Mmm.

I gave him the nine lives.

The CatWoman felt his body lose its sleepy languor as he pulled himself from cat dreams and human dreams alike, pulled himself deliberately toward her words until his arms loosed their hold and he propped himself up behind her. "Did you say something?" he asked sleepily.

"I said, I gave Eli the nine lives." When there was nothing but silence to answer her, she shook her head into the shadowed pillow. "I don't know what came over me—except I knew I wouldn't be able to save him. And it was all I had. It was all I had to give him."

"*Thank you.*" She heard Angelo's choked whisper as he slid down beside her again. His kiss on her shoulder was far too wet for anything but tears. "My dearest, sweetest Kat," he faltered, "if I didn't already love you, I would love you for that."

And with that, they cried, mixing their tears well on toward dawn until they both had exhausted themselves into a sleep beyond the reach of dreams.

⊂⊃⊂⊃

They're just now finishing up lunch—it's time to call them indoors, Kat thought, the pulse of her teacher's schedule ticking away as usual inside her, absolutely unsolicitous of her feelings. No firehorse ever had it worse, teased by internal bells she couldn't answer as she sat banished in Angelo's backyard on a day when she otherwise would have been teaching. Should have been teaching. Should have been there to give the exam, but instead was forced to sit idly by, forbidden by the board to ever be seen at the school again, leaving others to finish out the year with *her* students.

It'll take them a few minutes to get settled—how will they fit both classes in there at once? Her mind fretted over details much larger in remote control than they would be if she were there herself, until she had to rein her thoughts away, just like she had reined her eyes away from Angelo's cheeks these past many months.

My work here is over. It's as much in the past as my fourth lifetime. I wish those exams were in my lap right now. I want to be done with it all. It's not fair. I can't even say good-bye to them—

"Ahhh—" she groaned out loud, and went indoors to make herself a cup of coffee. "Stop feeling sorry for yourself. Being fired isn't anywhere near as bad as being burned at the stake. Ha." But even though she knew her words were true—that she would, for the first time in five lifetimes, be able to walk away from a tragedy on two sturdy feet—she was leaving with a heart firebranded forty-one times over with the faces of students who had come to mean so much to her. Would the new teacher next year truly appreciate Pilar's poetic nature? Or ride out Aaron's theatrics without losing patience? Or notice, under Travis' lousy spelling, a sense of social and historical injustice worthy of a great statesman? Fine things for me to worry over, she reminded herself. I'm the one who decided to leave a long time ago.

But today was the difference between thinking and doing, between planning a departure she knew she must take and actually unweaving the ties between her heart and each of her students. Ties of concern. Ties of hope. Ties of laughter and frustration and pride and joy.

Pride and joy.

These kids have been my kids, she thought. And Eli—ohhhh, Eli—

She had to step back from the stove to keep her tears for Eli from salting the pot of milk warming next to the coffee the way they had salted the soup Angelo made for dinner the night before. Except *those* tears had been Angelo's—silent tears a man will shed with his back to the world and sniff away before anyone notices. But Kat noticed, and Kat tasted them in the soup, and Kat kissed them away when they fell again in the dark, as he did hers.

Enough, enough, she told herself, wiping her eyes and carrying her coffee outdoors. At least I had the chance to say good-bye to Eli. I'll have to write good-bye notes to the rest of them on their exams.

Oso wandered over to lean against her where she sat, then rolled to the ground with his heavy jowled head in her lap of slow-healing scabs. "You'll like the canyons, Oso," she said out loud. "There's no mud. And Georgia guarandamntees there isn't anywhere prettier on earth." If Oso heard Kat's words, he gave no sign of it, lying hypnotized by her finger sliding rhythmically up the ridge of his long nose. "And we'll find a kitten after we get there, so you'll have a buddy." None of the cats on the mirage wanted to move with them. In fact, as both she and Angelo were informed very pointedly by the tortoise-shell, *Cats do not move by choice, and anyone who'd been born all-cat instead of half-and-half would know that.* "And if we can't get teaching jobs right away, Angelo can swing a hammer and I can—I can—hmm." Her finger stopped in its hypnotic path. I can tell stories and I can make things grow. An unlikely combination at best. "I'll get the job," she went on firmly, pushing her finger again to finish its path. A lavender perfume drifted through the yard from full-blossomed lilac stands all over the east valley, tickling both Oso's and Kat's noses. "I'll get the job and I'll grow things, too. I'll plant lilacs first off, right when we move in. Why didn't I plant lilacs on the mirage? They would have done well there—"

Kat's soliloquy was pierced by a ringing telephone from indoors, which she ignored at first. But when it insisted upon knifing a twelfth time into the lazy lavender afternoon, she figured it must be Angelo.

"Hey—love of my life—" came his teasing through the line.

"Love of your *fifth* life," she quipped.

"Damn right, and don't forget it." She could hear the blanketed ring of a hand cupped over the phone to mask his whisper. "And if I can just figure out a way to find you, you're going to be the love of my sixth life, too." When Kat laughed, the leftover salt of her tears crackled and fell away from her eyes. "Hey, I need your help. I'm on my way home to pick you up."

"What's going on?"

"The kids are on strike—they locked themselves into your classroom. They're refusing to take the rest of the exams because you've been fired."

"I can't go there, Angelo. You heard what the board said."

"To hell with the board, Kat. Nobody passes without taking the exams. Just ask yourself—do they want the entire student body flunking out?"

"I'll put on my shoes."

From the school parking lot, as Angelo steered his truck into an open spot, Kat could see no vestige of the lunchtime demonstration he had described while driving. "They found out from Mu. He announced after the science exam that he'd be seeing them after lunch for the history exam—fool to the bone, that guy. So, of course, they asked why, and he told them everything. He even said he's going to be headmaster next year, which is purely speculation on his part. But the kids took it seriously, and the next thing I knew I had an office full of irate students demanding an explanation." Angelo grinned wickedly across the truckcab at her. "A couple of them even said they wouldn't come back to school here next year if Mu's the headmaster."

"You think this is funny," Kat scolded him, even while giggling herself at the image of Mu's stupid posturing sparking a riot.

"You're going out with a bang, my dear." Angelo laughed. "You've obviously left your mark."

No, there wasn't a trace of disorder on the school grounds, where the same lazy lavender afternoon was napping on the empty benches and tables and gaming equipment. But the sudden furious pounding of a fist on a wooden door shattered the sleepy illusion, its erratic staccato accentuating the tension beneath the calm.

"That's Mu, being a headmaster," Angelo said dryly. "He's been trying to get in for an hour." They walked across the yard and around to the door of Kat's newly former classroom, where Mu stopped pounding the door to glare at them.

"You're not supposed to be here," he huffed at Kat, who only stepped past him to tap lightly on the door.

"It's Kat," she called. "Can I come in and talk with you?"

"You're the one who caused all this trouble!" Mu hissed at her.

"Then I'm the one to stop it, right?" she said calmly, holding his gaze glare for glare.

"You can't go in there. I won't allow it."

Angelo threw his hands in the air impatiently. "For Christ's sake, Mu, she's just going to talk them into finishing the exams. What—do you want your own son to flunk out?"

"Shanti will never flunk as long as I'm at this school—"

"Now *that's* a hell of an attitude from a headmaster," Angelo retorted, and Kat could feel a sudden, violent temperature rise in the air between the two men.

Don't you dare, she called silently to Angelo. *He's half your size. And I won't live with a bully.*

Meadow's voice came through the door to break the tension. "Just you?"

"No," Kat replied. "Me and Angelo."

There was a brief muffled debate from inside, then the click of the door being unlocked. Meadow slipped out and held the door closed behind her to address the three of them. Kat was surprised to see she had wrapped her hair in a shred of towel and wondered why her hair would be wet at midday. "Only Kat and Angelo," she declared firmly, "or we'll stay here all night."

Mu was stunned by her tone and said nothing as she opened the door just a crack to let herself and the invited guests inside. He was still silent as she locked the door again, but Kat wasn't; she caught her breath noisily as she scanned the crowded room of familiar faces, each and every one of them capped by shreds of cloth fashioned into turbans to mimic her daily bandanas.

Oh, Angelo, you didn't tell me this part, she gasped silently.

Does it make any difference? You should be flattered.

I am, but—She walked awkwardly, self-consciously to the stuffed chair at the front of the silent group and sat down. But it only makes it harder, she thought. Her mind slipped into an awed blankness as she gazed at face after face filled with precocious determination she hadn't noticed there before. Or had she? Hadn't that look been building gradually through the year, lesson by lesson, as they learned the hard knocks history was wont to deal? There it was now, in bloom as full as if they'd been rose-bushes in her garden, ripe enough for a rose chorus at midsummer. By her hand. In her name.

But—

—but *she* was the one who made the decision to leave, not the board of directors, as the unified protest before her assumed. She would have spent this day saying good-bye to them all anyway, even if the board hadn't fired her, even if Eli hadn't been too far beyond her grasp to save, even if Angelo hadn't gleefully agreed to run off with her. She'd have been saying good-bye to those she would miss a lot and those she would miss not quite so much, to those she felt were ready to explode out into the world to make their own history and those she wished could have a little more time under her tutelage. Today would have been a day of good-byes anyway because, deep down, she was ready to stop hiding on a mirage, stop hiding under a bandana, stop being alone. She was ready to go.

Even though she loved them.

Even though they loved her.

Slowly, sadly, Kat let out the breath she'd been perched upon, gazing at the faces of those trying to give back to her the very fruits of what they'd learned in her class—and she reached back to slip the knot on her bandana.

"I'd like to tell you a story," she began softly, pulling the cloth off her head and laying it out across her lap, smoothing it from center to hem in every slow direction, reluctant to look up until a whisper from Zephyr broke the breathless moment.

"Cool hair!"

Kat lifted her eyes to meet theirs, and her voice grew stronger in the shower of admiration—not repulsion, not fear—beaming upon her from all around the room. "It's a story about a woman who was—shy—and didn't much like being around other people because of some things she'd lived through." She let the thrill of Angelo's wink sizzle over top of the relief soaking into her after nine long months on edge. "And being shy, this woman decided, 'Well, the world won't miss me and I won't miss the world.' She had gardens and orchards that fed her in four seasons, and she had flowers to look at and coyotes to listen to. She had everything she needed, and she was content to leave the rest of the world to spin out its own life without her. Until, one day, a man came along and told her something that made her stop and think for a moment about the rest of the world."

The entire assembly jumped when the forgotten knocking suddenly began again. Without hesitation, Meadow strode across the room to speak sternly through the barrier. "Mu, stop being rude. We're having class in here and Kat doesn't allow any interruptions." When the rebuke went unrebutted from the other side, Meadow walked calmly back to her seat.

Look out world, she graduates next week, Angelo chuckled silently.

"So one day a man came along," Meadow prompted Kat.

"So, a man came along," Kat went on. "A special man. He was one of those people who takes what life dishes out and makes the very best of it. All of it. And that's why, when he found the woman hiding away in her gardens, he told her she was wasting her life and her talents. Instead of griping about how rotten the world was, she could be molding the next generation, making it better. And that made her think. A lot. Mostly, it made her think about cats—how they have to live nine times and jump back into the world regardless of how rotten or pleasant it might be. The woman wondered: What if, in a cat's third life, she joins a group that declares all tabbies should be put to death, and then comes back in her fourth life as a tabby? Or if, in her sixth life, she convinces all her fellow housecats that strays deserve to be on the street and starving, and then comes back in her seventh life as a stray? This is what the shy woman thought about when she decided to become a teacher—about how all the things a cat does in a life might come back to haunt her in the next. And she decided she wanted to teach the next generation to live as if the same could happen to them—to live as if they had to jump back eight times into the mess they'd created."

Kat gazed over their heads and out the window, where the very tip of Layira's pyramid poked above the western horizon. Her heart blew a silent kiss to Eli, whose leap back into the mess would be literal someday, not just a theoretical premise in a history class on a lazy lavender springtime afternoon.

"It was a tall order," she almost whispered, slow to move her eyes from the pyramid, "to think that she might have such an effect on the world by touching just a handful of students, in a small town, in a tiny school." She looked again at the resolute faces before her, seeing they had softened under her voice and with the dawning realization she hadn't come to rally their support but to bid a gentle good-bye. "But actually, that *is* what happened to this woman, and by the end of the year, she could see it written all over their faces, how they'd changed, how they'd heard what she said. And she was so proud of them—*so* proud—so glad they were about to burst out into the world and make their own histories."

Kat sighed and met Angelo's green-gold eyes, warmed not by a grin now but by the same glow she'd seen in them as she kissed his tears away the night before.

"And that's the funny thing that happened to this woman—this shy woman who knew her cherry trees so much better than she knew people. It was because of her students, and the sight of them ready to set out into the world, that she felt like doing the same. She was ready to leave, to go find another handful of students to touch, even though she'd grown to love the ones she was leaving behind."

The room had become so quiet with Kat's soft voice that Mu's sudden pounding—accompanied by a shrill "Your time is up! It's time to go home!"—landed like a grenade in the stillness. This time, Meadow was joined by all but Shanti as she strode across the room to open the door.

"Mu, you cut that out!" "We're not finished yet!" "Go away!" Kat looked at Shanti sitting alone, obviously aware of her gaze upon him and uncomfortably trying to avoid it. You, most of all, she thought to herself. I hope you learned something.

By the time the door was once again closed and the indignant crowd seated, Kat had lost the thread of her story and could only shake her head. "You have to take your exams," she told them. "If you don't, then all I've managed to do in my first year of teaching is to incite an entire school to cripple itself. I don't want that. Yes, the board fired me, but it was *my* decision to leave, and I made that decision long before any of this happened. But I can't leave without letting you know that I think what you've done here is wonderful, and it's exactly what I hope you'll do again if you ever see someone being treated unfairly—whether it's that they're being fired, or being left to starve on the streets, or whatever. If you believe it's wrong, then *do* something, just like you've done here today."

Kat turned to Angelo in the face of their mass disappointment. *I can't say anything else, Angelo, or I'm going to start crying.*

So will they. So will I.

Help me get out of here.

You haven't said good-bye yet.

"Good-bye," she whispered and saw several cheeks already streaked with tears. "And good luck." Her knees weren't working quite smoothly as she stood and walked to the door. As she reached for the doorknob, she stopped and turned back to them. "One last thing to remember, something I forgot to tell you this year: Don't let a whole lifetime go by without falling in love. Promise?" Everyone looked at her and then at each other much the same way they'd done on the first day of school, not sure what to do. "Promise?" she repeated, and waited until she saw self-conscious grins breaking up the disappointment on their faces. "Good." She smiled, and opened the door. "I'm finished," she said to Mu, his mute fury lending the only vibrance to the lavender laziness outside. She knew by his widening eyes that he was staring at her hair, even while trying not to show it. Angelo stepped outside and took Kat's arm to walk with her to the truck.

"But when will they take the exam?" Mu sputtered after them.

"Tomorrow," Angelo replied over his shoulder.

"But they were supposed to take it *today*—"

"*But*—" Angelo said firmly, turning to face Mu across the yard, "—I'm still the headmaster. The job's not yours for another week."

The tide of students streaming out the door only barely diluted Mu's venomous glare. It was Kat's turn to take Angelo by the arm and steer him toward the truck. *Please don't*—she started to say silently.

Don't worry, he replied, helping her into the truckcab and then leaning inside to add softly, "You're not living with a bully, Kat. But if he'd started something, I would have finished it. You need to know that."

She nodded. "I know, and I wouldn't have blamed you."

"Besides." Angelo grinned. "He's just jealous."

"Oh?"

"Sure—he gets the school, but *I* get to run away with the beautiful history teacher."

It was obvious from Zephyr's expression that she'd seen Angelo kiss Kat just then, for when they finally did notice her standing nearby, her face was glowing with a conspiratorial grin.

"What's up, Zeph?" Angelo asked casually as he closed Kat's door.

"You dropped this," she said to Kat, and held out the forgotten bandana.

"Ahhh, Zephyr." Kat sighed. "You know, I don't want that bandana anymore. Would you like it?"

"Sure—"

"But—" Kat reached out to pull the impromptu turban from Zephyr's head and to run her fingers gently through the curls underneath. "—you have to promise me you'll wear it anywhere but on your head. You have such delightful hair, Zephyr. Don't cover it up."

As the truck pulled out onto the dirt road, Kat could see in the mirror her old bandana fashioned quickly into an armband, tails hanging languidly into the lavender air as Zephyr waved good-bye.

SUMMER

Halfway between peas and tomatoes, halfway between early blossoms and late fruit, the summer solstice sat on the eastern valley—fat, hot, beyond perspiration or motion. The year's longest sunshine baked houses and fields and people into a rich corpulence, a loaf of risen bread, a beer in full froth, a seed eager to burst open to rain. The town was swollen with the solstice, chafing at its boundaries and nudging the very valley itself over the edge of the gorge rim and partway up the sides of the foothills. Plump, still, the solstice sat halfway between spring and harvest, halfway between promise and reward, halfway between rain—and rain.

A spindle in balance.

A marathon of sunlight.

A very long day for irrigating and tending and weeding everywhere in the world bordered by the eastern and western mountains, except on the mirage-mesa, where the CatWoman crept silently through her orchards an hour before the year's earliest dawn.

"Go to sleep," she whispered to each and every tree. "Go to sleep until the next person comes to take care of you." They stood as a dark army, pruned so severely that not a single brave shoot poked through into the heat of the summer solstice. "Go to sleep and wait for the rains, and go to sleep again when they stop," she whispered, touching each tree in the way her first mother had taught her. They were all alive under her hand but too drowsy to bear fruit or bud, too drowsy to do anything but soak up rain when it came. "For all the years of giving me fruit, now I give you the gift of sleep."

To the terrace of rosebushes, pruned nearly to the ground, she repeated her words and pricked her palm as she wrapped a loving hand over each one. "For all the years of giving me beauty, I give you the gift of sleep," she whispered, and let the blood from her hand drip onto the turned soil.

The morning glories she left alone. The cottonwoods she left alone. They would age and re-seed as they'd done for centuries without human help, pulling their lifeblood from the courtyard spring. But she did touch the house, its soft-plastered walls and carved posts, leaving faint spots of blood here and there from her rose-pricked palm. "I don't know if I have a gift of sleep for you, old house," she whispered to the kitchen wall, "but I thank you." Hours later, she felt dreams murmuring softly through the slate floor as she and Angelo packed the last of her mirage life into the buggy and paniers.

The cats watched in full-bellied silence following their latest— *Last,* complained the tortoise-shell—tuna feast.

Someone will come, Angelo told her as he dished out can after can. *We can't be the only ones who can open mirages.*

You could always come back, the tortoise-shell pouted.

We could always come back. Angelo smiled. *And if we ever do, it'll be with a load of tuna, I promise. But don't spend your whole lifetime waiting for us.*

So, considering their full bellies and their pouting hearts, the CatWoman and Angelo were both surprised when the cats followed them across the mesa at a trot, panting in the solstice heat. They pedalled their bicycles slowly so they might all arrive at the gorge rim together. The cats even walked down the long path to the river's edge and rubbed against their legs in farewell before the two of them wheeled their bicycles one last time across the mirage-bridge, letting the hidden world close silently behind them.

The river at solstice was crystal-clear and low, not even a distant cousin to the muddy torrent that had swept Eli into the twilight between his first and second lives. Innocent and inviting as it seemed, Kat couldn't bring herself to even dangle her feet in its coolness. She perched herself on a rock, waiting for Angelo to wade into the current and duck his head underwater, and then to come up shaking like a dog, as she knew he would.

"C'mon over here," he called, holding his hand out to her.

"I don't want to go in."

He waded back and lifted her from the rock where she sat. "Then I'll carry you," he said simply. "I want to show you something." He carried her downstream precisely to the boulder where Eli had been trapped, huge now as it towered above the low waters of summertime. "Here," he said, and set her on her feet between the rock and the stony bank in a shallow pool now eddying harmlessly between them. Angelo pulled Kat down to sit next to him in the cool water and guided her hand over the rock's face to a spot just above the water level where something had been carved into the stone.

"What does it say?" she asked.

"Read it." He nodded, and she braced herself to lie nearly flat in the river that had taken Eli's life. "Eli Papadimitriou was loved by Angelo Vittorio diVita and Meghan Katlin O'Malley," it read in letters deep enough to swallow a fingertip tracing them.

"When did you do that?" she choked.

"Last week, when you were packing your house and I was supposedly packing mine."

Kat shook her head, tracing and retracing the letters silently as the pool swirled in slow motion around them. "I can't believe," she said at last, "that I wasted so much time trying not to fall in love with you."

"Hey," Angelo teased, "so don't waste another minute. What— you think you're going to live nine times or something?"

As Kat teased him back with a splash that he quickly returned, neither of them noticed how the water drops reached the other side of the river and splashed the tortoise-shell, watching them from the mirage bank.

Humans! she grumbled, wiping her face dry and preening her coat fastidiously until it shone like autumn under glass. By the time her bath was done, she'd seen the bicycles and the humans disappear up the steep eastern bank, leaving just a faint, floating dust re-settling slowly in the breathless solstice heat.

Pobrecita mijita, the cat sang to herself as she turned to climb the long path to the mirage rim and make her way back toward the towering cottonwoods. *Brillarás como estrellita . . .*

While majoring in education and minoring in music at the University of New Mexico, **Kathleen Dexter** worked as a ghostwriter and producer for a children's storytelling program on KUNM (Albuquerque), an affiliate of NPR. This eventually led her to found her own company, Zephyr Tapes and Books, which specializes in stories from the southwest. She worked for fifteen years in the "movie industry circus" on various film projects while completing her master's degree in psychology. She began writing fiction when one of her professors commented that "the real students of human nature aren't psychologists—they're novelists."